THE VAULT

STUART Z. GOLDSTEIN

PEN PAPER PRESS

The Vault

Published by Pen Paper Press
Monroe Township, NJ

978-1-7366322-3-9 (paperback)
978-1-7366322-4-6 (hardcover)
978-1-7366322-5-3 (ebook)

FICTION / Thrillers / Suspense | FICTION / Thrillers / Crime

Cover and design by Pam Brooks, copyright owned by Stuart Z. Goldstein.
Interior design by Bryan Canter, copyright owned by Stuart Z. Goldstein.

DISCLAIMER: This book is a work of fiction. None of the characters in this story are real people. Any resemblance to real people or historical events is neither intended nor true. Americlear is not a real company. Please don't get lost in speculating about the details. This story was written to entertain, which I hope is made more exciting by its plausible nature.

For Eritt, Jessica, Adam, Brooke, Samantha Maren and Aaron Bennett *who I loved before we ever met…and who inspire me to reach beyond what may be possible.*

ACKNOWLEDGMENTS

Editorial: Steve Letzler, Steven W. Weinberg, Donald H. Harrison, Rosalie Jenkins, John Vrettos, Richard Bist, Jennifer Bisbing

Graphic Design Book Cover: Pam Brooks

Early Readers/Supporters: Patrick Donovan, Michael Falk, Charles Kaufman, Myrna Kimmelman, David DuPell

Publishing Advisor: Jeff Barrie

CHAPTER 1
THE THREAT

No one could imagine that down a rabbit hole near Wall Street stood the largest bank securities vault in the world, holding more than $37 trillion in assets. By comparison, the Fort Knox vault in Kentucky holds only $274 billion in gold bullion.

This huge steel structure is at the nerve center of U.S. capital markets, impervious to external or internal threats. At least that's what industry experts generally believed, until now.

Andy Russo had been there from the beginning in the 1970s, when the vault was initially built. Returning from his military service in Vietnam and with a college degree, Andy's uncle leveraged the "old boy" network to land him a job on Wall Street. He joined a technology group at Americlear, which focused on automating trade processing and recordkeeping for the industry.

He had seen it all. He had witnessed history as few would ever know. He was quickly groomed for leadership of Vault Operations. Every morning, he descended three levels down from the streets of Manhattan. The vault was housed in a building covering a footprint larger than three city blocks. As the elevator doors opened on level C, the vault stood there waiting for him.

In time, the vault became a vast wasteland with rows and rows of metal shelving filled with millions of paper securities (physical ownership records), including equities (stocks), corporate bonds, municipal bonds, money market instruments and bearer bonds. Andy understood that without automation, financial markets in the U.S. could not grow.

Getting the industry and investors to keep their physical securities in the vault would take decades. The tasks didn't require college degrees, just a large group of frontline employees and clerks. Andy embraced the challenges but hated the unwritten practices in the in the '70s and early '80s: if you were white you worked above street level in the building, but minorities and immigrants were relegated to work in a basement without windows.

Senior executives at Americlear reaped salary increases and large bonuses, as automation took hold. However, careers for vault staff were cut short, as fewer people were needed once documents were electronically recorded.

Over the years these loyal, hard-working and low paid vault employees never shared in the rewards widely known on Wall Street. As they toiled to safeguard the industry through market downturns and crisis events like 9/11, their sacrifice was followed invariably by patterns of layoffs, salary cutbacks, and reduced benefits.

Many would say their long hours and meager wages offered testimony to both the sacrifice and the hope that is America. But no one could ignore the disparities that existed between haves and have-nots.

Andy was highly respected for his leadership running the vault. His access to the CEO and status with senior management grew, along with his compensation. Yet he was increasingly disenchanted that he could not use his leverage to protect his people or get them better career paths. The C-suite often lulls themselves into a false belief that people can be treated poorly, and they won't rise up in revolt. They were wrong. Industry experts and regulators were certain nothing, or no one could threaten the safeguards created in the vault. But, what if? What if the computers failed, or worse, physical securities were stolen? How would the industry ever restore investor confidence?

It was unlikely that a steel vault, by definition, could ever fail. But people fail. Leaders fail. They fail in their values and commitment to the Golden Rule. And that can lead to disillusionment and betrayal. It is – and ever has been the dilemma of our time. Andy knew a reckoning was coming.

CHAPTER 2
DAEVA CONNOLLY COMES ABOARD 2010: YOU CAN GO NOW

The board's decision to bring in Daeva Connolly to become CEO would change the culture of Americlear in ways no one could have anticipated. Connolly was a 23-year veteran, in charge of technology and the back office at BNB Brokerage. She took preemptive action to voluntarily retire from BNB, anticipating the hard fought and well-known internal politics and purges that happened regularly at the firm.

Like Judy Jameson, one of her previous CEOs at Americlear, Connolly served on the company's governing board for several years, representing BNB's interests. But Jameson was seen as a reformer, pushing diversity, cutting edge technology and thought leadership in the industry. Connolly was politely referred to as "the hammer." During her tenure on the board, she had been the most vocal advocate for budget cutting and staff reductions.

Connelly was a complicated human being. She came from wealth and went to the best schools, graduating from Princeton University and completing her MBA at Harvard. But while imbued with a strong sense of entitlement, her detractors felt she was never comfortable in her own skin. Perhaps her physical looks contributed to what others perceived as her insecurity. She was described as rather short with dark black glasses and a round frame. She fit well into the BNB culture, a company with a reputation on Wall Street for being highly political and firing folks.

"Good morning," Andy warmly greeted Connelly during their first one-on-one meeting to review vault operations. "I've brought a deck of slides giving you some historical evidence of our progress on automating and centralizing the recordkeeping at Americlear. In addition, I have a copy of the plan I submitted after 9/11 to modernize equipment and decentralize vault operations away from New York. This plan languished because of the higher priority to decentralize data centers, but the goals here are significant to further protect the industry."

"Thank you for the material, Andy. You can leave that on the desk," Connolly responded as she turned to look at her computer. Andy sat patiently, hoping their meeting was not over so quickly. He wanted to plant seeds for the incoming CEO to consider during the early days of her orientation. Connolly continued scrolling through her email with the back of the chair facing Andy. Finally, she turned part way speaking over her shoulder,

"While taking steps to decentralize might be useful, I didn't join Americlear to spend money. Quite the opposite. We're just coming through the 2008-2009 financial crisis. I need every senior officer to help me cut expenses, regardless of whether the expenses are warranted."

Andy tried to explain that during Jameson's CEO tenure, she had broken down the cultural bias at Americlear limiting the ability of minorities and immigrants to work above street level. A small wave of vault employees managed to escape the basement through Jameson's sponsored internship program for executive assistants. Suddenly, Black, Latin and Asian faces began showing up in jobs and on floors they could only previously visit.

"Well, I'm not Jameson," Connelly indignantly responded. "I only care about the bottom line and how we're perceived by the board. So, get with the program Andy. If you're required to submit a 30% budget cut in vault operations, how will you achieve this expectation?"

The silence hung in the air. Andy felt a gut punch. The muscles in his neck tightened. His glasses began sliding down his nose helped along by the sweat forming on his brow. He worked hard to gain his composure.

"Daeva, if you look at my reports, you'll find our staffing of the vault has been reduced significantly. We are already operating on two shifts of employees working late into the evening. These folks have always performed in an exemplary way during a crisis, whether it's 9/11, the economic downturn in 2003 or the recent financial meltdown. While the markets may be in panic, the vault staff stepped up to manage the trading volume and recordkeeping. But at some point, our commitment to accuracy will suffer if our employees don't feel valued."

"Andy, you've been here a long time. I was told you are a "company man" so please remember your place. If you want to be an advocate for the frontline staff in the vault, consider switching careers to social work. I will not compromise on my commitment to show the industry tight fiscal controls, notwithstanding any collateral damage to our employees. Am I clear?"

"Yes," he responds.

"Ok, good meeting," Connolly responds. "You can go now," she states as she turns back to her computer.

Daeva Connolly joined Americlear in 2010 mid-year, almost 18 months before taking over as CEO. She was put in charge of the six major business units. This was intended to strengthen and broaden her command of the diverse financial sectors served by the company. There were many in Americlear's senior ranks that hoped the board's decision might change, after working with Connolly. It was clear she had a list of favorites among Americlear business leaders and senior staff, which often was driven by their tops-down willingness to follow their new leader. And if that message wasn't clear, it became so over her first year.

Connolly lived light years away from Americlear's history, values and employee contributions. She cared little for sacrifices made along the way in defining success. Through numerous downturns in the market and crisis events like 9/11, invariably these sacrifices by staff were met with patterns of layoffs, salary cutbacks, reduced benefits.

Andy finished dressing for work. He was up early today, but his wife Nancy would be there in the kitchen to greet him. The routine had not changed much since they were first married. As her husband sat down in a chair that allowed him to look out the back window, Nancy would bring over a cup of coffee and kiss his forehead.

"Andy, what's going on?" his wife asked. She had debated for several days about confronting her husband. It started with his tossing back and forth in his sleep. The restlessness only got worse as Andy began mumbling through the night. When the noise got louder, she would gently reach over to comfort and calm him. He had not experienced this disturbed sleep for almost a decade, following the 9/11 attack.

"You have to tell me so I can try to help you." This was classic Nancy, stepping in and standing by her man. She walked from the sink to put her arms around her husband's head and shoulders. Pulling him close, she kissed him again on the cheek.

"Nancy, I find myself going to work earlier, though I spend much of the time staring into space wondering about my purpose in life. I met the new woman, Connally, who will take over as CEO. It's a disaster. She's a disaster.

"When I came home from my tour in Vietnam, the world had changed for me. I was a different person having experienced war. Being one of the few who came home left me aware of how uncertain and yet grateful we should be when a light guides us to a safe landing.

"I wanted to do good things and be a positive force for my family – and in my job. But something is terribly wrong. The world I thought I knew is upside down.

My people sacrifice and trust me, because I feel like family to them. They know I will fight for them."

Andy sat silently for several minutes drinking his coffee. He could not look Nancy in the eyes. He feared she would see how despondent he had become.

After all these years, Nancy knew her husband needed time to collect himself. He wiped his eyes with the back of his hand. He set the cup down and looked to his wife for guidance.

"In my view, it's just a matter of time before Connolly turns her venom on us. She doesn't care about anyone. I'm angry because I doubt there is any safe landing now for me or my team. My staff's greatest weakness in this moment is their sense of loyalty to Americlear, beyond their own conditions and circumstances."

Nancy left the kitchen where her husband drank his morning

coffee. She didn't have answers to offer Andy. She prayed he'd find a way forward. She couldn't recall him ever feeling this way.

"I have to find a way to save them," Andy mumbled to himself. "I can't tell Nancy what I'm thinking. She doesn't understand and I know she wouldn't approve." The vault has been a source of safety for the industry, but it would be easy for a small well-organized group to walk the twenty feet from their mission to financial freedom.

He stood and put his coffee mug on the kitchen counter. "Could my team rise up and steal securities from Americlear?" he asked himself.

He didn't believe it was possible for those words to ever enter his thoughts. They certainly have the knowledge and expertise to do so. He quickly dismissed this idea as reckless fantasy. How could anything get so bad as to justify committing a crime. It was time to catch his train. For the first time, there was a restlessness in his soul. Andy didn't know the right answer – or the right path. Nancy was his anchor in life. She grounded him often, when he struggled with despair. He shook his head, as he put on his coat. He could only hope a sign would come soon to guide him.

CHAPTER 3
STELLA JONES 2010

Stella Jones went into a panic. She was fifteen minutes late for her job interview. She fumbled with her overstuffed purse at the security desk. It was unclear to her why the building had a security desk at the front entrance to the building and then the company, Americlear, had its own security desk and procedures. She looked at her watch again and frowned. I need this job; she kept telling herself.

Jose Ramos could see Stella was nervous as he approached. "Hi, I'm Joseph Ramos. I go by Jose. They sent me over to pick you up for your interview," he said with a smile. For a moment, Stella stared into space, tense and uncertain. "Look, it's ok," said Jose. "Everyone gets delayed by the security arrangements we have. You're not late. No one will hold this against you."

Stella took a deep breath and smiled. "I tried to make certain I was early for my interview. I had no idea there would be so many hoops to jump through."

"Welcome to our world," Jose responded. "This is the largest building on this side of lower Manhattan. After the terrorist attacks in 2001, everything changed. This building is the headquarters for Americlear and nearly ten other financial companies. Across the street is Goldman Sachs."

A puzzled look came over Stella. Jose had seen this before. "Don't worry, I didn't know who Goldman Sachs was either when I came to work here."

They walked almost the length of the building. Passing the four main banks of elevators that ran from the lobby to the 50th floor, Jose led Stella to a smaller bank of elevators at the rear. She stepped inside and glanced at the control panel and saw the elevator floors read lobby, SL1 (sub level 1), SL2 and C. Jose pushed C and stepped back. When the doors opened a minute later, Stella realized they were completely underground, several stories below the street.

She could immediately recognize a musty smell in the air. It was coming from the paper being stored in the vault. Her first thought was that it was like the smell of mushrooms.

"You smell it, don't you," Jose asked? "I did, too, when I first started the job down here. Now, I rarely pay attention. The good news is that the vault has very good temperature controls to keep humidity in the air. This helps reduce the smell. If there was no humidity, the paper stock certificates would smell like dirty socks. They'd dry out and the paper would chip and begin to crack into small pieces."

As they passed, Stella could see the two large steel doors. Jose stopped one more time to explain. "We can't physically open those doors by ourselves," Jose pointed out. The doors are three and one-half feet thick. I'm told they weigh nearly thirty tons. Computers instruct the vault doors to open and close. The walls are made of rebar-reinforced concrete, more than two feet deep."

Jose pointed down the hallway. "We'll have to go through one last security check at the turnstiles. The vault runs under more than half the entire building. Sorry, no windows down here. You won't know if it's raining, snowing or sunny outside."

By the time they reached Andy Russo's office, he was standing at the doorway smiling and chatting with two employees.

"Well, I'm glad you found your way," Andy said, as he extended his hand to welcome her. "Hi, I'm Andy Russo, but I usually go by Andy." He looked to be in late 50s or early 60s. He was short, maybe five foot six inches with thick wire rim glasses and a receding hairline. What stood out in Stella's mind, however, was the warmth she immediately felt in his presence. "Could I be this lucky to find a boss I could feel comfortable with?" she wondered.

Andy was struck by Stella's poise. She was a light skinned Black woman, nearly five foot eight inches tall, who had the posture and body of a dancer. He had been searching for an assistant for several months without success. He was hopeful Stella might be the one. He invited her into his office, and they sat down on either side of his cluttered desk.

"So, I know you have already met with our Human Resources department a few days ago, but tell me something about you I don't know," Andy asked.

"Ok," she responded as she sat up straight. "I'm 28 years old, a single mom. I live in the South Bronx. My mom is Italian, and my dad came to the U.S. from East Africa. Actually, it's southern Kenya.

"My mom's name is Bianca. Her family arrived here in the early 1900s from Italy. My dad, Kiko, came here as a teenager from Kenya. The story I'm told is that my father is a descendant of the Maasai warriors. He's a proud man who works two jobs to support the family. My mom named me after her aunt back in Italy. At home, my first language was Italian, which I still speak daily with my mom."

Andy laughed and shook his head. Is it possible he found an assistant who spoke Italian? He decided to test his newly found good fortune. Andy launched into asking Stella several questions in Italian. At first, a big smile came to her. Andy knew immediately what she was trying to say. "Ok, ok, I know my language skills are rusty," he responded. "My wife is Irish. It's been a long time since I had someone I could talk to in my native tongue."

Stella had a huge grin on her face. "No, you're Italian isn't that bad. Trust me, I hear worse here in New York."

"What else can you tell me about yourself?"

"Well, I really didn't learn English until I went to school. Got picked on a lot, but my parents taught me to keep pushing myself. I was dedicated in school, keen to read and learn. In time, my teachers thought I might go onto college. But I met a guy in high school. He was Italian and eight years older.

"His name was Nicholas 'Nico' Farentino. He had wavy black hair and broad shoulders. He literally swept me off my feet. He also had the most amazing black Pontiac Grand Prix, which we nicknamed "the rocket ship." I realize now the relationship was wrong. When I became pregnant, he promised to be there. But I think you heard this story before."

"Boy or girl?" Andy asked.

"A boy, Samuel. He's my pride and joy. He stays with my folks when I'm at work."

Andy listened patiently. Over his 35 years of working and managing people, he understood how life can trip you up from pursuing your dreams. What he admired in Stella was how direct and candid she could be. This young woman made no excuses for herself. Whatever mistakes she had made, she wasn't afraid to own them – and learn from them. As a boss, his first measure of an employee was their core values. The rest of the job, Andy knew, could be learned.

"Stella, since we're sharing, let me tell you something about my family.

I grew up in Bensonhurst, Brooklyn.

"My dad was a big strong working stiff, at six foot and two hundred twenty-five pounds. We looked up to him literary as well as figuratively. He spoke to us often about the discrimination his Italian parents faced coming to America. Did you know that more than half of the immigrants from the turn of the century eventually left and returned to Italy before WWII.

"My dad was my hero. He taught me valuable lessons about honesty and compassion. He managed a grocery store in Brooklyn and often missed dinner with the family. But we could feel the pride he took in his work. If someone lost their job or came up short with money one month, you could count on Tony Russo to meet you at the backdoor of the grocery store and quietly give you a box of food.

"Even the local mafia guys respected his commitment to helping families who needed it. They also accepted his unwillingness to cross the line or do anything illegal.

"Back in those days, I was a skinny, short kid with thick glasses. No one ever expected me to get in fights to defend my friends, but my father did expect me to speak the truth when it was required. The Bensonhurst part of Brooklyn where we lived had previously been Jewish. My father insisted I learn to respect folks who came from different cultures and religions. I didn't fully appreciate these life lessons until I was later called upon to defend them.

"Here at Americlear, my dad's lessons guide what I do here in the Vault. He taught me to value family and community. Luckily, we're down here in the basement away from those who may not share in these beliefs. Everyone here comes from somewhere else, but they all share a concern for each other."

After forty minutes, Andy asked Stella to walk with him so he could show her around the vault. "Leave your pocketbook and jacket here in my office. It's ok, it will be safe here.

"Stella, what we do down here in the basement of this building is routine, but important. I know it doesn't look like much, but it is a key part of what allows the financial system in the United States to function."

As they approached the vault, there was a steel cage blocking the entrance. Stella could see a turnstile on the far side, where Andy was headed. Inside the blocked entrance was a metal desk with a large man sitting behind it.

"Reggie, please say hello to Stella Jones. She's thinking about working here as my new assistant."

Reggie Seawright stood and came from behind his desk. He was a large man, with the shoulders of a linebacker. He greeted Stella as she passed through the turnstile. Her hand disappeared inside of Reggie's monstrous grip. But as big and strong as he appeared, she could tell there was a gentleness to his touch. He gave her a smile and a wink as he shook her hand. Then he turned back to his desk.

Andy walked nearly fifty feet inside the vault, before he stopped and turned to face Stella.

"We describe Americlear as a central securities depository. Maybe it's better that I explain we're like a bank, but instead of money, we keep paper stocks and electronic records of ownership. Many countries have a central securities depository, but none is as big as Americlear."

He explained to Stella that the vault held financial instruments or U.S. securities worth more than $37 trillion. Stella paused for a minute. She had never heard of a trillion dollars. How many millions of dollars were needed to reach a trillion? Her eyes rolled up to the ceiling, as she pondered $37 trillion. She could see the rows of files went for a far as she could see—and then beyond that point. There were also side corridors, with shelves lined with 8"x11" paper files filled to the brim.

Andy continued his introduction. "I know it looks like a maze down here in the vault, but there is a logic to how it's organized. These physical certificates represent the ownership record of major companies in the U.S. The certificates are held on behalf of millions of Americans who invest in stocks and other financial instruments. The securities industry has been moving away from paper certificates for over three decades. The financial regulators and firms we support are increasingly requiring investors to give up paper and accept keeping electronic ownership records on computers."

Andy's speech slowed and his voice became more dramatic. "If anything happened to these physical certificates or our ability to change the ownership of securities traded each day – or completing the payment of trades with financial firms – the U.S. markets would come to a screeching halt. That's a doomsday scenario no one in the world wants to think about.

"You'll see computer terminals both inside and outside of the vault, where a few designated employees have a security clearance to make changes in the certificate ownership records held in the vault. These changes are made based on a set of procedures you'll learn about when you come work here."

Andy's comment was not lost on Stella.

"When you come to work here?" she asked.

Andy smiled. "But only if you want to."

CHAPTER 4
AMERICLEAR'S CRITICAL MISSION: HOW U.S. MARKETS WORK

Stella Jones was attending the three-day orientation session with more than sixty other people. She felt certain she was the only person who didn't understand half the information being presented. As she poured some water and grabbed cookies during a break, she heard comments from other new staffers. She soon realized she was not alone.

Stella heard one new employee say, "I must have found 800 pages on the Internet about Americlear. Some of it said they were a secret company, but it looks like this cat's out of the bag." Stella promised herself she would do her own search of Americlear, as soon as she could afford to buy a computer.

During the second day of orientation, employees learned how their work contributed to the company's mission. Stella smiled at the number of eyeballs that rolled up toward the ceiling, as the HR folks used slides to introduce acronyms to identify each business unit. For most people attending the class, learning about Americlear was like an alphabet soup. Few had financial experience, so they didn't understand even the basics about the trading of financial instruments.

For most of the new employees, the third day turned out to be the best. Ben Klein, Americlear's Managing Director for Corporate Communications, explained the company's history and purpose. Ben had a gift for telling stories. He was able to describe Americlear's role in plain English. He didn't use a formal presentation, and his relaxed nature won over folks in the audience. Ben showed enthusiasm for how Americlear created certainty and reliability—and essentially helped grow the U.S. economy.

Ben enjoyed showing segments of old movies. "You see traders screaming and running around on the floor of the New York Stock Exchange (NYSE). Pieces of paper were thrown in the air, as trades were completed. By the end of the day, the floor was littered with trash." He used these visual images in describing how by the mid-1970s, the New York Stock Exchange was in total chaos. The exchange had to close one day a week, on Wednesdays. They needed a full day to catch up with the paper records keeping. In those days, they traded only 15 million shares of stock daily. "Today," Ben pointed out, "across stock exchanges and electronic trading platforms more than 2.3 billion shares of stock are traded each day in the U.S.

"During the 1970s," he explained as he strolled back and forth in front of the attendees, "our financial markets – and the U.S. economy could not grow unless the industry tackled automating the process.

"Before Americlear, the streets of lower Manhattan were flooded with an army of runners or part time employees who would deliver large envelopes or satchels filled with paper stock certificates. Financial firms sent checks for payment of trades.

"They called this period of history the 'paperwork crisis of the '70s' and, if not solved, everyone agreed the trading markets in the U.S. could not continue.

"It would take decades to convince small investors and brokerage firms to keep their paper stock certificates at a central location and not under the mattress at home. The anxiety and fear during the Great Depression in the 1930s when banks closed, were deeply ingrained in U.S. culture.

"True, no one really cares about Americlear's arcane process, but everyone understands that trading would come to a stop in the U.S. if payments for trading obligations were not completed each day and ownership records were not updated."

Ben stopped and turned to face everyone. "Let me end this presentation explaining a very basic principle of economics. The point is that people who invest money will always look to invest where it is cheapest to conduct business. Right now, the U.S. is not only the largest, but the cheapest market for investing and completing stock trading anywhere in the world. This flow of investment to our country helps grow our economy. People all over the world look to conduct their business and trading in the U.S. versus Europe or Asia. Automation has really allowed the U.S. to be more efficient, safer, more secure – and cheaper for trading stocks.

"After the break, I'll tell you the Americlear story of September 11, 2001. We don't really talk about this horrible day, but after I share this with you, you'll understand your purpose working here."

During the coffee break in the orientation program, Ben mingled with new employees. Stella Jones was standing with a group of other new hires when Ben interrupted to say hello. He wasn't like anyone she had known before. His blue suit, white shirt and red tie fit so well across his six-foot frame and broad shoulders. The mustache may have seemed odd, since few men she saw at Americlear had facial hair. He seemed so confident and spoke with such authority. She hung on his words, before realizing her attraction.

After the break, the employee orientation resumed. Ben walked into the audience and remained standing there as he shared the story of what he called "Americlear's finest hour."

"Ok, I want to share with you the details of an event that must stay within this room. The events of 9/11 are well known and tragic. Everyone would remember where they were, what they were doing and the shock they felt as the buildings came crashing down. We can never forget these events or the loss of loved ones and friends we all suffered."

Ben paused for a moment as he saw the audience nervously shifting in their seats. He wasn't consciously trying to scare these folks, but he knew it was critical for them to understand what was at stake. Americlear may be less than a household name, but without the security and safety provided by this organization the financial industry would cease to function.

He knew this event would be especially hard to talk about with these New York employees. He doubted there was anyone in the room who was not impacted or touched by the events of that day.

"When stocks are traded," he began, "investors and financial institutions have three days (T+3) to pay their trading obligations. If the payments are not made or if the ownership records aren't changed, the entire financial system in the U.S., and in other countries, will freeze up. No one will trade if there's uncertainty in the market about whether trading partners will complete paying their obligations. I hope that makes sense to you. You wouldn't keep selling or buying stock if you weren't certain you'd be paid.

"Yes, a question from the young lady on the right?"

"But I thought the stock exchanges didn't open on 9/11? Why was there a threat, if no one here was trading stocks?"

"Good question," Ben responded.

"Yes, on 9/11 the New York Stock Exchange and Nasdaq markets did not open or opened and then immediately closed after the attack. But U.S. trading had been going on for three days before 9/11, with billions of dollars owed for the payment of those trades. Everyone in the U.S. – and the world – feared the system would breakdown.

"In the midst of this chaos, Judy Jameson, our Chairman and CEO at that time, made a critical decision to keep Americlear open and operating after the 9/11 attack. Our location downtown was ten blocks from the World Trade Center. The cloud of dust from debris filled the air. The National Guard was sent in to seal off Lower Manhattan. If Americlear employees did not immediately leave the building, they would be prevented from exiting until calm was restored in New York City. No one was certain if this would be days or weeks.

"Judy Jameson asked 350 key employees to remain in the building and at Americlear's backup data centers, to staff critical areas, including the vault, and to help financial firms who lost their workspace. Americlear had long ago prepared a backup facility in another location in New York, which their bank and brokerage customers would use to regain control of their operations. The bulk of our employees were sent home before the troops arrived on the evening of September 11."

Ben could see his audience was transfixed. In some instances, employees were sitting on the front edge of their chairs, fearing they might not hear the details. He could also see their eyes widen as he talked.

"Please keep in mind that in the aftermath of the initial attack, no one was certain if the danger was behind us. No one knew the sound of jets over New York was the National Guard flying Combat Air Patrols. The uncertainty led some Americlear executives to dive under a desk when the planes roared outside.

"But our CEO rallied her team to focus on the task before them. Americlear could not immediately verify whether the electronic method of sending payments through the wire service run by the Federal Reserve was working. There was also the challenge for banks and brokerage firms who were located at the World Trade Center to internally issue instructions for payments.

"Judy Jameson started hourly calls with the Federal Reserve to ensure the Fedwire system was able to transfer payments. Calls by Americlear senior executives with financial institutions would verify their ability to send payments. Down in the vault, employees were entering ownership instructions and pulling physical certificates.

"On 9/11, Americlear stayed open and settled $180 billion in trading obligations. Between Tuesday, 9/11 and that Friday, Americlear settled $1.8 trillion in payments for completed trades that were in the pipeline. The goal of reopening U.S. financial markets required that all trading from the prior three days was settled and paid for. By the following Monday, the trading markets reopened, and a clear message was communicated globally about American resilience being achieved. The story is rarely told, but this goal was accomplished behind the scenes through the efforts of Americlear."

Ben Klein stopped at this point to catch his breath and took a long pause to emphasize his message.

"So, as you come to work here as a new employee, you can take pride in the critical role Americlear plays in the financial well-being of our country, our economy – and the admiration this company inspires around the world. We are not a household name. That's ok. No one here is in it for the glory. This is a company where people's passion and commitment are the driving force. You may not succeed in explaining the arcane nature of what we do to your family, but what is more important is that you're here to make a difference."

When Ben finished his story, the audience erupted with applause. As the spokesperson for Americlear, he so enjoyed the story telling part of his job.

CHAPTER 5
EDITH COLON: ACCURACY AND ATTENTION TO DETAIL MATTERS

"Look Stella," Andy explained, "the best way to learn and build relationships down here in vault operations is to work side-by-side with your colleagues. That may seem old school, but even after my long tenure at Americlear I'm still gaining insights and knowledge from the folks who work in the vault.

"Let's start by having you spend part of each day working with one of your colleagues," he told her as they walked down the corridor to the vault.

Reggie Seawright took Stella to the locker room outside the vault, which was where employees were required to keep all their personal belongings.

"Stella, there are a lot of security precautions down here. No one can wear a sports jacket, bring a purse, backpack or briefcase into the vault. Our security procedures are like a gold vault inside a bank. Employees and visitors may be subject to periodic spot inspections to ensure no physical securities are removed. You'll also see cameras covering virtually the entire area inside the vault."

Reggie returned with Stella to the vault turnstiles. He introduced her to several of her new colleagues. Aside from learning about her job, Andy wanted her to see that each of these employees had their own back story of struggle and survival. He turned her over to Edith Colon, who took her on a quick tour.

"Before we head back to my section of the vault, we should show you the breakroom they created for us. The idea was to reduce the traffic going in and out of the vault. The decision to have a breakroom was largely driven by our Corporate Security folks on the 32nd floor of the building."

Edith Colon was a senior clerk in the vault. She was a warm, gregarious person. In her late 50s, she had worked at Americlear almost two decades. Stella's first impression was that she looked like the actress Rosie Perez. Edith essentially pulled and placed physical certificates in the designated files arranged by the financial firm. Her job also involved helping others make digital copies of the certificates. She did not have permission to enter a change of ownership on the computers.

"So, here's where I spend my day. Our jobs down here are routine and boring, but it does require accuracy. The next three rows of shelving that you see are where I primarily work supporting dozens of major financial institutions. Beyond this area, the shelves go back as far as you can see. My section includes Jumbo stock certificates, which are organized by the financial institution they belong to. At the stock exchanges or on the 50+ electronic platforms that trade stocks in the U.S., for example, American Express stock may be sold throughout the day. So, you're looking at millions of shares of stock sold or bought each day.

"Goldman Sachs, for example, may own 100,000 shares of American Express for its customers. At Goldman's request, we hold a Jumbo certificate for the 100,000 shares. Goldman Sachs then has its own computers that will tell them Stella Jones owns 100 or 1,000 shares. It is so much easier for the institutions to have these large Jumbo certificates, though looking ahead to the future we're trying to keep these ownership records on computers versus having paper certificates."

"But I still don't understand your job," Stella said. "What do you have to do with these certificates?"

"Well," Edith explained as she motioned to Stella to walk down the aisle, "every day as the ownership of stock changes, we must pull these Jumbo certificates or smaller individual stock certificates and update the physical piece of paper and the computer records. Yes, it's tedious as hell. Yes, we get tired doing these repetitive tasks, but there's no alternative way to keep these records. All day long, we're either pulling certificates from the shelves or filing new or amended certificates back into the files. Updating the computers is a lot easier.

"But the process of pulling individual stock certificates off the shelf to update the owner's name, the company's name or the number of shares being held takes enormous patience and time." Edith paused to reach for a file on the shelf. She then continued walking, "Today, brokerage firms charge their customers extra fees to cover the expense of holding paper certificates, but this is because many small investors don't trust electronic records.

"The work here is truly menial, as are the wages we're paid. However, no one disputes that without the physical work we perform, the markets aren't ready to rely solely on electronic records. So, I guess we keep the ship afloat and the trading markets operating seamlessly.

"I'm done with my current batch of filing," Edith said. "Follow me. We can grab a coffee or tea in the break room."

Stella reminded herself that Andy encouraged her to learn the job but also ask her colleagues about their back stories. "You need to understand how folks got here to understand their families and their values," Andy would tell her.

"Edith, were you born in America?"

"Why, do you hear my accent? Don't worry, I'm not offended."

"I came to the United States in 1960, during the "Great Migration" from Puerto Rico. I was only five years old. Usually, you lose an accent if you're younger than 12 when you come, but we only spoke Spanish at home. The Colon family had for a century worked in agriculture, but this all changed during World War II (WWII).

"Industrialization had taken root in my country. My parents told me our island was often called the Pearl Harbor of the Caribbean, supporting Navy ships and the Army's Borinquen Airfield. Men left the farms and flooded the mechanical trades. Women also left farming to provide support in factories supporting the American war effort.

"After WWII, our family struggled. The farming life had been abandoned. My father, Luis had joined the more than 65,000 Puerto Ricans who signed up for the Army to fight for the United States. But coming back from WWII, with two children born after the war, the family only had an income of $3,000 annually.

"War preparation and automation changed our agricultural society. Immigrants slowly left Puerto Rico over time to find new opportunities in America. Between the 1950s to 1960 nearly 21% of the island's population (470,000 people) desperate for jobs surged northward.

"We had relatives living in New York who promised my dad that finding a job would not be hard and he could make a better living. The Colons said their goodbyes to their parents and left. No one was certain if they'd ever return. In the U.S., our family shared an apartment with a cousin's family for two years, until we could afford renting a place of our own in East Harlem.

"My father, Luis, found it difficult finding a job. The market for Puerto Ricans workers who barely spoke English was not good. And much to his surprise, Luis' Army service during the war did not open doors. The contributions and sacrifices made by his island community were quickly forgotten. Alondra, my mom, found work at a local clothes cleaner, ironing shirts and dresses. Luis eventually found work at a small bodega in the neighborhood. While most children were oblivious to the world around them, I was not that child. I still remember hearing my parents arguing about their financial difficulties.

"I was a good student at school and learned English quickly. However, my older sister Val (short for Valencia) was not so lucky. At 14 years old, Val struggled with speaking or reading in English. East Harlem soon became her island away from home. Most neighbors only spoke Spanish, and our families remained isolated from the world beyond 96th street."

"Wow, that's an amazing story," Stella responded. "Are you still close with your sister?"

"Yes, Val was like a mother and sister, because our parents

worked to support the family. If I got sick, Val would stay home from school to care for me. Our parents never let go the dream that their children might one day have a better life. But Val eventually quit school at 15. She took a job sweeping floors at a local hairdresser's shop. It took her several years to learn and work her way up to cutting hair. I was determined to finish high school, but going to college was just too costly. Life was not kind to our struggling immigrant family from Puerto Rico, but nothing could dampen our pride and love for each other.

"Ok, break time is over," Edith said as she got up from the table. "Stella, you haven't told me your story.

"Wait. If you didn't go to college, how did you get your job at Americlear? And you didn't tell me if you have a family of your own?"

The two women continued talking as Edith grabbed a stack of certificates to put on the shelves.

"Enough about me," Edith told her, "Let's focus on our daily routine."

Stella didn't wait to be told what to do. She charged ahead placing certificates in the files on shelves. "Look, I'm sorry Edith," Stella explained, "I may make a mistake, but I don't want to stand by while you do all the work."

Edith smiled. Stella was more mature than she expected. "Do you see these shelves over there on your left?" Edith asked. "These shelves are color coded. The green ones are home to the certificates of Zicron Technologies owned by Bobbie Yates. I remember. It was somewhere in the mid-1980s when Yates came to Americlear. There must have been three vans filled with his certificates and two carloads of security personnel. We made the guys with guns wait outside."

Stella wasn't quite certain what to make of this story about Zicron. She had not heard of the company.

"Look Stella, the green shelves go up to the ceiling and they cover the whole length of two bookshelf rows. I understand from Andy, when Zicron launched its IPO. Wait, I'm sorry, you may not understand. The letters for IPO represent when a company first starts to sell stock or ownership in their company. It's called an initial public offering (IPO), and it can be worth millions of dollars.

"This guy Yates was only thirty-five years old. When he came to Americlear, he was a young, skinny boy with wire-rim glasses, and he was surrounded by Cinco giant 'chicos fornidos.'" Edith and Stella started laughing.

She explained that Yates at that time owned forty-nine percent of the company. The carts loaded with stock certificates kept coming off three trucks parked at the side entrance to Americlear's building. Yates dropped off stock certificates representing over 11 million shares of Zicron. "Andy told us within two to three days, those stock shares were worth $258 million. And today, those shares are worth billions of dollars."

Over the next several days, Edith and Stella grew close and laughed often. While more than two decades of age separated them, they still could relate to a shared immigrant experience of struggle. There was enormous pride working for a company like Americlear, but Edith also talked about friends who lost their jobs in 2003. After the 9/11 attack, the country faced a financial downturn.

Americlear would not be immune from staff reductions. However, it was clear employees who worked below the street level of the building fared worse than jobs defined as "professional" or "technical" positions. The vault staff was cut from twenty-four to fifteen employees.

"Morale sank to a new low. It was so wrong for management to eliminate our jobs. The workload down here in the vault didn't diminish. The volume of paper grew. Our management could have found those cuts upstairs. We felt the vault was targeted because no one really cares about us. The stress to keep up with the physical workload was always on everyone's mind."

CHAPTER 6
BEING MENTORED: BRUISED AND BONDING

A month passed. Stella came off the elevator one morning wearing a big floppy hat and dark sunglasses. Reggie Seawright was standing at the turnstiles greeting employees and instinctively knew something was wrong. He begged off from his conversation with Jose Ramos and followed Stella down the hall to her desk.

"How are you today, Ms. Jones?" Reggie asked. He towered over the young woman, who sat down with her coat on. Stella was crying, which caught him by surprise. In her short time at Americlear, everyone on staff called her "a ray of sunshine," and "one of the most upbeat and personable people I've ever met."

But on this morning, a wounded Stella Jones showed up to work. "Hey, you ok?" Reggie asked quietly. "You can talk to me. I got your back. You don't need to be hiding anything. We're family here, and we look out for each other."

Stella wasn't certain what to say or do, but she knew keeping her situation a secret was not an option. She raised her head and took off the hat and sunglasses. Her left eye was swollen and circled by a dark purple ring.

The tears rolled down her face.

"Who did this to you?" he asked angrily. "Were you mugged coming to work?" Reggie's fist clenched when she responded. "It was Nico," Stella responded. "He came over to see our son yesterday. Sometimes, he just can't control his anger. He can't stand it that I'm strong and independent. And he's bothered that I'm working and trying to move on without him. The crazy thing is that he's had a girlfriend for a very long time now, but he still thinks he owns me."

Reggie knew it was better to just listen. But he couldn't accept the idea of a man hitting a woman, for any reason or at any time.

Reggie Seawright fit the image of a gentle giant. At 37 years old, he stood six foot five inches, 290 pounds. A former NFL football player from a small college in New Jersey, Reggie was so close to his dream as a defensive linebacker when he blew out his right knee. A college degree and two kids later, Reggie was happy just to have a job at Americlear.

"Stella, I'm sorry you have to deal with this guy," Reggie said. "It's so difficult to cut the cord when you share a child together. But you can always talk to me when you're down or struggling. All of us think you're quite special. We're here for you.

"I'll give you some private time this morning. When I see Andy, I'll suggest he keep you out of the vault for a few days. Everyone doesn't need to know your business. Is that ok?"

When you're at your absolute worst, the simple kindness of words or an outstretched arm can help make your troubles more bearable. She wiped the tears running down her cheek with the back of her hands. She then nodded in agreement to Reggie. He had no idea how special she felt at that moment.

Andy arrived fifteen minutes later. It was unlike Andy to reach the office after his employees. His office lights were usually snapped on by 7:30 a.m., almost an hour before employees normally arrived. He was the sort of boss who enjoyed walking down to the elevator and hanging out with his morning coffee as he greeted employees. He always wanted to have the pulse of his staff; to understand what was going on in their lives outside of work. In a stuffy, hierarchical organization like Americlear, it was uncommon to find bosses or supervisors who were this genuine.

The news about Stella shocked him, but Andy realized his best response was no response. He decided not to acknowledge her swollen eye. He would keep Stella close to her desk, and he'd focus on being her friend.

He decided to try and distract Stella with some of his own stories. His young assistant sat in his office, as Andy talked about the early years. He was now 61 years old, but his career started with the Central Certificate Service (CCS) in 1972.

After completing a college degree in Art History, Andy told her his dream was to one day work at the Metropolitan Museum of Art. He recounted how his parents would take him to the museum as a child to reward his progress at school.

"I just fell in love with that place. I couldn't draw, but the beauty of the paintings lifted me up in ways I could not express.

"I considered myself one of the lucky ones. I couldn't avoid the Vietnam War draft, but my brother was also serving, so I was assigned jobs behind the front lines. Knowing what I know now, I considered it a blessing that I made it home in one piece. My brother also came back, answering our parents' prayers. But finding a job during a very tough economic period in the 1970s had me depressed for months. It was like no one cared for those who served.

Finally, my uncle, Lou Ragano, offered to help my family find me a job after nine months of unemployment in 1973. My Uncle Lou was a big shot in the back office of Shearson. He served on various industry groups and committees working on the so-called "paperwork crisis."

Andy explained that the 1960s and 1970s were the glamour years, when major corporations in America used their stock certificates as branding tools and, indeed, many looked like works of art. Companies paid huge sums to create the most colorful and compelling graphic images on these paper certificates. Small investors were motivated to buy stock simply to gift drawings of Disney's Mickey Mouse or Coca Cola's logo to a loved one. The growing competition among Fortune 500 companies to advertise their brand on physical securities would eventually run counter to the financial industry's need to eliminate paper. But no one cared. Companies didn't worry if stock certificates were lost. Not their problem.

Stella listened patiently. She welcomed the distraction. Some of the stories seemed to track closely with Ben Klein's presentation at her orientation. But Andy's version had so much more color to it. "Thirty years ago, the Vault didn't exist. Wall Street was threatened with chaos.

Andy paused to sip his coffee and continued. "I joined a small group of recent college grads who were hired at CCS to figure out how to introduce various new computer technologies. My sub-group would focus on the first IBM personal computers introduced in the mid-1970s for bank recordkeeping and innovative copying equipment from Xerox. How could this technology be used for duplication of documents from brokerage firms?"

Andy sat smiling as he reminisced. "I know it sounds silly now, with all the automation that has followed. I probably sound like a relic from the Stone Age or something, but I was part of a team that changed the world of financial services forever."

"You know what?" Andy paused. "I think you need to spend a day or two with Ben Klein. He's worked at the clearing corporation side of the business and can better explain this relationship with the vault. Besides, it will get you out of the basement for a few days.

"I'll call Ben and see if he can do this early next week. In the meantime, I'll let you work on these management reports that I must turn in on Friday. You can take a break from meeting the staff in the vault."

CHAPTER 7

BEN KLEIN: TRUST BETWEEN FRIENDS

It took Stella a good fifteen minutes to find her way to the 48th floor. It didn't help that there were six banks of elevators in the building. Each bank serviced floors belonging to different companies, including Standard and Poor's (one of the largest credit rating agencies in the U.S.), Mercer and a dozen more firms.

Trying to find Ben's office on the executive floors of Americlear reminded her the building where she worked was enormous.

Ben Klein was talking on the phone to a news reporter when she arrived. His assistant, Natalie Rodgers, greeted Stella. She could tell almost immediately that it was Stella, because she seemed a little lost. Stella kept looking down each of the many side hallways trying to find her way.

"Ben, Stella is here," Natalie casually said poking her head in the office.

"Okay, great," Ben responded. He didn't wait for the formalities. Ben sprung from his chair to greet her at the door. "C'mon in. Welcome."

Stella followed Ben back into the office. It was one of the largest offices she had ever seen. There were two walls of windows looking out on New York City. At one end was a huge desk with two black leather chairs in front. At the other end, there was a green suede couch against the wall with two beige side chairs and a large oak wood coffee table in the middle.

She stood motionless for a minute, looking at the impressive art collection that adorned the two walls. Over the couch was an eight-foot-long Chinese watercolor painting of waterfalls and the countryside. On the coffee table sat a large green verdite elephant from Zimbabwe, maybe two feet tall. Near Ben's desk was a bookshelf, where he had a brown bust of a female Maasai warrior. Above the bookshelf hung another Chinese watercolor painting of a tiger.

"May I ask about the bust of the Maasai woman?" Stella inquired. "Did you get it while you were traveling?"

"No, I haven't traveled to any of these places," Ben responded. "But I do have an interest to explore the world someday. Right now, I'm limited to the business travel I do in Europe. I love the Maasai sculpture. I do believe there is beauty in every culture."

"My father is a descendent of the Maasai," Stella said.

"I'm confused," Ben replied.

"Well, my skin isn't that dark because my mom came from Italy," Stella responded.

"Fascinating. I know there's a story there, which I hope you will share at some point. Oh, and just to be clear. I didn't ask for an office this big," Ben laughed. "So, don't think this really matters to me. There are some outdated customs at Americlear that the size of your office is automatically linked to your title and role at the company. You should see the executive offices on the 50th floor. These customs from the banking industry disappeared more than a decade ago. I'm certain in the not-too-distant future this will change here as well.

"Let's sit over here by my desk, if that's ok," said Ben. "I have to keep an eye on the phone in case our CEO calls."

Initially, Stella felt fidgety and nervous sitting across from Ben. He had an intensity in his eyes, which at times felt like they could see through her. "How is this possible?" she thought to herself. "Why am I attracted to a guy I don't even know?" she wondered to herself. "Get a grip, girl. Klein is out of your league."

Ben engaged in small talk for a half hour. He let her know Andy was very high on her – and that endorsement counted.

"Stella, I have a surprise for you," Ben said. "I wasn't certain if I could get us on the schedule, but we're due to visit the New York Stock Exchange (NYSE) at 10:30 this morning. If I'm going to explain clearance and settlement, it might help to see a trading environment."

Stella sat up in her chair. She was in shock. No one told her she was going on a field trip. She had no idea what happened on a trading floor. The video employees watched during their orientation program were borrowed from old Hollywood movies. She recalled one with the actor Eddie Murphy, with traders shouting their instructions and throwing paper in the air as they ran across the floor.

When they arrived at the stock exchange, the security was even more challenging than at Americlear. Alice Cantor, a friend of Ben's, from the Corporate Communications group at the exchange, came down to the entrance of the building. Yet even her presence as an escort could not force any easing up on the strict security procedures. By 11:15 a.m., Stella Jones found herself walking across the trading floor. Surprised, she didn't see any of the chaos from the orientation videos. Men were dressed in blue NYSE jackets. They calmly huddled around computer screens. Ben explained how changes in technology had automated the trading environment. Traders now use PalmPilots and iPhones to conduct trading.

"Stella, that Eddie Murphy film you watched, well that was at the height of the so-called 'paperwork' crisis. In the mid-1970s, traders filled out paper tickets when they bought or sold a stock. The paper ticket was handed to a runner, who ran back there," said Ben pointing to the rear of the building, "where a data clerk sat and entered information into one computer.

"The whole purpose of selling stock, Stella, is to help companies raise money, so they can invest in their products and grow their profits. The value of using computers today seems obvious, but at one time folks were truly skeptical that technology would change anything."

After touring the trading floor of the stock exchange, Ben took Stella up to the balcony overlooking the entire exchange. This was the vantage point most people see on TV when the exchange opens or closes. He explained how a bell rings to open the exchange. The balcony is usually filled with people from companies who have their stock listed (or traded) on the exchange. That same honor is extended at the end of the day, when the bell rings to end trading.

Stella had never seen TV coverage of the stock exchange. She thought it must be exciting that everyone on the balcony and the trading floor started clapping at the opening or closing bell. It was especially cool to hear Ben describe how, on occasion, the exchange might invite celebrities, i.e., actors, rock n' rollers or other famous political leaders, writers or scientists.

The walk from the exchange back to the company was only six or seven blocks. Ben invited Stella to stop at the local Starbucks to grab a coffee. His afternoon would be filled with meetings. He promised to take her to lunch on Thursday. For now, he was desperate for caffeine.

As they sat down, Ben paused for a moment before he spoke.

"So, tell me about you," Ben said. She described her son, Sam, as a gift she had been given in life. The bruise on her left eye was still visible. Ben didn't want to pry, but Stella also didn't want to hide the truth.

"If you noticed the eye," she pointed out, "I have an overly possessive ex-husband, Nico. I'm dealing with it." Ben could see Stella faced some tough challenges. He wasn't in a rush to go beyond what she was willing to tell him. As she talked for ten or fifteen minutes, He could feel himself being drawn in. Ben was nearing 40 and had been on his own too long.

"Ok," Stella leaned forward in her chair. "What can you share with me?"

"Stella, my job is mostly telling stories to help news reporters understand what we do as a company; both its complexity and the important contributions we make.

"With employees, I help communicate our CEO's vision. This was Judy Jameson's reason for appointing me to the job. At the time, the senior management team was all men at Americlear. She knew the men resented the idea of a woman being in charge. I believe Jameson saw herself as a change agent.

"Now I know you met Natalie. I hired her through a special intern program started by Jameson, which allowed minority employees who worked in the vault or other operations areas to train and become executive assistants. It was one of Jameson's first initiatives to signal change at Americlear."

Ben pointed out that the executive team at the company finally realized Jameson was serious about transforming the company, when she later appointed a Black man to become the Chief Financial Officer (CFO), and she promoted a woman to take over as General Counsel.

Stella sat shocked at Ben's candor. This guy was more real and direct than she could imagine. He was likely a valued contact to have at the company. He had personal integrity.

But she wondered if Ben could be as open and honest with her about his life? He talks about business. Is he afraid to talk about himself?

"Look, if we're going to be friends...and I hope that will happen," Ben told her, "You need to trust that I'll always be honest with you. I won't pull any punches. I don't want you to think Americlear is perfect. It's not. A company is only as good as the folks running the organization. I may be the firm's spokesperson, but I can tell the difference between the PR positioning and the bullshit."

Stella was in a good mood after returning from her morning with Ben. She let go of wearing the hat down over her face and the sunglasses that shielded her black eye. Luckily, none of her colleagues working in the vault saw her before she returned to her desk near Andy's office. Her boss had left for meetings upstairs. She wouldn't see him the rest of the day, which gave her some time to think to herself.

Two days later, Ben sat at the round table in his office with Stella to explain Americlear's role in clearance and settlement. She found it funny how he drew pictures on a white pad to help him explain the company or how trades were paid for. The man had no artistic talent. He tried, however, using boxes, circles and stick figures to illustrate his ideas.

"In the 70s, 80s and into the 90s, computers would 'match' or 'compare' the computer records from the firms and the exchange. Each day financial firms would get one report 'confirming' their trades and how much money they owed or was owed to them. This report was also sent to Americlear, which waited for financial firms to deliver checks to pay their obligation. We would change their ownership records, once a check for payment was received. Does that make any sense? I've tried to explain this as simply as I can," Ben told her.

"What's amazing is that each financial firm makes only one payment to our firm each day. Think about the trillions of dollars spent on trading each day, but it all gets boiled down to one check payment per firm. Today, as the system has been further automated, the payment of trading obligations at Americlear is done electronically over something called the Fedwire system," he explained.

Ben could see Stella's eyes were starting to glaze over. He knew she wasn't going to be an expert in clearance and settlement. But she could see how enthusiastic he was to explain why Americlear plays such a critical role.

"Let's take a break," Ben suggested. "We can go for an early lunch. I think I should be fair since you shared so much the other day. What do you want to ask me? Come up with 10 questions and I'll do my best to give you answers, I promise. In the meantime, we can walk over to Delmonico's. It's three blocks from here. They have great salads and steaks, if you prefer meat."

As they walked, the silence between them was deafening. Stella's mind was racing with questions she wanted to ask. If this was her only opportunity, she was not going to waste it.

Entering Delmonico's near Williams Street was like a trip back into the 1940s, with white tablecloths and waiters wearing black ties and tuxedos. Along the entire back wall was a bar, where some patrons enjoyed a liquid lunch before going back to work. But the excesses of 1980s on Wall Street were gone, and few settled for a two-hour cocktail break. Delmonico's proximity at the cross streets of dozens of financial firms kept the restaurant a perfect venue for networking and good lunch conversation.

"Ok, so why aren't you married?" Stella blurted out before they were fully seated.

Ben shook his head and started laughing. "Wow, I didn't see that question coming." It was his turn to blush at her directness. He paused to collect his thoughts.

"Well, I was married once," Ben said.

Stella was shocked. She expected some long story about being obsessed with work and never finding the right woman. "I'm sorry. Do you mind explaining," she responded.

"We met in college. Both of us were English majors. She was blond, a terrific dancer, great sense of humor and had a killer smile. We started dating in our sophomore year and got married going into our senior year. We were favored by the professors in the English department who thought it was cute that we attended Shakespeare classes together. We were together almost 10 years. But as we were nearing our 30s, we discovered we wanted different things.

"So, did you leave her?" Stella asked.

"No." Ben responded. "It was actually the other way around."

"I'm sorry I asked," Stella said. "I didn't mean to bring something up that might seem hard to talk about."

"It's okay. The sense of loss does soften over time. Besides, I believe if you truly love someone," Ben stated, "I mean truly love them…it never stops. I believe love is unconditional. We don't own people in life. We separated and then divorced, but we talk once or twice a year. We remain close friends."

"I hope I didn't cross any lines asking that question?" Stella asked. "You sort of surprised me the other day when you were critical about racial attitudes at Americlear. I guess I was curious how real a person you could be. I'm beginning to understand why Andy has such trust and faith in you."

"Tell me about some of the people you're meeting in Andy's group," Ben said.

Stella launched into her descriptions of Edith Colon, Jose Ramos and Reggie Seawright. "Reggie Seawright is a prince. He's like an older brother who looks after me. I really love that guy so much. And then there's Jennie Li Zhou.

Ben was fascinated by Stella's description of her new hero, Jennie Li, who was a deputy administrator of vault operations responsible for the computerized record changes of stock ownership. They had worked together only a week, but the two women bonded. Jennie Li was a strikingly tall Asian woman, almost 5' 8" tall with natural curves "in all the right places," according to Stella. Jennie Li was a role model at 31 years old. She had never been married and wasn't certain if she ever wanted to be.

Jennie Li's parents brought her to the U.S. as a young child with her brother, Jie.

In the late 1970s, the Chinese government started to go after families that violated its one child policies. The Zhou family fled Communist China in the middle of the night. They were hidden in the bottom of small Sampan junk boat that crawled along the coast from Shenzhen to Hong Kong. The trip was only 35 miles, but the boat captains (usually women) were not keen to get stopped hauling stowaways. These refugee boat trips were more lucrative than fishing. But they were fraught with the danger of capture and having your boat seized by the government. By midnight, the waters were calm. The trip could take several hours. The goal was keeping the speed and engine noise at a minimum.

Jennie Li thrived after arriving in America. Her father is a 'Sifu' or master of martial arts. He gained a following soon after his arrival. Both Jennie Li and her brother Jie trained every day, to learn discipline and fighting skills. The Zhou family rejected the often-common decision to avoid learning English. In New York's Chinatown in the outer borough of Flushing, Queens, one could live their entire life speaking only Mandarin or Cantonese. Families lived this way for several generations. But Jennie Li and her brother were sent to a school that required them to learn and speak English flawlessly. At home, the children spoke to their parents in Cantonese, having come from Guangzhou in Southern China.

Jennie Li graduated from City University of New York with honors. She was hired by Americlear to manage a staff of computer input clerks, who updated stock ownership records each trading day. She still lives at home with her parents near Main Street in Flushing.

Stella paused while eating her salad, "Ben, every time I think about my life's challenging twists and turns, I think about Jennie Li fleeing with her parents to escape a very different life in China. I'm so excited to talk to her. And can you imagine her kicking the butts of boys she fought with every day? She's such a badass."

Ben and Stella laughed for several minutes at her calling Jennie Li a badass.

CHAPTER 8
GIULIA SAMARTINO: COPING WITH LIFE AND LOSS

After two months, Stella finally met Andy's favorite person in vault operations. However, it took her some time to truly understand why.

At 62, Giulia Samartino was a senior vault supervisor and the oldest veteran on the team. She had been with Andy from the beginning and was responsible for Americlear's large collection of money market instruments, corporate bonds and bearer bonds.

Working with Giulia, Stella began to see that what set Giulia apart was her quiet, reserved and soft-spoken nature. Giulia represented a different perspective on life. She discovered her family had immigrated from Naples after World War II and settled in a small apartment near Little Italy in Manhattan. Giulia finished high school and married Enzo, a nice neighborhood boy.

She rarely missed a day of work. Even during snowstorms, Giulia could be counted on to show up. Other staff members living in Manhattan would call in and be absent, but she would not disappoint her boss. He had given her a job that helped her provide for her family. Andy was her hero.

Giulia's husband, Enzo, died prematurely from cancer. She was dedicated to helping Mia, her grown daughter, who struggled to care for her own special needs child. Mia worked at a local restaurant in Brooklyn. Giulia's financial support was critical helping Mia pay for caregivers and special education tutors to help Giana, her grandchild. She was grateful beyond words when Andy protected her during employee layoffs. Loyalty to Russo was never discussed, but to her he was family.

"Stella, our days are filled with pulling physical pieces of paper out of the files on the shelves. Much of this activity is related to the change in ownership after trading is completed. But there are other functions performed here. For example, when a company changes its name or merges with another company, we call this a reorganization. We are required to remove the old certificates and then replace it with a new one.

"We all struggle with some level of boredom associated with the job. The younger members of the vault team listen to music while they file or pull certificates from the shelves. This isn't really permitted under the security procedures in the vault. Senior management wants us to concentrate on our accuracy. If Jose, for example, incorrectly files a certificate, Edith Colon will spend days going through their files to find the missing certificate. You can tell when something like this happens. You'll see Edith looking up at the ceiling and saying out loud, 'Lord give me strength.'

Stella and Giulia laughed at the story, but Stella knew there was a lesson there about not taking the work for granted. Edith was committed to helping reinforce the vault team's reputation for accuracy.

"We all love Jose Ramos," Giulia told her. "He just a good soul, well-meaning and hard working. If a cart holding hundreds of files breaks, Jose will be there in milliseconds to help retrieve the files strewn across the floor. He'd never let Edith or Henry Wong struggle with such a mess on their own. Yes, he makes mistakes. But we hold out hope he will get better at this with time."

They walked the rows and shared stories as they went along. Like Andy, Giulia was impressed with the fact Stella could speak Italian.

Giulia stopped to show Stella the floor locations in the vault marked X, Y and Z painted on the floor.

"According to urban legend," she began, "these three areas are the only places in the vault where the security cameras cannot record the staff." Each of these floor areas were painted light gray and none of them are larger than a dining room table.

"But who knows if it's true!" said Giulia.

Ironically, the area marked X is near the yellow coded shelving. Giulia pointed out that this is where Americlear keeps the remaining bearer bonds that still exist in the United States. "These bonds are unlike any other financial instrument. These bonds are the same as holding cash."

She could see Stella's eyes roll up toward the ceiling. "Okay, let me try again. There are no actual owners of bearer bonds. Giulia pulled a piece of paper from one of the files. "Here, look at this bond. There's no number on the bonds to identify an owner. And there's no central registry anywhere in the world where you can see the names of the bond owner."

"But why is that?" Stella asked. "Why not have ownership records?"

Stella kept turning the bond over as if looking for a number or name.

"Bearer bonds go back to the Civil War period in the U.S. The bonds could be issued in very large sums of money," Giulia pointed out. "Stella, that one piece of paper you're holding is worth over $1 million."

Both Giulia and Stella stared at each other and began laughing for several minutes. The thought that you could just grab a piece of paper worth so much money truly boggled Stella's imagination.

"During the Civil War and through the World War II period, private investors and businesses liked bearer bonds because it was an easy way to move and hold money without relying on banks," Giulia explained. "Many wealthy folks kept bearer bonds hidden in safes at home, so they never had to go to a bank. Since these instruments were not registered with the government or banks, they also protected the anonymity of bond holders while conducting business deals.

"Overtime, some saw the opportunity to avoid taxes or launder money using these bonds. The bonds became a new form of currency to commit theft and other crimes."

"Well, if that's true, why are these bonds still around?" Stella asked.

"Bearer bonds are still around because many of these bonds have a maturity date of 50 years. In the U.S., the government passed a law in 1982 to outlaw the creation of new bearer bonds. But no one really knows how many of these bonds are still circulating here or overseas.

"Since these bonds are like cash, banks and brokerage firms felt it was more secure to keep their remaining bearer bonds centrally in the depository's vault. At Americlear, we currently house more than 700,000 bearer bonds for the industry worth more than $560 billion."

As Giulia finished her explanation, she gently leaned over toward Stella and took the bearer bond she clutched in her hand. Stella smiled, not realizing she was holding the paper so tightly. After a second tug, she opened her hand, and the bearer bond was put back on the shelf.

At the breakroom, Giulia was quick to show her new colleague photos of her grandchild. "Giana's just so bright and loving," Giulia pointed out.

"The doctors tell my daughter that her child is on the autism spectrum. It can be hard at times," Giulia stated as her eyes filled with tears.

"Giana rolls on the floor, but I'm not able to hold her. She doesn't like to be touched.

"I'm told the autism does not impact her ability to learn, but she needs tutors at home to give her one-on-one counseling. She also needs specialists to help improve her ability to communicate feelings or allow others to support her when she's in distress. I might have retired from Americlear at my age, but I need this job to help Mia pay expenses. I desperately need resources from medical insurance and the benefits I'll get when I retire. Each time they announce more layoffs, I go into a panic. There are also rumors about Americlear changing its retirement policies. These issues are important to all of us. What happens now will one day affect you and your son as well."

"Excuse me, but we have a situation," Edith Colon stood by the break room door and interrupted Giulia's conversation. "I don't know what to do. Bea is at it again. She's in the ladies' room crying and out of control. Should I get Andy?" Stella didn't understand but left the breakroom and followed the two women.

Beatrice 'Bea' Siegel in her late 50s is currently the deputy vault supervisor. She is a 27-year employee with Americlear. She and her husband lived in Brooklyn. Together they raised three kids, now grown and on their own. A gregarious woman, Bea was also known to be very religious. "Yes," she explained to her vault family, "I wear a head covering to underscore my modesty in the presence of God wherever I go."

The three women approached the ladies room located outside of the vault and just beyond the turnstiles. Reggie Seawright stood guard by the door. "I can't get her to come out," he told Giulia, as they approached the door.

"Why?" Bea was crying uncontrollably. "Why, God? Why did you take Louise? My poor friend is gone. Why did this happen to her? Why not me? Why did the company let this woman die? What will become of her child? Oh, merciful God, where are the answers? Who will be next? No one cares. We can't all just go on. How can we forget our dear Louise?"

Bea's voice grew loud and then softened to a whisper. "We thought she was over this already," Giulia turned and confided to Stella. "Her emotional outbursts had diminished in the past eighteen months since our colleague Louise died during the summer of 2009. Each time she has one of these episodes, everyone feels like it's cutting the wound open once again."

"Giulia, did Louise die at the company?" Stella asked. "Is that why Bea is so upset?"

Giulia's voice was almost inaudible. She confirmed that Louise died a horrible death in the vault. "Violent death is especially difficult to accept," she told Stella. "Life can be unpredictable and cruel. While the entire staff shares Bea's pain, most of us are just too scared to allow our feelings to surface." Tears welled up in Giulia's eyes as she faced Stella, "No one goes to work expecting to die on the job. How much more awful can it get?"

"I'm going in," said Stella, as she walked past her colleagues.

"But she doesn't even know you that well," Edith called out.

Looking back over her shoulder, Stella responded, "Yes, that's true. But maybe she just needs someone who doesn't know the story, someone to just listen – and help her calm down."

Stella pushed through the door of the lady's room. She was not about to wait for permission. "Bea, are you in here? Bea, it's Stella. You know me, I'm the new girl. I work for Andy."

She combed the bathroom, which was unusually large with 10 stalls. This was the only ladies' room on the floor, near the vault. Bea was still talking to herself and crying when Stella reached the sixth stall.

"Are you in there, Bea?" Stella asked. "Please come out here so we can talk. I am alone. No one will bother us. Forgive me, but I don't understand why you are so upset. Can you just come out? I want to help, but I haven't been here long enough to truly get it."

A silence came over the bathroom for several minutes. Bea had met Andy's new assistant several times, but she was taken off guard by Stella showing up at the door of the bathroom stall. Her eyes were red and filled with tears, as she opened the door. Her hair was matted down on her head, as if she had been rubbing her wet hands through the short crop. Stella slowly reached out to take her hand.

"Let's go over here," she motioned to Bea. "We can sit on the small bench there against the wall."

"What's going on, Bea? Why are you so distraught?" Stella asked.

Sitting down, Stella decided it was best to let Bea find herself in the moment. If you have the patience, time is a good antidote for sorrow.

"She's dead," Bea said with tears streaming down her face. Her head shook from side to side. "My best friend, Louise Taylor is dead. She was only fifty-three years old. Right here in the vault. It was horrible. Just horrible. I try to move on. I try to forget. Yet there are days when all I can do is think about her. None of this would have happened if the company modernized our equipment and didn't cut staff so often.

"Have you ever known someone who was crushed?" Bea asked as she looked down at the floor shaking her head side to side. "I can't imagine the sense of panic. I wonder if Louise had time to think about her daughter…to say a prayer…and to ask for God's mercy?"

"Wait," Stella replied. "I don't follow you. How could someone die here in the vault?"

"I just have these terrible days when thinking about her overwhelms me. I'm so sorry. I want to let it go, but I still can't accept that she's gone. In my heart, I believe the company let us down. They insist it was an accident. I'm so afraid. I need this job. If I lost my pension now or if I was fired, my husband and family would truly suffer. I keep hoping these anxiety attacks will go away."

"Bea, it's just the two of us. Whatever you tell me stays between us. You can trust me not to tell anyone," Stella told her.

"Louise and I joined Americlear at the same time back in the 80s," Bea explained. She was a divorced woman with one teenage daughter. Louise held onto her strong religious beliefs to cope and raise her child. She'd go to church every Sunday, trying to provide her kid with a good role model, and guide her toward the right path in life."

"I'm sorry," Stella stopped her. "Why do you think the company caused her death? Are you talking about Andy Russo?" Stella asked.

"No, not Andy. He's the only one who cares about us. I know he mourns for Louise as well. When we talk about her, I can see his eyes get red. He's tried for years to modernize the vault, to get new equipment and to generally improve the working conditions. But we are all out of sight down here – no one cares.

"When the company eliminated jobs, they didn't eliminate the work. Often, we had to work double shifts in the vault just to catch up with the paperwork, with filing or refiling certificates. This was especially true after the financial crisis in 2008 and 2009. Yes, we occasionally earn some extra pay but the compensation for clerks is low to begin with. The money doesn't really compensate you for the long hours of tedium and the loss of time with family. And it certainly doesn't justify being killed on the job.

"Louise was on the second shift before the vault closed at 9 pm. The President of Americlear told us in a memo that a security officer walked through the vault to check if employees had left.

"Yet I have my doubts they did a proper check," said Bea. "You've seen the rows of shelves in the vault. It is easy for a person to be working there and not be seen. She was working in section eleven, near the north side of the building. It's one of the oldest areas of the vault. Our equipment down there is ancient.

"Suddenly, it appears one of the shelves collapsed on top of her. She may have been reaching up and leaned on the shelf. A second shelf across from her also toppled. The weight of these two shelves filled to the ceiling with files of financial documents crushed her and caused serious injury. No one heard the noise of the shelves coming down.

"That poor woman laid on the floor of the vault by herself all night. Only one other staff person, Neil Regalo, was in the vault. Neil, a young guy, was wearing headphones listening to music while he worked. He didn't hear the shelves collapse from his location. He also didn't check on Louise as they routinely do. Once the security guard saw Neil leave, he assumed that was the last employee and locked up the vault.

"They found poor Louise the next morning. She had died from her internal injuries. The fire rescue crew had to come in to remove the heavy steel shelving off her. Many of us believe she could have been saved if they found her when the shelves collapsed. What a horrible death. Neil couldn't forgive himself. It wasn't his fault. But after the security officers interviewed him, he left the company the next day and never returned."

Bea calmed down as she explained the events to Stella. However, like the ocean tide, her emotions overwhelmed her again as she talked of her friend's death.

"All I see when I close my eyes at night is her face, calling out for someone to save her. It's there in my sleep. The image sometimes comes to me when I'm in the vault working. I still look up nearly 100 times a day at the shelves that surround us. When will it be my turn?

"Stella, I still don't understand why this happened to such a good person. The Callahan brand of steel shelves in the vault are the 'gold standard' in the industry. But the shelves in section eleven were more than twenty-five years old.

"An investigation was done, but it concluded the death was an accident and no one's fault."

In the retelling of the story, Bea became exhausted. Stella moved closer to Bea on the bench and wrapped her arm around her shoulder, gently hugging her.

"I'm so, so sorry for your loss," Stella told Bea. "I just can't imagine what everyone down here in the vault must have felt or still feels. I know how important faith is through a horrific experience like this." Stella knew nothing could ease the pain Bea felt. Her loss and fears for her own safety might never get resolved. Stella could think of only one thing to try and comfort her colleague.

"Can I pray with you?"

Bea looked at her young colleague with surprise. She had not anticipated Stella's offer. Bea bowed her head quietly, as Stella grabbed her hands. Others clearly mourned Louise in their own way, but Bea now felt a special bond with Stella. The two women were different in so many ways. Yet, on this day they bonded in prayer.

As the door to the ladies' room pushed open, Stella walked out with her arm still around her colleague. Edith and Giulia took over escorting Bea back to the vault. The situation had been alleviated, at least for now.

Reggie waited to check on Stella as she walked back toward Andy's office. "Are you ok?" he asked. "You were quite brave to talk with Bea, who is many ways a stranger. What you did here today will not be forgotten by anyone down here in the vault. We all say – and try to treat each other like family. But today, you refined this high standard."

"I'm tired," Stella confessed. "It doesn't sound like this tragedy has changed much."

“I won’t soft pedal this Stella. Working under ground, most employees are resigned to the conditions. They often feel like second class citizens. We’re on our own most times and so we try to look out for each other. You cannot see sunlight from below the street level. You also don’t expect to be seen by anyone in upper management. I’m not certain I have a better answer for you,” Reggie admitted.

CHAPTER 9
HENRY WONG: HUMAN CENTERED VALUES AND MORE LAYOFFS

It was nearly seven months before Stella was introduced to Henry Wong. "He is an unusually kind and soft-spoken 58-year-old," Andy explained, "who grew up and lived in New York City's lower east side Chinatown his entire life. But he has this special quality about him. I call it human centered values."

Stella wasn't quite certain what Andy meant by this description.

Henry Wong came to America from Hong Kong in the 1950s. His family had deep roots in Lower Manhattan going back almost to the turn of the century. When the time was right, his relatives sent letters encouraging Henry's family to emigrate to the USA.

Giulia told her, "I believe there is good and evil in the world. Henry is the sort who looks to focus only on the good in people. I don't really know if that's a religious perspective for someone Chinese, but I find he thinks deeply about the world. In the nearly two decades since he began working at Americlear, I can't recall Henry having words or disagreements with anyone. He brings a quality that makes each person feel special."

Stella helped Henry pull certificates from the files piled up on his desk. He showed her how the new advanced copying machines made his job so much easier than when he arrived at Americlear. "You just feed the paper in this slot. The machine pretty much does the rest. One side and then turn it over for the other side. You won't see a paper copy. These advanced machines are copying everything digitally."

"Has the job changed much since you started working here," Stella asked?

"I guess it's been about eighteen years since I joined Americlear. The job is pretty much the same routine." Henry explained, "The newer technology does help make the process easier and less time consuming. But I don't mind doing these tasks each day. I try my best to remember how lucky I am to be here.

"My family lived in a very small apartment near Mott Street here in Lower Manhattan. At the time, New York had the largest Asian population outside of China. Where I grew up, most of our neighborhood only spoke Mandarin. If you didn't leave Chinatown, you never had to learn English."

"Weren't you forced to learn English in school?" Stella asked.

Henry started laughing. "The short answer is no. The Chinatown schools would offer classes only in Mandarin. And unlike today, few of us ever finished high school. We left school to work and help our families as teenagers. I resisted learning English, but my parents and my uncle who lived here his whole life pushed me to learn both languages.

"Why don't you speak Chinese?" Henry jokingly asked. "Do

you know Mandarin is likely the most widely spoken language in the world. Everyone will also tell you it's the toughest language to learn. You can understand, yes? I guess one's perspective depends on where they sit or which language they grew up with. I still tell my children that learning Mandarin was a piece of cake, next to English."

"Well, Henry," Stella began, "If I closed my eyes, I don't think I'd guess you were a Chinese American speaking English."

"Young lady," he replied, "There is a Chinese proverb that teaches us, 'Gold cannot be pure, and people cannot be perfect.' I think you are being kind. Thank you. But when I go home at night, I'm glad I can speak Mandarin."

Both Henry and Stella began to laugh.

"Our parents are gone now, and our two daughters will soon finish college. Yet we remain here in Chinatown. There was a large eastern migration of people from the West Coast. Mostly, they came from San Francisco. The Chinese population in Manhattan was still small by today's standards.

"After my parents passed away, my wife and I remained in Manhattan. We have two daughters going to college. Today, I believe there are eight or nine Chinatowns that have grown within the boroughs of New York. I'm told the largest number of Chinese now live in Queens and maybe Brooklyn. The neighborhood near me is shrinking in population."

"Henry, I was thrilled getting this job. You told me you also felt lucky working here. Can I ask why?"

"Well, growing up I had worked an assortment of odd jobs for different Chinese retail merchants. As a teenager, I carried heavy boxes of stock goods from the basement upstairs to the small store front. Later, I got a job as a cashier. Neighborhood store owners learned from each other that I was hardworking and honest. When I wanted to move on or earn more money, I just let folks know I was looking. The jobs came to my door. But I wanted to find better pay and a secure job, especially after I decided to settle down with my wife, Mei.

Like so many of the people she had met in the vault at Americlear, Stella started to realize their shared immigrant backgrounds taught them an unusual lesson about life. Most came from somewhere else. Few of them had the opportunity for much schooling. But the common bond they shared, if any, was having come from very close families. They saw their parents' struggle. None of her colleagues complained or felt they were entitled to a better life. In finding a job at Americlear, they felt their life was a blessing. Stella knew her path now was different from the South Bronx and her two years with a difficult husband.

Henry and Stella grew close over the week working together. Henry was surprised that she responded to a story, he told her about raising his children.

"Wǒ wèi nǐ gǎn dào jiāo'ào," Stella said in broken Mandarin. Her pronunciation was awful, was Henry's first thought. But he told his wife, Mei, "she's trying to tell me she's proud of me. I'm not certain if that's as a father, friend or colleague. "Tài gǎnxièle" Henry responded. "I said thank you."

Richard Gordon, head of IT Tech support, visited the vault several times a week, sometimes even more often. He was tall and very athletic, about six-foot one inch and quite muscular. Stella took note of this good-looking guy.

"Henry, is everything going well today?" Richard asked.

"Yes. My temperamental digital copying machine is behaving today," he responded. "I'm guessing it's because Stella Jones is here assisting me.

Have the two of you met before?"

"Hi, Stella, I'm Richard. Aren't you Andy's assistant? Welcome. It you get frustrated with any of our technology, you can always call me to help."

With his chiseled face and dark brown hair that layered perfectly without a comb, one would expect to find conceit. But Richard had grown up as an Air Force brat, traveling with his family throughout Europe, including Germany and Italy. He and his brother Tommy were bicyclists, who would take off in their teen years to ride hundreds of miles on backcountry roads.

His IT job at Americlear had him leading a team focused on resolving PC and data base problems impacting the staff in the vault and nearby operations areas of the company. One would expect this level of responsibility would cause him to be impatient. But his affable, laid-back nature was endearing – and even attractive in Stella's eyes.

"So, Mr. Wong, what's his story?" she asked smiling.

"Well, Ms. Jones. He might be a good catch, but for the last year I see him coming down here more often to visit Jennie Li. My colleagues tell me he has a serious crush on this young lady."

"Henry, it's ok. I think right now I'd be better off focusing on my job helping Andy. Love may keep you warm at night, but as you know it doesn't pay the bills."

As they finished their conversation, they could see Richard heading in Jennie Li's direction. Richard wasn't responsible for Americlear's main computer systems. His expertise focused on the LAN network of PCs used for data input. It gave him an excuse to talk with Jennie Li. She rarely let on whether these visits were welcomed or just tolerated.

Andy suddenly appeared, "Henry, I see you and Stella have been working well together. I came to rescue this young lady for a timely project, if you can continue without her."

Henry was not too surprised at the sudden interruption. His boss had a habit of walking around the vault throughout the day.

"I apologize, but today I need to pull you away, Stella. I have two reports that must be prepared for my boss in Operations and for our CEO. I'll need to closet you away for the next few days until we can finish this. Then we can start the rotations again. Can you stop by before lunch so I can explain?"

Even when it was obvious that Andy was under the gun, he never imposed this pressure on others. He was always low-key and matter of fact. His team could tell the seriousness of the situation when Andy's face seemed redder and flushed with tension.

"I've seen that look before," Henry told Stella before she followed Andy out of the vault. "Something important must be going on. He's not just following his normal routine today. He really needs you."

Like so many things down in the vault, Stella would try to pick up and follow the cues of her colleagues. She acknowledged Henry with a nod and headed back to her desk.

Stella decided to work through lunch and get ahead of the material needed for Andy's report. She wasn't certain, but it appeared to be a response to another planned staff cut. Thankfully, she told herself, no names were listed in this report. Andy included nearly 20 pages of charts and timesheets to support his arguments that further layoffs might sacrifice vault operations – both in the area's timeliness and its accuracy.

During the afternoon, Stella called her mom and asked her to pick up her son. She rarely missed spending time with Sam in the evening. But being there for Andy was a commitment she could not ignore. The two of them worked back and forth for hours, fine tuning the report due the following day. She could not remember seeing Andy labor so long on a report.

Andy didn't have to tell her what was at stake. She could tell by the endless set of questions he would ask out loud. He apparently needed his story to be airtight and convincing. None of his employees ever doubted how far Andy would go to protect them. Few, however, got to see up close the sweat he spent and hours he labored to achieve his purpose.

The documents were close enough to being final that Andy felt a fresh look in the morning was sufficient. He knew it would take over an hour for Stella to get home. She had proven her mettle this day, leaving her desk only for quick bathroom breaks. He called for them to break at 8 p.m. He did not mention that he, too, had responsibilities outside the office.

His wife, Nancy Russo, was waiting at home alone. Her weekly medical treatments for the thickening heart muscle had stolen her strength and dampened her will power. For the past year, Andy had been wrestling with fears over Nancy's health. They met as youngsters in the Italian section of Brooklyn. They had been married almost 40 years, with two grown children and three grandchildren who lived some distance from their home. Andy still delighted in arriving home in time to feed Nancy or just sit with her and talk through dinner time. Her condition could only be described as in decline. Andy would confide to his brother, "I worry that we're in a race with time. The drugs don't seem to be helping her. My dear wife keeps growing weaker. I just don't know what more I can do."

The trip home to Dyker Heights for Andy would take an hour. He felt good about the report he worked on that day and hoped it could save employee layoffs. But sitting on the train this night all he could focus on was Nancy. She was the center of his universe.

He first met her in a math class in high school. Their families lived on the same street. Andy thought of himself as short and skinny with glasses. He could not get over just how beautiful and angelic she looked. Her white porcelain-like skin never required makeup, and she had black hair that flowed down past her shoulders. She was petite and wore blouses outside of her pants as a teenager to hide her rather large hips. However, Andy never saw any flaws in the woman he would grow to love. She was perfect and he was won over by her quiet demeanor, modesty and grace. Looking out the train window, the ride home went quickly.

As Andy walked into the house, only a dim light greeted him. He looked down the hall to the kitchen. He realized Nancy had gone to bed. Her excitement to see him had been overcome by fatigue. The light next to her side of the bed was still on. He went over to her. At first, he was certain she had fallen asleep. But as he turned to leave and not disturb her, Nancy lifted her hand.

"Andy are you ok?" she asked. "I tried to wait up for you. I really did try." She finished the sentence, and Andy could see she was crying.

"Nancy, I'm so sorry for not getting home sooner. Please don't cry. I know how tired you get. I don't blame you. I missed you so much today. I'm going to take the day off on Thursday, once I'm done with this report I've been writing. I want to spend my time with you.... only you, my love."

Andy went to sit by her side in the bed. He gently reached down and softly ran his hand through her hair. He had not eaten, and his stomach gurgled. He ignored the hunger. "I'm here now Nancy. You can rest. I won't go anywhere."

She quickly fell asleep. There just wasn't any strength left in her. Her friend Agnes would go with her to the hospital for checkups. The doctors claimed for months the treatments were working. Privately, however, Andy only saw loss of breath and weakness.

This was a woman filled with such vitality, he told himself still rubbing her forehead. "What's happening?" he kept asking. "She barely has enough energy to get through her day. We've been to three doctors. None of them has been able to help her."

CHAPTER 10
NANCY RUSSO

Andy Russo was a very private man. He almost never talked about Nancy and her health issues to anyone at work. However, the next morning, when Stella came in early to help revise and finish the report they worked on, she found Andy at his desk. His head was buried in his hands. He was crying.

At first, she backed away. She had never seen a grown man cry. Her father was from Kenya. He knew how to work, how to fight, how to travel long distances without food or water – and how to persevere pain without showing emotion. In her experience, men did not cry. Her mother was different. The Italian side of the family was very expressive, quick to hug, even quicker to slap and laughing throughout the day was quite common.

However, she had been taught to respect someone's privacy, when you saw them struggling. But Stella could never hide her humanity. It was her nature to show compassion and comfort to another person. She purposely dropped her purse near her desk and kicked the garbage can as she sat down to signal, she had arrived.

Andy started to wipe his bloodshot eyes, but not quickly enough before Stella entered his office, closing the door behind her. "Are you ok?" she asked. He looked pale and his clothes were unkept. Moving to his side of the desk, she reached out with her arms hugging him around his head. He wanted to hide. The pressure and emotions had been building inside him for so long. Suddenly, Andy just let go.

He was sitting, but he could feel his head collapse into Stella's embrace. He cried without control. She was thankful that no one came to the office before 8 a.m. She didn't know how long it would take Andy to regain his senses. She prepared herself to hold on no matter what. Something very difficult was going on. This kind-hearted man was hurting. She knew this is what he would do if the tables were turned.

"I don't mean to burden you," Andy began as he tried to regain his composure. "My wife, Nancy, has been in treatment for cardiomyopathy, which affects the heart muscle. It's inherited and it can't be cured. In the past two months she seems to be getting weaker. I fear she has given up, not seeing the end of the tunnel. I'm not stupid. I know what's coming. I just can't think of life without her."

Stella instinctively pulled Andy closer. At 29, she was no expert on life and death. She couldn't imagine the loss of someone she loved. She stood in silence holding onto Andy and tried to console him. Her ex-husband, Nico, had never risen to this feeling of love and devotion. He may have represented possibilities, but sadly, he no longer was someone important enough to truly care about. Stella, however, did draw on her fear and loneliness, always feeling uncertain about where she was headed.

Before Americlear, there were many tear-filled nights asking herself – and asking in her prayers what life might hold for her.

Andy deserved her support, her loyalty, and her love. She instinctively knew a parent in time would become the child again, which is so true as we get older. She was determined to help her boss not lose his way, or his faith, after caring for so many people in his life and career.

Stella slowly stepped away from Andy as he calmed down. She knelt on one knee beside him and grabbed his hands with hers.

"Andy," she said looking up into his eyes, "I'm here for you. I don't have answers on why this is happening. I don't have words to make it easier for you. I can't honestly tell you that things will get better."

Stella's eyes began to fill with tears. They ran down her cheeks. Andy could not get over seeing the emotional response from his young assistant.

"I'm here Andy. I am here for you. I will do whatever I can to lift you up. Please remember you have your children; you still have your wife — and you have me."

Once again, Andy wiped his eyes with the back of his hands. He took several deep breaths. He lifted his glasses and put them on. He was regaining his composure. He paused for several minutes looking beyond Stella's shoulder into the empty space beyond. Then, without warning, he pulled her close with his arms tightly hugging Stella.

"Thank you. Thank you." he said.

She returned to her desk to get settled. Ten minutes later, she returned to Andy's office with a black cup of coffee. Saying nothing, she set it on his desk and left. By mid-morning the pain traveled across Stella's shoulders from the stress of finishing

Andy's report and dealing with the awful news. She downed Tylenol to help with her mushrooming headache. Your boss tells you his wife is dying. He's beyond distraught.

Life and death are not a debate you can win. The words will not be there, because the mind cannot comprehend what's coming. When will it be your turn? Who will you ask for forgiveness? Who will you argue with to reconsider the divine plan? When you look in the eyes of strangers, how will they know the suffering you have witnessed and the love that still inspires you? Death completes us in a way without challenge or competition.

By 11 a.m., Stella had finished the report rebutting proposed layoffs. She was now sworn to secrecy on who might be impacted. Andy was resolute that he would fight to protect his people. He often felt the employees in the vault were scapegoats in the slow turning of the screw. The most deserving, loyal and hardworking folks should not be the first ones tossed into the sea.

His state of mind was such that for the first time he planned to confront his friend and CEO Richard Ashton. He had taken over after Judy Jameson, but Ashton had been with Americlear for more than two decades. He knew the people, the history and the disparities that existed. During the meeting with Ashton and the senior management team, Andy gave his presentation. Daeva Connolly, the CEO in waiting, was adamant about cutting staff. At a critical point, Andy pulled out all stops. He went out of his way to invoke the loss of Louise Taylor. Connolly was tone deaf. She urged Ashton to avoid any special treatment of the vault staff.

Ashton was taken aback when Andy responded aggressively, slamming his hand on the table, "when is 'enough' enough?" He had stood up to Connolly, which no one had previously done.

The Andy Russo everyone knew at Americlear was jovial and calm even in the worst of times. The raw emotion in Andy's comments cut the air like a knife. It was not like him to buck management. "Let's move on," Ashton said as he redirected the meeting to proposed cuts in other areas of the company. Andy sat back in his chair; his arms crossed. Ashton sat back as well, trying to figure out what he had just witnessed.

It would be two weeks before a response came back from Ashton. Layoffs would be made in other areas of Operations, the technology group and several folks who worked in the budget/finance department. For the first time in several years, the vault would be spared any cutbacks. Andy knew this victory was fleeting. Once Connolly took over as CEO, his ability to get concessions would be gone. He would not tell his team the behind-the-scenes details. He now turned his full attention to Nancy, leaving early two days a week to spend time with her. Stella made certain his whereabouts were a secret.

CHAPTER 11
MORE THAN FRIENDS: SUMMER LOVE BLOOMS

Giulia stopped by the security desk outside the vault to set the tone with the staff.

"Look Reggie," Giulia told him, "I know everyone has been talking that Andy's wife is ill, but please make a point of coaching everyone not to say anything. The man deserves his privacy, especially during this difficult time. Ask everyone to not to initiate a conversation. Unless he brings up the subject, no one knows what's going on."

"I agree, Giulia," he responded. "I'll talk with everyone over the next few days. And I will also ask them for their prayers. I only wish we could do more."

Another secret had also surfaced down in the vault, as rumors started to spread about the budding friendship between Stella and Ben Klein. No one could truly say that they had been seen together. Yes, Ben had been stopping down more frequently though many argued he was just checking on Andy and his wife.

It appeared that the information leak in the group was not from Vault Operations.

Richard Gordon would often stop by to talk with Jennie Li. He'd comment seeing Stella on the same floor where Ben had his office. Jennie Li was not a gossip, but other staff members were in ear-shot of their conversations. When asked, Bea Siegel would shoot down the rumors. She had grown close to Stella following her melt down. She claimed Richard came around not because he really knew anything. He just wanted to hang out by Jennie Li's desk. "That man is shameless," Bea was quick to say with a smile.

But it was true. An attraction had been growing between Americlear's spokesperson and Andy's assistant. They worried their informal lunches might feed gossip. Ben was protective. He did not want Stella to get static over their growing friendship. He suggested it might be better if they met after work. Initially, Stella would meet him at Gotham Café on 68th Street and 2nd Avenue. Their conversations mostly involved small talk. They just seemed to enjoy being together. Stella felt conflicted, losing track of time and periodically missing dinner with her son Sam.

Ben asked about how Andy was dealing with his wife's illness. They would compare notes on their interactions with him. The two men had grown close following Louise Taylor's death. He admired the way Ben handled the situation. Andy played a key role in briefing Ben on the vault and the accident. Andy could be counted on to keep their discussions confidential. He knew and respected the job Ben had to do in protecting the company's reputation, though the company may have ignored aging equipment as a factor in the accident.

"Stella, a critical part of Ben's job is to never lie to the press," Andy told her. "We all have different roles and functions to perform. Reporters must ferret out the truth and facts. Ben and his team of corporate communications professionals must respect the facts as they are and try to put them in a larger context. If Ben ever openly or purposefully lied to the press, he understands they would never trust him again."

"Ben," Stella would ask, "Andy says you'd never lie to the press. Is that true?"

"Stella, folks in management just don't understand. The trust and credibility with press folks is what allows me to help shape how reporters decide what they will report. Some seniors at Americlear will tell me, Ben just give them some 'spin.' It doesn't have to be true. I don't engage with these folks. They don't get it. I just keep to my own values and those of my CEO. Now, if a CEO asked me to lie, I'd walk away. I'd quit. My reputation is worth more — and it extends beyond my current job."

He explained that luckily, Judy Jameson was still CEO when the vault accident happened. She would never ask Ben to make up a story.

"More than forty calls came in from newspapers across the country. In situations like this, someone in my position often delegates these calls to their staff to avoid their own job exposure. But I trusted I had more experience in crisis situations than my staff, so I refused to delegate these press conversations.

"Five TV network camera crews showed up late that morning. I went down and met with each of them. Some insisted on waiting to speak to employees at lunchtime. I can't control the press. No one can. No one should control them. Yet, I knew at lunch, there would be thousands of people who worked at companies in our building milling around in the lobby. Finding our employees for comment would be like finding a needle in a haystack. We're in the largest office building on this side of downtown Manhattan."

Ben told Stella how important it was to be accessible and not defensive in a crisis. "After Louise was found in the vault, I went down to meet with each TV crew, handing out a written statement I prepared. What began as a major media story was contained. We were successful and we were lucky, largely because we were forthright and direct during this tragic event. This kept the situation from spiraling and resulting in negative news stories."

"Okay," Stella asked, "I'm going to put you on the spot. I know we talked about this before and I promise not to get emotional. But looking back, could folks in management have done more? Could this situation have been avoided?"

"Boy, you're tough! The short answer is yes," Ben responded unflinchingly. "All of us must accept the principle that if something could have been done, and it wasn't done, someone must be accountable. However, it's never that simple in life. You can argue the issue of 'who' contributed to this tragedy, but aside from a general notion of fault, it's hard to pinpoint one individual."

Long ago, Andy had proposed a modernization program that would have changed the vault equipment, decentralized our locations and added new safety procedures, but it got shot down over cost and other priorities.

"I will say, in the months following the accident a range of safety changes and inspections of shelving were completed in the vault, many of which were needed. Maybe at some point, Andy will be able to raise his larger modernization plan again."

Neither Ben nor Stella planned a relationship. Both feared the impact of the dating on their jobs at Americlear. The defining moment came one early evening in summer after they met for coffee. The conversation that day was light and filled with laughter and sarcasm. Stella was sharing gossip about Jennie Li and Richard Gordon, which at this point was widely known in the vault. Colleagues in the vault claimed to have seen them kissing behind shelves. Another claimed that Richard was found in the ladies' bathroom stall with Jennie Li, but Ben poked holes in this story. It didn't seem credible and came from secondhand sources. Neither Ben nor Stella was judging these employees, but the stories were so filled with energy that it certainly heightened the sexual tension growing between them.

Ben had always been very careful around Stella. It wasn't like he could hide his attraction or his growing feelings, but he did not want some quick office affair. He had been on his own for more than a decade. Never a monk, Ben was not frivolous with his affections. He often worried that he was too "old school" for the current generation.

"I guess I better let you get home, so you can see Sam before bedtime," Ben told her as they were leaving the café. Stella paused for a moment. She could no longer hold back from letting Ben know how she felt. She responded, thanking him for their nearly two hours of fun conversation. Her hand was extended to shake Ben's hand, as was their custom when leaving each other. And then, she stopped shaking his hand and pulled him close. On occasion, Ben had gotten used to the casual light kiss on the cheek. This night was different. Stella went for it. She turned her head slightly to the right, so her mouth covered his. As their lips met, she pulled his waist closer to her.

"When you kiss someone," Stella would tell him later, "it should be the best! Give him the most passionate kiss your lips, tongue and mouth will allow. He needs to know from the depth of your soul…how you feel."

Ben dropped his briefcase on the street and embraced the moment. He finally abandoned his concern about where they were and who might see them. This was different now. She was different. They had crossed into new territory.

Ben and Stella would eventually tire of these clandestine coffee conversations after work. By late July, Ben invited her to dinner at his apartment on the Upper Eastside. In a rare move, he took a day off from work to prepare and cook for his her. She arrived at 6 p.m., leaving work early to have dinner and still arrive home before her son went to sleep. Stella's mom stayed with Sam just in case she was delayed.

The chemistry and tension between them were intense, but the couple tried their best to contain their emotions. Like two kids afraid of being caught at school, they acted very formal in public settings.

The doorbell rang at Ben's apartment. The chicken tetrazzini casserole was still in the oven. Ben smiled at the sight of Stella wearing a yellow sundress. He could not imagine a more gorgeous looking woman. The dress draped comfortably across her tall and lean figure. Stella rarely wore much makeup. Her skin was beautiful. The scent of her perfume hung in the air.

Ben tried to break through his nervousness. He offered Stella a glass of white wine. His favorite was a Gewurztraminer from Dr. Frank Konstantin's Winery in upstate NY. "Hmmn, this tastes so good," she told him. "I don't know much about wine. What is it?"

"Well, I guess some call it a Riesling wine, but it's a little different. It has a light taste of oranges and lemons." With a glass in hand, he gave Stella a quick look in the oven and a five-minute tour of his rather small apartment.

Once again, Ben's signature love of art was present, except the subjects were not Asian or African like his office. He had filled his walls with a mix of figurative art, including paintings of boxers by Steve Huston and female portraiture by a Scottish artist, Stephanie Rew.

"Stephanie Rew is my all-time favorite painter," he explained.

Ben loved to talk about the art he purchased, and Stella was a good listener. "I found Stephanie's work in 2000 while looking at artwork online. She was part of a movement of women painters in Scotland who only painted women."

"That sounds so cool," she responded.

"I really love this black and white nude oil painting," he said pointing to far wall. "The painting focuses on the woman's back, with nothing too detailed showing. But what's special is how the light on the painting changes the image as you moved from left to right. The large painting in the living room, was done by an Israeli artist, Avi Ben Simhon. Hang on a second."

Ben went to the kitchen to check on the food. Stella followed him. She was almost done with her second glass of wine. She started to feel a little tipsy, but didn't want to let go of her glass.

"Excuse me, Ben," she asked as he closed the oven door, "do you mind if we eat a little later?" With that, Stella filled the distance and kissed Ben. Taken by surprise, Ben still held his ground.

"Yes. Ok. Let me take this dish out and leave it in on the stove."

Ben followed Stella into his small bedroom. He kissed her again and again. Ben decided it was his favorite thing to do. She arched backward and he bent down to continue kissing her neck. After several minutes, they each moved to one side of the bed. Facing each other, there was nothing accidental or impulsive in this moment.

Stella reached up to pull the straps of the dress off her shoulders. The dress fell to the floor. She unhooked her bra while staring across at Ben. He had unbuttoned his shirt and set it on the end of the bed.

Their movements were slow. This was not a race to a destination. As the bed sheet was pulled back, they crawled under, naked and holding each other in a long embrace. Once again, Ben slowly kissed Stella. Whatever happened from this point on would take its own course. They both used their lips, their hands and moved their bodies as if in some rhythmic exercise. Words were not spoken. In this silent movie, all the angst, nerves, and pent-up passion were swept aside. No one was leaving this moment to chance. Each of them acted with purpose and commitment.

Almost an hour would go by. The two lovers were still locked in a sweaty embrace. They pulled the sheets over their bodies to stay warm, as the AC gave them chills. On several occasions, Ben would break the calm by pulling Stella close and kissing her neck, cheeks and her swollen lips. Stella had decided she would never leave Ben's arms.

"Are you hungry?" Ben asked.

Stella finally nodded in agreement. She lifted her head and rolled away from Ben's embrace.

"Look," Ben told her, "Rest here for fifteen minutes while I go heat up the food. I'll meet you at the dining room table."

Ben pulled on a clean white t-shirt and tan shorts. He was setting the food on the table when Stella joined him. She had borrowed one of Ben's long sleeve blue shirts from the closet and rolled up the cuffs. Her black thong underwear was visible when she sat down. They began eating. Ben poured an extra glass of wine with dinner. Each of them ate, but the conversation soon took over.

"Stella, you've had a challenging time these past few years. I don't doubt raising Sam on your own, working and not knowing the future has been hard on you. Can I ask what you want now? Where do you see things going?"

"I don't want to be alone," she replied. "I know I want to share my life with someone. I just hope it will be with someone who cares and values me."

"What about you?" Stella asked. "You've been on your own a long time. Maybe getting involved with a single mom, with a crazy ex-husband and child, is not the package you were looking for. I can understand that. I just want you to always be honest with me."

"I've been on my own perhaps too long," Ben replied. "The job consumes so much of my life I forget why I'm doing the job. I think I know something has been missing, but until now I wasn't certain what it looked like. But I think, Stella, it looks like you. I believe you're what's missing, and I'd like this to be more."

"And what would you do, if you weren't working at Americlear?" she asked. "You always come across as if this is the only place you'd ever want to work. What would you do without this job?"

"Well, maybe I could write," Ben answered. "I never really entertained the idea before. I never thought I had the skill or discipline. I know that may sound silly. Yes, I've ghost written for several CEOs, but speeches or bylined articles in newspapers are still very different than writing a book. At this point in my life, however, I feel less afraid about letting go of my 9-5 job.

"Oh, how's the casserole? I'm guessing women today expect their partners to share everything, including the laundry and cooking," Ben started laughing.

"This is actually quite good," Stella commented, "but I liked your suggestion of having dessert before we ate the main meal."

"Wait, was dessert my idea?"

Stella and Ben continued laughing together. Each of them took turns making mocking gestures. Eventually, Stella reached out for Ben's hand and off they disappeared to spend the evening in each other's arms.

CHAPTER 12

NOTHING GOLD CAN STAY: FINDING PURPOSE

News of Nancy Russo's death arrived on a Monday morning in September 2010. Andy had planned to be on vacation, but this was just a cover to take more time with Nancy during her final days.

He would describe later how she would go in and out of consciousness. In July, he decided it was time to tell his children, Anna and Emily that their mom was losing her battle. The doctors had performed a second ablation more than a year ago, but their mom's condition didn't improve. He sat them down at the house. Nancy had gone to rest. The pills she took literally knocked her out.

Anna and Emily came home when their father called. Andy tried his best to put off this talk. He had always been very protective and loving with his children. Yet as he talked, they realized Andy had been carrying this sadness on his shoulders a long time. "Dad, I'm sorry we weren't here to help you," Anna told him. "I guess we've been too self-absorbed the past year.

We should have done more. Mom has always been there for us."

"Her love was unconditional," Emily added. "I don't know what to say."

Andy nodded. A partner in life, she had been there from the beginning sharing the ups and downs. When they were very young, Andy's salary was modest. Nancy would juggle to buy the children clothes and books to read with them at night. She rarely bought a new dress or makeup. She would tell Andy there was little she needed while staying home with the kids.

Her husband knew better. Every woman needs to be reminded how much they are valued; how much they are appreciated for giving so much to their family. They ought to get something new on occasion. The contributions of a good woman can't ever be adequately rewarded, especially in proportion to the sacrifices she makes along the way. At times, Andy was certain even the most special women, like his Nancy, could become invisible. He would never let that happen. Every Friday, he brought her flowers. Every holiday, he'd write and leave cards on the kitchen counter.

On Sundays, Nancy was fond of making an early dinner. These family get-togethers took on added importance to her as the children moved out to live on their own. Sometimes the kids would come home with college friends, later with spouses and now, with grandchildren. Andy was the family greeter, always relaxed in conversations with their guests. However, he would not follow his father's example. When the meal was finished, Andy could not sit there and watch Nancy clean the table. This was just not right. He figured it was a small gesture. He wanted Nancy to feel his love as often as he could find ways to express it. He never saw helping his wife as a big deal. He helped clear the table. He helped wash dishes and the pots. And in time, he taught his children do so as well.

As his career grew more successful, Andy would insist on taking short trips with Nancy. Sometimes it could be a Saturday drive to upstate New York or down to the New Jersey shore where they would walk on the boardwalk in Long Branch and get Wind Mill hot dogs for lunch. He wanted to shower Nancy with gifts, but she was much too modest for fancy coats or jewelry. She did love traveling to Maine. He had not anticipated how much she'd enjoy seeing the trees change color in the fall. Nancy also loved lobster, much to Andy's surprise. He'd sit at a small roadside restaurant laughing as Nancy pried, poked and pulled apart the shellfish. Always with a piece of corn on the cob on the side.

Andy told stories to his daughters to lift their spirits. "I want you both to know that the time your mom and I spent together was enough. I am grateful." Well, that was a lie. The time you spend with someone you love is never enough. Regardless of how much you celebrate being a couple, there are moments when all seems lost. Andy was trying his best to follow Nancy's example and make it easier on the kids. He wanted so much to embrace and honor the values she lived.

By the end of their talk, Andy had taken off his glasses to dab his eyes with a tissue. They all sat and cried, without speaking. Each of them in their own way let out the deep emotions they were feeling. They sat in silence for the longest time. They hugged Andy, one at a time. Emily had trouble letting go of her dad. Without saying more, they then left home. Each of them needed time to cope with this news.

On the second Monday in September, Nancy Russo died in the bed she shared with Andy for almost 40 years. Andy had gone to the kitchen for a cup of coffee. He stopped over on Nancy's side of the bed to kiss her good morning. This was a custom that increased with frequency the last year. Nancy opened her eyes momentarily hearing Andy's voice and feeling his lips against her cheek. Andy was careful not to linger too long. He wanted her to rest. He'd return in a half hour to see if she could sit up. He would bring her coffee with two sugars, another custom he embraced.

The house was very quiet, Andy thought to himself. He resisted putting on the TV, so he could hear Nancy if she called for him. He searched the kitchen cabinet for her favorite mug. It was not Valentine's Day. It was not Nancy's birthday. Christmas was still a few months away. Andy, however, felt a certain giddiness come over him as he added two sugars to her cup. He looked out the window as he had done some many times, before walking down the hall to their bedroom.

Andy started to make small talk as he walked to Nancy's side of the bed. He would never understand the feeling he had, but he realized almost instinctively that she was gone. He stood silent and still. "Nancy, I brought you coffee." But he knew. He knew she would not – she could not respond any longer. Something made Andy believe in that moment if he didn't accept the silence, she would come back to him. At the time that death arrived, Andy's knees wobbled. He put the coffee down on the nightstand. He felt confused and powerless.

For several minutes, he held onto the bedpost to steady himself. He was never a very religious person, but in this moment all he could think to do was kneel by the bed. He bowed his head leaning it next to Nancy's body.

He prayed. "Dear God, please don't take her now. Please give me just one more day…this is all I ask…to say our goodbyes."

He asked in his prayers to revive her…to escape the horror of losing his wife. Then he prayed for the strength to bear her loss. And while he had been a skeptic his entire life, he prayed his wife was in heaven. He prayed that Nancy was no longer in pain.

Andy sat on the floor at the side of the bed weeping for more than an hour. He eventually fell asleep. His head rested awkwardly against the side of the mattress. When he woke up, he struggled to get up. His legs hurt so bad. He looked at Nancy who seemed so peaceful. It was time to call for an ambulance and to contact the children. But Andy would not be robbed of this last private moment with her. He leaned down one last time and kissed her lips. He told her several times how much he loved her, how much he would miss her. Slowly, he pulled himself away to make the phone calls that would tear them apart forever.

As the news reached Americlear, Stella could not bear the thought of Andy being alone. She wasn't certain what funeral arrangements were needed. Even if it was just answering the phone, Stella decided she wanted to be there. She asked her mom to bring Sam to their apartment, while she headed to Andy's home in Brooklyn.

Before leaving the office, Reggie asked her to keep in touch so he could update the staff. "I believe these folks would do anything for Andy. We need to allow them a chance to show him their love."

Stella arrived before Andy's daughters. She began making phone calls at Andy's direction. Aside from an initial hug, Stella kept her emotions in check. She gave her boss time with his children and grandkids. The house was ghostlike. The grandkids were corralled in the far den in front of the TV. Stella tried to ensure Andy would eat and rest before the funeral.

The wake and funeral seemed like a blur to Andy. He was

going through the motions. He did his best to smile and thank friends for their support. The line of Americlear employees lined up outside the funeral home and down the block. Anna and Emily were surprised at how many people came from the company to pay their respects to their mom. Both CEOs, Judy Jameson and Richard Ashton attended the church service. However, Daeva Connolly was absent. Andy did his best to be polite and introduce his children, but the look in his eyes told you he was somewhere else.

When it was all done, Andy sat in his house for days by himself. Initially, Stella pulled back from visiting. She believed he needed a few days of privacy during the grieving process. She spent time at home explaining to Sam what had happened. It was hard for him at ten years old to grasp death. Sam still had his own grandparents so the idea of someone missing or gone forever wasn't easy to process. He did understand, however, the feeling of being alone. When a home is broken and parents separate, it's not unusual for a child to be left alone. It doesn't really matter if they stay with a relative or friend, it isn't mom or dad. In Sam's case, the burden of his loneliness would always fall on Stella since his dad was so absent in his life.

A week after the funeral, Stella returned to Andy's home to help her boss get back on his feet. She'd cook and sit with Andy during dinner. She was very pleased the night he finally agreed to drink a glass of wine. If only he could talk, she thought…it might allow him to heal.

"You know Stella, I'll never understand what Nancy saw in me. We lived on the same street. I used to play stickball with the boys. I was so awkward. I don't believe anyone would confuse me with being very athletic. I think she liked that I seem to get along with everyone. I never used foul language, even when some of the boys cheated."

"How did you know?" She asked. "You were so very young. When did you realize that Nancy was your soulmate?"

Andy sat back and smile. The use of the world soulmate really appealed to him.

"If I'm honest, there was something I felt inside the day I met her. Yes, I worried for the longest time that she might not see me the same way. I mean, there is nothing about me I thought was so special. Why would she ever want to be with me?

"There was this boy in the neighborhood, Frank Celentano. He was the tallest and most gifted athlete. Most of the girls were drawn to him. I'm not sure if it was his strong, silent personality or the beautiful wave of black hair. Frank could be rough around the edges, but I knew him in a way that many did not. Underneath the gruffness, cursing, and occasional brawling, he was really a sensitive and caring guy. He looked out for those of us who were smaller and not able to defend ourselves. But Nancy didn't care about his looks or his demeanor. She wanted someone with fewer rough edges."

"What ever happened to Frank?" Stella asked.

"He grew up," Andy responded, as he turned his head and stared at the backyard.

"We all grew up," he said quietly. "Frank settled down with a terrific girl, Angela Savino. They had two children. He never went to college, but he made a good living driving trucks across the country. He became a great dad and a family man.

It seems silly now that I worried my Nancy might see the potential in Frank, just as she saw the potential in me."

Andy put his wine glass down. His eyes filled with tears, as he struggled to finish his story.

"I remember so clearly when Nancy told me, as a young teenager, that I was special in her eyes. She said, 'I hope one day you'll marry me.' I'll never forget that day. I was just a kid. I was so stupid. I sat there and didn't say a word. Maybe I was in shock. Perhaps I feared she might change her mind.

"Now, not every dream in life ends as we plan. My Nancy, however, had her faith. She kept her prayers close, and she waited for me to find her. I grew up not truly realizing how blessed I've been to be with her."

Andy seemed to finally find some peace that night, but their conversation ran very late into the night. Stella slept on the couch at Andy's home. She didn't want him to be alone in the house or feel alone the next morning. He woke to find Stella cooking breakfast. His spirits were lifted by her kindness. They ate and then took a long walk at a nearby park. She let Andy guide the conversation. If he wasn't ready, she'd allow the silence to keep them both company. On the way home, she made some small talk. She grabbed onto his arm and held on. Andy looked down. He could still recognize love when it found him.

In the weeks and months that followed, the vault staff rallied to Andy's side. He returned to work, though he kept to himself. He'd focus on year-end reports he had to complete for management. Connolly had rebuffed his requests for year-end bonuses for his staff. He had hoped, once again, that Ashton might intervene. Some bonuses were eventually approved but it was half of what he recommended.

On occasion, Ben would stop down to check in on Andy. He'd sit with him, drink coffee and talk. Ben would thank Stella for being so caring, but he wouldn't linger too long. They had both agreed to continue being discreet about their relationship.

The women in the vault decided to start a Sunday tradition at the Russo home. For six-weeks, they would all travel to Brooklyn to cook and enjoy lunch with Andy. The male employees joined as well, often bringing desserts and wine. On some weekends, not everyone could make the trip. But they made certain the dining room table was full – and no office business was ever discussed. On several occasions, Andy's children joined the Sunday lunch. They were thankful their dad was not alone. To them, the turnout for lunch reinforced how much people respected and valued their dad.

The lunches took on a certain ethnic flare, depending on who agreed to cook and what part of the world they came from. Each week, there was one chef and many helpers. The meals became a source of conversation by themselves, with back stories about parents and a shared celebration of food. Reggie Seawright was not about to be left on the sidelines. He was not a cook, but he knew where to buy the best barbequed ribs and fried chicken, with all the trimmings.

The upcoming Christmas holiday season would present its own unique challenge. No one wanted Andy to be alone. So, the group cooked up a scheme that had him traveling each week in December and January to someone's home.

Initially, he was resistant. He didn't want to intrude with their family time. However, they were all so welcoming that Andy soon started to accept his role as Santa Claus and the ultimate gate crasher. By early January, it was clear he had gained weight from all the good meals. Everyone also interpreted this as a sign of Andy getting back to normal. They were reassured he found his footing when Andy started making his rounds going through the vault in the morning.

CHAPTER 13
NO BONUSES, NO LEGACY

By February 2011, Andy was back, fully engaged working on a new management Task Force. This group of key executives at Americlear was put together to guide the implementation of a new repository for trading data on credit default swaps (CDS). The financial industry was often lauded for its ability to innovate and create new trading instruments to raise investment capital or to mitigate risk associated with financial transactions. However, in their rush to launch new products, the industry too often relied on manual recordkeeping. The technology supporting innovation always lags, creating new types of risk.

The *Financial Times* wrote often about CDS trades even before the 2008 financial crisis. Julie Ripmeister, a rising star at the *Financial Times* in 2003, was the first and most frequent critic talking about the danger these new instruments could pose:

"CDS trades allowed two financial firms to enter a contract that helped mitigate risk and buy insurance protection against losses for a distinct period. So, a trader in the UK could agree to a trade, or contract, with a trader in the U.S. The traders would scribble the details on a piece of paper and hand the trade details off to a clerk to be filed. It wasn't unusual for traders to then sell some of their risk exposure on a new CDS trade to someone in Asia. This process could go on for several more trades to spread the risk around. But all the records and details of these trades were written on pieces of paper and held in different countries.

"During the 2008 crisis, it became clear that regulators had an impossible task trying to figure out the scope and value of CDS trades; essentially who had exposure to whom? If a single firm failed, would it create a ripple of financial exposure across the industry globally?"

Ripmeister was the only financial journalist focused on the risks CDS trades created at those firms, the lack of regulatory controls and the possible impact it could have on a global basis.

One bright spot was Americlear seizing on the opportunity to automate the process of record keeping. Leveraging their experience as a central securities depository, a multi-year effort was launched to focus almost exclusively on tracking these trades to help global regulators and financial firms reduce risk.

Andy worked on this project for six months. At home, he always had his nose in the task force paperwork that sat on his desk at home. He rarely looked up from it. About the only time he wasn't turning pages was when his children and grandkids were over for Sunday dinners, making noise in a house that was usually silent. He was grateful the work kept him distracted, but Nancy and the family were always in his thoughts. Sundays helped him keep his priorities in perspective.

Ben was also appointed to the Americlear Task Force on CDS, to help guide and support the announcements and communication needed to win industry support for a CDS trade repository. He butted heads with Connolly at these meetings. She didn't understand the value of lobbying in Washington and Brussels with regulators or the importance of a media strategy.

Ben tried to avoid meetings with Connolly. He realized she would be his new reality as CEO – and as a boss at some point. Luckily, his absence at Task Force meetings was overlooked by the discussions that were dominated by a review of operational details, technology procedures and backup data recovery issues.

Meanwhile, Stella had started to legally pursue getting full custody of her son. Her ex-husband, Nico, was rarely around. He had stopped contributing any financial support. And she feared that if Nico did show up, he could lose his temper with her. She had gained confidence in her job at Americlear and the growing feeling of financial independence.

Andy, Ben and Reggie had all coached and supported her decision. They helped her find a lawyer. With clarity on the steps required for custody and the timing, she began the process. She did have some reservations, however. The lawyer told her to keep a distance from any relationship she might have with Ben. Stella and Ben discussed the issue several times.

"I trust you know how I feel about you Ben. I can't recall a happier time in my life. If you doubt that, I'll have to sneak over one night to remind you."

The smile stretched across his face, "Stella, I get it. Really. I don't see this as a test of our relationship, just a detour. It won't be easy for either of us to keep our distance. I just speak for myself. I may be tempted by your offer of clandestine late-night meetings. But Sam must be the priority right now."

Privately, he knew staying apart while the custody battle was going on would be tortuous. Ben trusted and believed; however, all roads would always lead back to Stella.

Ben and Stella stayed separated for almost eight months. Their bond was strong, but would the time apart harm to their relationship? Stella was determined to shape her destiny. She would surprise Ben, periodically showing up at his apartment near midnight. But these stolen trysts were infrequent and kept discreet. Though they both accepted the time apart was necessary, an isolated moment of passion was sustaining – for both.

By the fall of 2011, a gut punch was delivered to all Americlear employees. "Did you see the memo?" staff members were asking as they walked down the hallway. "Check the mail." The mail room was overloaded and backed up delivering envelopes throughout the company. This type of communication, delivering paper memos, was reserved for executive announcements. Folks were shaking their heads in disbelief heads. "This sucks," a junior manager shouted across the desk to a friend standing several feet away. "Are they kidding us?" another employee asked. "Why did they wait for us to work the whole year, before giving us this news?" A pregnant staffer grabbed her stomach and sat down reading the notice.

The memo from CEO Richard Ashton described the challenges the industry was facing after the financial crisis. He spent considerable time hailing the good work and sacrifice Americlear staff made, the long hours, and weekends and vacations given up managing the risks their customers faced.

After nearly two years of chaos, he cited the improving economic climate.

But as occurred in the past, Ashton dropped the hammer. "The Board still believes in this period of recovery, Americlear should set an example by curbing salary increases and reducing the bonus pool at year-end 2011."

The reaction to the memo was swift and uniform across the

company. No one was happy. An online forum setup by HR was flooded with anonymous electronic messages. While no one could be certain if the site would protect their anonymity, no one held back. It felt like a mini rebellion was underway.

The string of negative feedback filled the forum:

> "We sacrificed during this financial crisis, with no promotions or salary raises in 2010."
>
> "We absorbed two rounds of layoffs since 2009. Now, they are cutting bonuses again. When do our sacrifices end?"
>
> "Why isn't Ashton a more effective advocate for us with the Board? When the economy took a nosedive after the crisis, our families got hurt as well. Our expenses also increased."

Within a week, the online forum was blowing up. Ashton realized even his oldest and closest colleagues at Americlear were giving him negative feedback. He decided his only recourse was to try and appeal the Board's decision. However, Connolly opposed this move and Ashton feared he was losing his ability to shape the final decision.

Ashton sat down with Ben to ask his help in writing a new memo to staff, once he went back to the Board. However, the meeting started differently than Ben anticipated. "Ben, I have made a decision to retire early from Americlear, at the end of the year." The news came out of left field. Ben sat quietly trying to process the information.

"I've been dealing with several health issues. The announcement of my stepping down from Americlear at year-end could wait two months, but it may help you understand why I wasn't successful on the bonus issue. Connolly would soon be taking over. She's already throwing her weight around," Ashton said somewhat sarcastically.

"I've started treatment for blood cancer. The pace of this treatment will become more aggressive in the coming months. I really don't want this information shared with anyone. I trust you'll keep this confidential."

It was clear from the conversation that Ashton really cared about his legacy with employees. "I have a lot at stake when I go back to the Board. But however this turns out, I'd value your help making certain our employees understand I pushed very hard."

Ben stood up. He could see Ashton needed a break from their conversation. "I will do my best on this memo, once you have clarity from the Board," he promised Ashton. "Even if there is only a small concession on bonuses, I believe we can write something that our employees will see this as a win."

With that, Ben left Ashton's office. He walked down the hall thinking about how unpredictable life could be. It didn't matter that Ashton worked his whole career to reach the job of CEO. Does the job really matter? Does the money he earned matter, if his health is threatened? His attention then turned to the reign of terror he anticipated with Connolly taking over as CEO.

At the October meeting, Ashton pulled out all stops and the Board finally agreed to modify their decision. A bonus pool for year-end would be authorized. The total pot of money would be reduced by fifty percent, which meant many employees at the lower end of the pay scale would likely be left out. Since senior personnel take up more of the bonus money, based on their higher salary, the pool gets drained quickly. Within weeks of bonus recommendations, it became apparent that none of the money would reach the employees working in vault operations.

Ben knew this would happen. He understood after many years at Americlear how these decisions get made. At the front end, no one in senior management consciously decides "no bonuses for frontline staff." The Board simply cuts the bonus pool. Managers throughout the firm are then forced to re-prioritize their bonus recommendations.

Over the next week, Ben closeted himself away to try and artfully craft the CEO's second memo on bonuses. The goal was to highlight Ashton's success with the Board based on the commitment of Americlear staff during the financial crisis. He credited employee efforts across the firm as a plausible rationale for getting bonus money restored. The best Ben could do was to persuade most employees that everything possible was done on their behalf. He considered this to be one of the shittier jobs he was given. But considering the circumstance of Ashton stepping down, Ben felt a loyalty to help his CEO go out a hero instead of a villain.

In early November 2011, Ben stopped down to check on Andy. Ben felt bad each of them had been running in different directions. Andy slammed a book he was holding onto the desk and got up to close the office door. Ben could tell he was beyond irate, and he understood why. The second memo from Ashton had been sent out. Many felt that Ashton had gone to the wall for them. Some employees felt slighted and angry. As he returned to his chair, he launched into a tirade.

"Ben, you did a great job on Ashton's memo. But I don't really give a twit about that. My people down here in the vault are my family. Once again, these people down here are the forgotten ones. They're getting fucked over."

Ben hesitated to respond. He had never heard Andy Russo use foul language. His affable friend was quite aggressive, and hell bent, but his true purpose was unclear. Ben couldn't mention Ashton's planned exit. And he didn't think it mattered whether Ashton was still in charge. Andy was right. "Andy, you know I agree with you. We've talked about this issue many times. The folks at the low end of the totem pole don't get the recognition or the rewards they deserve."

"Well, I'm really fed up," Andy said, his voice loud enough to be heard down the hall. "Maybe I've been here too long. Maybe losing Nancy has changed the way I feel about stuff. I went up to see Ashton. We've known each other over twenty years. Until now, I considered him a friend. He gave me some bullshit story about the Board. I feel bad about what I said. I spoke very bluntly about his failure to look after the folks at Americlear who are most vulnerable.

"Ben, you can't just keep fucking people over without a response. We're going to have a rebellion on our hands. Since Jameson left the company, you know those employee feedback surveys have plummeted. The person at the top sets the tone."

Ben sat with Andy for a half hour. He did his best to calm his friend, but there was something different about him. This man, who always had a filter and rarely showed emotion, was acting out. He certainly had been around long enough through good times and bad times. He knew the score. This wasn't the first time employees on the front lines were squeezed. Why was this time so difficult for him?

Stella wasn't at her desk when Ben emerged. He shook his

head seeing her empty chair. He turned and headed toward the elevators. "Later," he muttered to himself.

Andy made his usual rounds of walking through the vault. He expected to hear feedback about year-end bonuses. He wanted to hear his employees complain. He relished the opportunity to join them in complaining, even if it was rare for him to do so. Andy had always been a company man. He may not have agreed with actions being taken, but he worked at Americlear so long that he accepted the crumbs being offered. To his surprise, however, there was no feedback from his staff, not even a snide comment.

He lingered by Reggie Seawright's desk asking about the upcoming football season. Reggie chatted, but he did not comment on the recent news. He now felt a responsibility to be an advocate for those he considered to be voiceless. Andy had decided it was his time to push back on injustices he saw at Americlear.

The second Ashton memo had quieted down the negative feedback from many staff members above ground. Most in middle or upper management positions figured they would now get some sort of bonus, even if it was less than the prior year. Everyone had been hurt by the freeze on salary increases and promotions in 2010. If an employee got a bonus in 2011, they might not fall too far behind in their overall income.

Of course, Ben knew the financial firms represented on the Board of Directors did not see any cuts in their own bonus programs. Some firms saw reductions in the size of bonus pools, but like Americlear the pattern was the same. It was always the folks on the front lines who suffered the most. The disparities in pay by race and gender were well known, even as efforts on diversity grew in the upper levels of management.

The announcement came in December that Richard Ashton would leave the company at the end of 2011. This was a year earlier than his five-year contract as CEO. However, it was rumored he was given a golden parachute bonus at the end. No mention of his health was included, which only stoked the fires of the rumor mill.

The head of Human Resources (HR) was there – and then he was gone. No one knew the details, but rumors were very strong that Connolly would not tolerate those who might offer differing opinions. The back story on the managing director of HR was that he expressed concerns to CEO Ashton and a few Board members that senior officers were increasingly unwilling to share their views at high level meetings or with their own direct reports. The first question at meetings was "what does Connolly think?" or "what does Connolly want us to do?" The era of silence had truly begun. If anyone doubted her resolve, their opinion changed when the announcement came out the head of HR was retiring.

A half dozen other senior management changes were included in the announced news of Richard Ashton's planned departure. Most Americlear employees saw this as a natural changing of the guard, with Connolly taking charge of the organization. And if the rumors about Connolly were true, no one who wanted to keep their job was talking.

CHAPTER 14
RECKLESS MOMENT: UNCERTAIN FUTURE

The mood at the company was best described by R. Lincoln Smith, head of Americlear Security, while talking with Ben Klein. One of Ben's most valued qualities was his ability to listen and reflect employee opinion across the organization.

"Unsettled," was the word used by Smith during their conversation. "Do you think that's because of the year-end bonus decisions?" Ben asked. "Do you think folks were surprised Ashton stepped down at the end of 2011 versus what some believed would be the end of 2012?"

"I believe it is all of those things," said Lincoln. "I can't recall so many issues and circumstances impacting the mood of staff since I arrived more than a decade ago. There's no question the bonus cuts hurt how employees see the future."

No one really wanted to think about what might be coming in 2012. While large Christmas parties at the company were replaced by small gatherings and lunches, employees still looked for any excuse to hug and celebrate together.

The vault employees historically experienced a large volume of work in the closing weeks of December. Investors were either trading to lock-in profits before year-end or they were dumping stocks they considered losers, so they could take tax deductions. Andy tried his best to avoid having his employees working double shifts filing certificates in the vault this time of year. A skeleton crew of two would be asked, on a volunteer basis, to cover the second shift from 4 p.m. to 9 p.m.

While it was unusual for Jennie Li to volunteer to help in the vault, most of her colleagues chalked it up to her good nature. Jennie Li never minded stepping in if it lessened the burden on others. During the year, Jennie Li's job supervising the computerized transfer of ownership records rarely involved removing or replacing certificates from their files.

But this year, Jennie Li had a reason to hang out in the vault past normal business hours. She and Richard had slowly moved beyond their flirting and the strong visceral attraction that pulled them like magnets. Richard had a high level of security clearance which allowed his employee ID card to get him through the turnstiles by the vault.

Jennie Li and Richard were texting each other on their phones the entire day. Fantasy and a reckless desire were consuming them. Jennie Li was a tough, outspoken woman. She was not some quiet and shy Asian caricature. It was not unusual for men to underestimate her intelligence, self-confidence and her passion.

She knew Giulia would be working nights in mid-December. But the filing of bonds and money market instruments would keep her on the far side of the vault. Further back, near the floor marked zone Z, Richard and Jennie could hide away without interruption and out of the camera view.

This moment of recklessness had been building for months. Richard quickly walked back through the vault and moved toward Jennie Li. He took her hand and pulled her close. He slowed his advance, gently kissing her lips. As she responded, his right hand reached behind her lower back to bring her closer. Their arms and their bodies were lost in this embrace. Their kissing moved between their mouths and toward their necks.

After several minutes, Jennie Li and Richard were lost in their passion for each other. A sense of privacy seduced them as they saw the letter Z written below them on the grey painted area of the floor. Richard felt this could be his moment. Jennie Li was not the reserved image of an Asian women in the movies and stories Richard had seen or heard. She didn't hesitate to express herself openly and aggressively.

Jennie Li reached back with her hand to find a table and rest her body. With her balance secured, she brought Richard to a new state of consciousness. She grabbed his head with both hands and forcibly pushed him down to where her dress rose up on her thighs.

This woman wasn't holding back about what she wanted. In the moment, Richard kissed her inner thighs, and he found rewards in places where underwear soon disappeared. For the longest time, Jennie Li leaned back and simply enjoyed Richard's earnest efforts to please her. She worked hard not to allow her moans to get too loud and echo down the hallway where her colleague was working.

Richard was shocked that his partner was so direct about what she wanted and where she found satisfaction. She would not rush her lover's sacrifice, especially when she could close her eyes, look up at the ceiling of the vault and imagine that this moment could last into 2012.

Her hips bumped up and down numerous times before her back fell limp against the wall behind the table.

But Jennie Li was not done. The two lovers had found a connection which transcended place and time. She pulled Richard up from the table and kissed him with all the passion she could muster. His face was still wet, but she didn't care. Her hand reached down and pulled on his belt. In minutes he found himself inside of her. He lifted her off the table with his hands. It would take ten minutes before they were done. As he set her back down, they began to laugh at their circumstance and their discovery. Fantasy had become a relationship before the night was over.

When they were done, Richard told her he would be waiting outside of the building near Pier 11 and the East River. The second shift ended at 9 p.m. She walked slowly down the sidewalk leading to the pier where the ferry would pick up passengers for the ride north on the river to the Upper East Side or south back toward New Jersey. She could see Richard waiting in the cold December air. He was shivering and moving in circles trying to generate some heat. Jennie Li jumped into his arms. Together, they floated on the promise of finding new love. Laughter filled the air, as they talked about what they did in the bowels of the vault. "I can't believe you," Richard said as he set her down and then looked into her eyes. "Do I have to tell you; I don't want this to ever end."

"You are full of surprises Richard Gordon. I'm not certain how I could resist," Jennie Li confided. "This will certainly be a story (not told) for the ages," she smiled. Both Richard and Jennie Li were reluctant to characterize the relationship. The new year was coming, and they greeted it with all the energy they could find. Life was about new beginnings. And the more unexpected, the more blessed they believed these new beginnings would be.

CHAPTER 15
ENOUGH IS ENOUGH: A REASON TO ACT:

Daeva Connolly took over as CEO of Americlear early in 2012. The press announcement of her appointment gave an appropriate send off and acknowledgment of Richard Ashton's more than 20 years of contributions to the company. Connolly tried to edit out accomplishments attributed to Ashton in the press announcement, preferring to claim some of them later during her own tenure.

Ben Klein could immediately see the character flaws at a very human level.

In writing the press release, he could tell almost immediately that Connolly would be a very different leader to work with than any he had known during his long tenure at. Connolly never asked Ben if language or a proposed press strategy was appropriate. She didn't care. There was only one approach: Hers.

When asked about the new CEO, Ben would tell his staff "Buckle up your seat belts."

Connolly restructured the senior management team within the

first month, after taking hold of the reigns. She demoted eight long-term executives and reassigned them to smaller roles at the company. This had never been done before following other CEO transitions. Americlear's role in the industry was to bring certainty and stability and this mission had always been reflected in the long tenure of senior managers. Connolly was determined to turn the place upside down. New and younger executives were promoted to the firm's management committee. Some argued the new team did not have the same depth of experience, but all agreed this was her way of ensuring they'd be unlikely to challenge Connolly's control.

With the new management team in place by February, Connolly got them to approve the most significant change since the origins of the firm. Connolly had been the most vocal advocate for reducing budgets and cutting employee benefits. She favored rewarding the upper ranks of the organization, even if it came at the expense of the lowest paid employees. She did not share with Ashton before he stepped down her plans to eliminate Americlear's pension program and end the retiree medical benefits program. It was her way of avoiding any effort by Ashton to interfere with her decisions. A majority on the Board were ready to give the new CEO a free hand, as was the custom, even though a few members raised concerns.

Connolly confided to one of her closest management team supplicants, "Let's take some steps to get rid of older employees so we can reduce medical costs. I don't really care if the company loses this historical experience. We can hire new and younger middle management folks at lower salaries. And eliminating the pension program will save millions of dollars. Our HR department estimates these policy changes will impact fifteen percent of the population who might be nearing retirement.

Andy Russo waited until the end of March, five or six weeks after his staff received and digested the memo from the new CEO. While not telling anyone, he had privately hoped that the companywide reaction from executives and staff might force Connolly to modify her policy changes.

Stella shared with Andy feedback she received from the vault staff, "I am paraphrasing comments, but many said the memo landed like a punch below the belt."

The memo gave employees until mid-October to either retire early with the pension they earned to-date or accept a payout from the company to a designated private retirement plan.

It didn't take folks long to figure out that the move to privatize the retirement plan could cause long time employees to lose twenty-five percent of their money. Employees furiously emailed each other with information and rumors on the impact of this new policy. The loss of retirement savings was based on how the pension fund might be valued by an outside accounting firm and the loss of investment growth in another retirement plan.

The end of retiree medical benefits for employees was also a bitter pill, especially for those who had satisfied the requirements: working twenty-five years and were fifty-five years or older. Many financial firms in the U.S. had been reducing health benefits and increasing co-pays for several years. However, Americlear employees were in shock their new CEO did not grandfather existing staff who paid their dues and earned their benefits. For any employee with a loved one having serious medical issues or requiring long-term services or treatment, the retiree medical plan was a lifeline to protect their savings.

Periodically, Lincoln Smith, Head of Security would stop down to grab coffee with Andy. The two men had an easy rapport and worked closely for many years. “Well, you got the memo Andy. What was your reaction?”

“Lincoln, I believe Connolly could have rolled out her changes in stages over several years. This decision is just stupid. And she could have spent a year educating employees on industry trends and creating more of a rationale for the policy changes. Why did she spring this on employees nearing the end of their careers? These staff members sacrificed long hours and showed loyalty to the company.”

“Andy, as long as I’ve been doing my job, it is never easy escaping the wrath of employees. So, like you, I’m really confused over this move. We underestimate the impact these decisions may have on people. We take for granted that even the lowest level staff among us will push back, if they feel aggrieved or their families are threatened.”

It was gratifying for Andy to get Lincoln’s take on the Connolly decision. After weeks of silence, he realized he was not alone. Other long-term seniors did not agree, even if very few would speak out. After his colleague finished his coffee and conversation, Andy sat in his office stewing.

When he returned to work after his wife’s Nancy’s death, something about him had changed. He no longer saw his job as being a defender of the company’s message and direction. His employees had always felt like extended members of his family. However, now he felt his mission was to look after them, with the same commitment they showed him.

In the months following the announcement, small acts of sabotage and rebellion were found in different areas of the company. An open-source application being developed in Americlear’s large IT world was found to have bugs in the programming. The accounting department found irregularities during some of their audits, with some financial firms paying too little or too much on their trading obligations. The math errors on payment instructions sometimes favored Americlear but more often favored financial firms. These errors began to raise red flags. There was at least one IT system shut down that occurred near June that was unexplainable. The problem became a nightmare to resolve in eight hours before morning resumption of daily trading.

While rumors about sabotage were growing, no one wanted to attribute these events to the policy decision on privatizing pensions. Increasingly, there was an undercurrent of uncertainty, but no one dared to speak out publicly. No one could be certain any longer who to trust.

Lincoln Smith and his team had their work cut out for them. When several financial firms in June found accounting errors with millions of dollars in unwarranted deposits into their accounts, Smith asked Ben's help to head off any news leaks from appearing in the press. But whether the Security department investigated the finance group or the IT department, none of the issues they found could be attributed to a specific employee or group of employees.

Andy's planned meeting with the entire vault staff was highly unusual. The only prior meetings were when Louise Taylor died in the vault – and the days after 9/11. Andy was on a fact-finding mission and to take the pulse of his team. He arranged with Lincoln Smith to have security personnel standing outside the vault.

Jose and Reggie brought in additional chairs. The room was very tight as the team gathered in Andy's office, some decided to stand behind others who grabbed the few chairs in front. Bea Siegel had a nervous habit of sneezing when squeezed together with other staff members. Since the hallway was clear of staff walking by, Reggie kept the doorway open so there was some airflow in the room.

"Ok," Andy opened the meeting, "you know why we're here." The sound of chairs shuffling could be heard, as the staff tried to settle down for the discussion.

"We're here to discuss the CEO's memo on privatizing pensions and eliminating retiree medical benefits. At the outset, I want you to know that I will also be impacted by this announcement. Like some of you, I will have to decide whether I take the early retirement offer. I will also be losing certain medical benefits. So, rest assured, I'm just as frustrated and disappointed as you must be. I've talked with most of you one-on-one, but I wanted this meeting so we can share your concerns within our family.

"Yes, I said within our family. I know we've done that before during some very challenging times. But I'm looking beyond the company. The world around us is changing. We've all sacrificed time with our families and accepted less in pay than others at this company – and in the industry. So, I'm no longer defending the actions of management. Who wants to start this conversation?"

"The CEO's announcement has left me without hope for the future," Bea volunteered. "It's too soon for me to leave my job. I'm fifty-five. No one will hire me at my age. Yet, I can't live on the pension I'll get at this point. My husband, Barry, retired several years ago when the store where he worked closed. We still have a mortgage on the house. We have more than a decade to go before we file for Social Security. Why? Why are they targeting us? For years, we've given our all to this company. Now I'm looking at a life of struggle."

"Jose," Andy called out. "You may not be as impacted by the changes announced. What's your take?"

"I think this is awful," Jose replied as he slowly looked around the room. "Yes, I'm here only seven years. Once they transfer the little money I have in the pension plan to a 401k, I guess it will recover and grow. I believe that's true, assuming the market performs. But many of my colleagues here have served this company for decades. They are the heart of Vault Operations. I've learned so much from their insights and experience. The idea they might lose money by staying at Americlear when the pensions are privatized or being forced to retire early which they can't afford to do is really a slap in the face.

"My parents came to this country from Puerto Rico when I was a child. They taught me that if I worked hard and sacrificed, I could make a good living and have a better life for my own family one day. What I see going on is that sacrifice doesn't matter to this company anymore. My friends and mentors in this room are getting screwed, forgive my language. It's not right. And I'm not afraid to stick up for them, even if it means losing my job."

Jennie Lie stood up from her chair. "I agree with Jose's comments. We may be among the younger members of Vault Operations, but we have seen first-hand the contributions of our colleagues. I've worked very hard in my life to go to college and get a good education.

"I've read that HR memo a dozen times. I understand how in the past few years during the financial crisis, management felt we had to share in some of the industry's sacrifice. So, we lost bonuses. We lost ground in our lives, due to freezes on salary increases and promotions. We all adjusted our thinking and moved on. But now I feel like we're all paying a price once again."

"Why are older employees and those of us who come from immigrant roots in this country being targeted?" Edith Colon asked in a calm, measured tone.

I know why non-whites always worked below street level at Americlear. Let's not waste time or ignore that once again, we're being targeted. Maybe Judy Jameson tried to change that, but she's gone. I am very sad right now."

Andy and the group sat up in their chairs when Edith spoke. She had always been a spark of upbeat attitude on the vault team, sometimes singing quietly as she worked. No one ever heard Edith speak a cross word about other colleagues in the vault or the business units that she talked to on a regular basis. Her workmates considered her articulate, but tough in her own way.

"Look, you all know my story," Edith continued. "I had nothing coming to America. My parents struggled. My older sister Val, who has been like a mother to me, has struggled without a good education. Luis and I also vowed when we married to not let go of this dream of college for our children. I have one son accepted to a small college in Maine next fall. My other son planned to apply to schools in 2013.

"This announcement has thrown my life into uncertainty. Our combined income will not cover the expense of living in NY and paying college tuition. Like Bea, I can't retire at my age. However, staying at work will rob me of retirement resources when I leave Americlear. I don't honestly know how Luis and I will manage, even with Social Security. So, my life and the life of people I love is now uncertain – and all our planning, all our hard work and dedication doesn't matter any longer."

"Edith," Andy stopped the discussion to reach across his desk and hand her a box of tissues. “Please don’t cry. I didn’t call this meeting to upset you or anyone in this room. We’ve all been together a long time. There are few secrets among those of us who work and live in the vault. I had hoped by talking through the situation, there might be insights to help me figure out how best to guide you and to champion your concerns up to management. But I didn’t realize how personally deep and painful this decision is impacting each of you.”

Reggie was standing in the back. He raised his hand. “Yes, Reggie,” Andy responded. “Do you want to speak?”

“I guess from an age point of view I have time on my side. While I may lose money from the elimination of pensions, Jose is right that there is a fifteen-year window of time for the 401k to grow and recover whatever may be lost now. As a younger team member, I never truly believed the Retiree Medical benefits program would last. What I read suggests healthcare insurance expense is a huge issue for companies in the U.S. and it’s growing non-stop. I guess the only exception is in the IT industry, which offers great benefits and pays well because of the competition to find talent.

“However, there’s something else going on here,” Reggie said as he waved his hand in the air. “I’m no different from many in this room, who joined this company because of the stability of my job and the benefits. I wasn’t unrealistic when the company did periodic layoffs due to market conditions or the financial crisis. I wasn’t happy about it, but I accepted the decision to hold back raises and bonuses, even though so many people in this room and at the firm committed long hours to safeguard our customers. But the timing of this announcement has me rethinking the decision I made almost a decade ago. I’ve lost faith that this company can or will provide the certainty during the rest of my career."

He stood up straight, his height towered over the room. "I doubt I'm alone in this thinking. If the environment isn't predictable, why should I be loyal to this company...or any company for that matter? What prevents this company from pulling the rug out from under me when I'm nearing retirement? I swear this decision speaks to the values of people who are in leadership positions. I loved my time at Americlear, but I can't trust my life and the future of my children to this company."

"Wow," Andy responded, "Thank you Reggie. I don't know if the views of mid-career professionals have been fully considered. You offer a good perspective.

Andy asked the group if they needed a break. He could sense the emotion in the room was growing stronger. He knew better than many company executives the impact of Connolly's decisions on front line employees. However, his staff wanted to continue their dialogue. The meeting had given them a chance to voice their objections. No one wanted to break the rhythm.

Giulia Samartino began, as she always did, in a soft, but strong voice, unwavering voice. "I've been working at Americlear for 30-plus years. I know many of you see me as this senior member of the team. Yet, I'll be blunt. At sixty-two, I don't really want to be here. You all know that I need to be here for the sake of my daughter, Mia, and my granddaughter, Giana. Since my husband passed away, I'm needed financially to help Giana get the special needs expertise and counseling that she requires. Mia works her tail off as a waitress at a local restaurant, but she struggles as a single mom without an education.

"I've given this company all that I can give. Whether it was coming in when I was sick because of work demands or not taking vacation time to cover another employee being absent. You do in life what you must do for those you love. I never cared about recognition. I only cared that I could support my child and grandchild. Is that too much to ask of Americlear?"

Moving from her chair, she walked to the front of Andy's desk. Giulia turned and faced her colleagues. "Look, losing almost twenty five percent or more of my pension following the privatization is not likely a decision I'll make." She began shaking her head from side to side. "Medicare won't kick-in for at least three years. This means my pension will pay me less each month and I'll have to pay medical expenses before I'm even eligible for Medicare. I don't see how the company can promise retiree medical benefits and then take them away, as they force me to retire. My world is coming apart right in front of my eyes.

"I believe the company I worked for – and loved for a good part of my life has lost its way. From where I am here in the vault, I don't know if this disease of moral rectitude is from the CEO or how deep it has affected our senior management. I do know that I am not invisible. This decision threatens me, and I cannot ignore my fears."

The room remained quiet after Giulia spoke. She had thrown down the gauntlet. Regardless of their diverse backgrounds, they all shared a common belief in hard work and respect for the Golden Rule. These minority and immigrant employees understood sacrifice, but they rejected being treated poorly.

Andy wasn't certain if the employees wanted to continue. Giulia had always been the senior spokesperson the staff looked up to in representing their truths. She didn't need a title. Her honesty cut through the air when it was needed.

"Have you all had a chance to express your concerns?" Andy asked as he walked around his desk and stood next to Giulia.

Standing next to her, he hoped his team would see he supported her assessment of the situation.

"Wait, I don't think in the last hour Henry has said two words," Bea responded.

Henry Wong was considered one of most reflective members of the staff. At this point in the meeting, Henry was strangely silent.

"Do you want to say anything Henry," Andy asked?

"A bird does not sing because it has an answer," Henry responded, "It sings because it has a song."

The room fell silent as Henry leaned forward in his chair. It was unlike him to ever talk about his family or personal issues. Suddenly, resting his elbows on his thighs and clasping his hands in front of his face, he took a deep breath.

"I have not told anyone," Henry began. "My wife Mei has not been well. The doctors tell us that she needs heart surgery, and she will need six months afterward to recover and rebuild her strength."

Henry paused, looking at his colleagues. "I have no choice. I simply have no choice. I am forced to stay at Americlear to ensure we have health insurance to cover these medical expenses. As someone suggested, we may lose twenty-five percent of our pension during the conversion to the 401k plan. I am too young to retire at fifty-eight. I can only hope that I can keep my job and work another eight to ten years to get back what I may lose.

"The loss of retiree medical benefits will impact me. My income will have to pay more for supplemental medical insurance, even after I qualify for Medicare. I did not expect that we'd have so little retirement income. Mei and I have always lived very modestly. I am powerless to change the journey. I only hope that Mei can get good doctors for her surgery, and we can grow old together. I feel despair at this moment. As the Chinese proverb says: I have a song to sing, but not the answer."

No one moved for several minutes. He lowered his head. Henry Wong was not an educated man, but everyone found he shared valued life lessons. Calmly, he could see beyond the pettiness or bias that can cloud judgment. It was a surprise to the group to hear about Mei's heart surgery. A simple nature does not mean a person lacks the depth of insight about life, love and so many of the issues he shared with colleagues.

At Nancy's funeral, Henry told Andy: ***"Although you may lose someone, the remedy to death is to live a life of value."*** Henry was a man of deeply held feelings and beliefs. His openness in the staff meeting brought some of the women to tears.

Stella could sit no longer. She did not feel it was her place as the newbie in the group to comment. It had been almost two years since joining Americlear. She struggled like so many of her colleagues to reconcile the company's proud reputation for safeguarding the industry and the degree to which employees were not treated well. Were other folks worse-off at other financial firms? No one was ready to entertain that debate.

"You are where you are. You feel the curse of circumstance without comparison," Ben Klein had told her.

While everyone sat still after Henry spoke, Stella walked over to put her arm on his shoulders and comfort him. The tears welled up in her eyes. This man of slight build and gray hair was despondent. He could not share his fears until this moment. Stella's good nature would always shine through at times like this. She did not have Henry's grasp of life or of words. But her heart wanted to reach out to Henry. There is nothing she believed was worse in life than feeling alone.

It was not Henry's custom to physically touch or hug someone. Yet he knew from day one that Stella was a person who "walked among others only to light the way." He did not say anything in response to Stella's arms around his neck, but Henry could not deny the weight of silence for him had been lifted.

Andy had gotten what he came for – and more. The emotional feedback was overwhelming. These were his people. No, he didn't own them but next to Nancy and the kids, they had been his family for more than two decades. He felt powerless and disturbed as the staff meeting ended. He could not look away.

Weeks would go by quickly. Andy followed his usual routine of walking the floor both inside and outside of the vault. But a strange chill came over him. There was a distance between him and his team that had never been there before. The weeks turned into a month. The distance remained. Surely, he thought, the team could not possibly blame him for the actions taken by senior management at the company. These folks had been so important in his life. He would not have survived losing Nancy if the team didn't embrace him. However, Henry now faced losing his Mei. The others talked of fears. Soon they would all face choices harming their futures.

The sense that he was personally responsible weighed on Andy for almost eight weeks. He embraced the idea that if he wasn't part of the solution, then he was part of the problem. He had failed in the promise he made to protect his team. He had sleepless nights tossing and turning. He could visualize the worst of circumstances. He stopped eating regularly. Ben stopped by and asked if he was on a diet.

One of Henry's Chinese proverbs kept playing over in his mind: "The remedy to facing a death is to live a life of value."

This well-read man of modest heritage could always be counted on to offer insights about human nature.

Andy walked around in a daze now. He was lost in his own frustration of not knowing what to do – and the struggle to find a way forward. The conflict growing inside of him disappeared for a moment, when Stella showed up to work with signs of a fresh beating by her ex-husband. Andy might have missed it at first. She arrived once again with dark glasses and a floppy hat covering her battered face. He walked past her desk twice on his way to the vault that morning. On his second return to his office, he could see Stella had not removed the glasses. She had not bounded from her chair to greet him, which had been her custom.

"Oh, Stella," Andy froze in his tracks. "Please tell me this has not happened again. Didn't you have the lawyer file papers to keep him away from you? I know Ben and I both agreed this was so important to protect you – and Sam. I realize the custody decision has dragged on, but this husband of yours is clearly a threat."

She began to cry. "Andy, I've done my best to avoid him. I did file papers to keep him away, but without full custody of Sam, he still has a right to visit. I tried to have these visits at my parent's home. Last night, he just showed up at my apartment. He had been drinking. He broke the chain on my apartment door to get in. He punched me in the face. The man cannot control his temper."

"We have to find a way to stop him," Andy replied. Once again, the feeling of paralysis and fear welled up in him. This young lady had become like a daughter. No, she would never replace his own children. But Stella was the spark of positive energy that greeted and inspired him each day. He often wondered what his life would be now without her.

Andy stayed with Stella that morning, until a new unanticipated crisis called him away. Near 11 a.m., Reggie Seawright was at his office. The commotion could be heard down the hallway. Andy got up from his desk and met Reggie at the door.

"It's Giulia," Reggie yelled to him. "She collapsed inside the vault. I called for an ambulance, and I notified Security."

"How bad is it?" Andy asked.

"I honestly don't know," he replied. "She's been really stressed about her daughter and grandchild. Giulia rarely talks about personal stuff, but Bea and Edith told me she been openly upset since our staff meeting. They said she's been talking to herself. Does that sound like our Giulia?"

Reggie could see Americlear security personnel administering CPR on Giulia as he ran into the vault. Andy was close behind. Andy looked for someone in security to see if he could tell him anything about her condition.

It would be almost eight minutes before an ambulance and medical staff arrived. Lincoln Smith's deputy, Sal Perez, had put the security staff on high alert. This required multiple staff members to leave their current post and assemble at twenty feet intervals from the front of building to the elevators in the rear that would take them down to the vault. The priority was to get the medical staff to the injured employee as fast as possible. Sal called the building security so the medical team and Sal's staff could get around the normal building security procedures.

Andy kneeled next to Giulia. She had regained consciousness, but she labored to breathe. The small group of colleagues and medical staff were a blur. Andy held her hand. He would not let go until they reached the ambulance near the front of the building. "Giulia, I got you," Andy kept trying to assure her. "You're ok. I promise you it's going to be ok. I'll track down your daughter so she can be at the hospital. Please, Giulia, please just hang in there a little longer."

The medical staff forced Andy to let go before they loaded her into their vehicle. Andy's eyes were filled with tears. He wasn't proud of himself being so emotional, but he didn't care. Giulia was with him from the beginning of his work life at Americlear.

The ambulance pulled away. Andy stood alone on the sidewalk. His eyes would not leave the vehicle until it was out of sight. Stella and Reggie finally met Andy at the curb. They gently put their arms around their boss. He was in shock seeing his favorite employee struggling for her life. His hands were trembling. His head kept shaking side to side. He apologized, though no apology was needed. He then returned to get his suit jacket downstairs.

Andy came back and hailed a taxi. New York Presbyterian Hospital in Lower Manhattan was a short cab ride. The hospital had a well-regarded emergency room and one of their departments specialized in cardiac care. Giulia was not the first Americlear or Wall Street employee to require intervention during a heart attack. Andy kept telling himself she was headed to the best place possible. The traffic made the trip seem like forever. Two streetlights away, Andy could see the hospital. He feared going in. He feared what he was about to see. He feared facing death once more.

He paced back and forth looking at his watch. "Mr. Russo," the desk nurse told him, "It's only been an hour since she arrived. "The doctors need time to treat and evaluate her condition. Please try to be patient."

Andy walked back to the waiting area. He sat down, closed his eyes and quietly prayed to himself that she would survive.

After twenty minutes, he walked back looking through the small glass on the doors entering the ER. He could see six people huddled near the corner bed. He assumed they were Giulia's doctors and nurses. Finally, an orderly came into the waiting area and asked out loud if someone was here from the Samartino family.

"Wait," Andy called out. "I'm Giulia's boss from work. Her daughter is on her way. Can I help? Is she going to be ok?"

"Excuse me," the orderly responded. "What's your name?"

"Andy Russo. I'm her boss at Americlear down near Wall Street."

"Ok, yes. She's awake. She asked for you. Please come with me."

Andy could barely contain himself. He hustled over to the orderly and followed him through the ER door. The blue-green curtain was pulled around her bed, but he could see Giulia was awake and sitting up. An oxygen mask covered her nose and mouth. Her hair was a mess. It stuck up in several different directions. The lipstick was gone. Andy knew she would be mortified if this stylishly dressed elegant Italian woman saw herself in a mirror. His eyes filled with tears.

"I'm so grateful you're ok," Andy said repeatedly. "How do you feel?"

"I'm better," Giulia whispered. "I had trouble catching my breath at the office. Then I felt this numbness and pain in my left arm. Edith came over right away to try and help. When I got dizzy, they ran and got Reggie. That man is the sweetest person I have ever met. He asked Edith to call 911, while he put something on the floor so I could lay down and not fall. The women took over at that point. He told me he was going to get you."

"Did they tell you what happened?"

"Yes, the doctor said I had a heart attack, but I'm lucky it wasn't too bad. They don't believe there's too much damage, at least from the tests they've done so far. He wants me on several medications. He also wants to insert a device in me to calm and regulate my heart. It's all good. Andy, this is not your fault."

He was so relieved to hear Giulia letting him off the hook, but he knew better. He told Giulia that her daughter, Mia, was called and she was on her way to the hospital. He wasn't certain who called Mia or when they called her. But from Brooklyn, he assumed it might be another 30-40 minutes before she could get to the hospital. Andy sat down next to Giulia's bed, "Don't worry, I'm not going anywhere," he told her. "By the way, did I ever tell you how important you are to me?" he said smiling.

Giulia turned her head toward Andy and smiled back. She never doubted how much Andy favored her. She had learned over her working career about bosses who say they care – but don't. Her connection to Andy was deeply felt. Often a partnership at work was driven by a boss who had expectations of loyalty and a one-way commitment to their success. But Andy had always been there to help her, to find support resources for Mia and for Giana. How many times had she brought her grandchild Giana to work over the years, because Mia couldn't be at home? Andy broke the rules. He'd set up a section of the break room for Giana to color and draw. He encouraged others on staff to engage with Giana as they would their own children. His humanity and commitment to each person was never worn on his sleeve, but it was clear in his eyes.

Mia would arrive within the hour. With tears of relief, she cried seeing her mom sitting up in bed. Andy stepped away so Mia could have some privacy with her mom. As he wandered down the hall looking for a café at the hospital, he saw Reggie coming from the opposite direction. "Andy, how is she doing?"

Andy paused before responding, "She dodged a bullet. But I'm not happy. No, I'm not happy. We need to have a talk, Reggie. I'm done. I have had enough. I'm no longer going to play by the rules. We could have lost Nancy today."

"Excuse me," Reggie responded. "You meant to say Giulia" he asked?

"Oh, I'm sorry. Did I not say Giulia?"

"Maybe, I didn't hear you correctly," Reggie answered. But he knew what he heard. Did Andy get confused? Or maybe he was just so stressed seeing Giulia on the floor. And then, maybe using his wife Nancy's name reflected his worst fears. Reggie watched Andy carefully. He couldn't be certain if Andy was okay?

"Reggie, is this what it all comes down to, for those of us who worked and sacrificed all these years? And who's next? They are pulling the rug out from under folks. This is criminal in my judgment. I tell you, honestly, I'm done. I've kept my end of things for forty years. It's time to find a new way."

Reggie listened patiently. He had no idea what Andy was thinking. His boss was never rash or impulsive. He spent long hours quietly looking at situations when faced with a challenge. At the same time, Andy would always find clarity at the end – and he could be relentless when it was required.

"Please go give Giulia a quick hello," Andy instructed. "She's waiting to get assigned a room. She kept thanking you for helping her this morning. When you're done, we need to talk on the way back to the office. We can walk."

It was clear Andy had reached a tipping point. The sky had turned grey, signaling the rain predicted for that afternoon. A light breeze cooled the men down as they crossed Beekman Street. The hospital dominated these backstreets.

Andy suddenly stopped as they reached Gold Street two blocks away and looked up at Reggie. He had not said a word, walking quietly in his own thoughts.

"This company has fucked with the wrong guy," Andy began. "I'm tired of it. I'm not going to accept these decisions. I'm no longer that guy." His voice grew louder. Reggie stepped back shocked at Andy's demeanor and his language. What was happening to the guy he had been working with for nearly a decade?

Andy and Reggie continued walking toward Fulton Street without speaking. The tension continued to build. Andy stopped a few times, muttering to himself. He snapped his fingers several times. His fist punched the air. Eventually, he just stopped on the corner of Fulton and Pearl Street and walked around Reggie several times. His arms were still flailing. Then he pulled Reggie's arm to bring him closer.

He began in a whisper. "What's coming will be risky Reggie. It's something that's never been done before. But I cannot stand it any longer. I will not see the lives of my family threatened – and do nothing. I never thought I could ever come to this point, but the way forward is becoming clear."

Reggie waited for the punchline. It did not come as quickly as he expected. Andy continued walking two more blocks before stopping once again. He took Reggie's left arm gently to signal he was ready.

"We're going to steal $100 million in bearer bonds from the vault. It will require everyone on our team to make this happen. But no one will ever have to worry about Americlear doing the right thing any longer."

"Andy, you're kidding," Reggie said. "I've never seen you like this. Are you sure you're not just upset over Giulia? This is radical if you ask me. Maybe you should give this a few days before deciding a course of action. Besides, what makes you think this could really be done?"

"Yes. It can be done Reggie. And I may be the only person who could pull this off. Yes. I agree. I would be risking everything I ever worked for, including my good name. But my life is different now. If I don't step up, I'll never be worthy of the people who believed in me. Trust me, with careful planning this can be done."

Reggie stood silent for several minutes. He walked to the traffic light by himself. "What the hell is happening here," Reggie said out loud. "Andy is not Robin Hood, I'm not Little John and our team of employees in the vault employees were not the Merry Men." Reggie was convinced his boss had lost his mind. "You see these stories in movies, not in real life."

Still muttering, Andy caught up to Reggie, "I'll have to find someone to fence the bonds. They'll have to distribute the money through a network of banks directly into accounts set up for each of our people. But it can be done, Reggie. It's not as complicated as you think. The bearer bonds are the safest to steal, because they are so fungible. There's no specific person listed on the bond as an owner. Whoever holds the bearer bond essentially owns the bond. This is unlike any other securities we hold in the vault.

"Stealing $100 million, we're only talking about removing about 100 pieces of paper. That represents maybe .002% of the $560 billions of bearer bonds we safeguard in the vault. Those bonds are rarely checked or moved these days. While we do perform an audit of bearer bonds to verify how many bonds we're holding for each financial institution, this is only done once a year in January. We'll have almost six months to take the money and run. It's possible they may not even realize the bonds are missing. Miscounting during audits is common."

Reggie held out his hand as if to force his boss to stop talking. "Andy, if we go down this path, they'll be no turning back. All of us will be done working at Americlear. We may all be done working forever. Our families might face the worst of circumstances if we're caught. Are we all ready to take this dramatic step?"

"You were there," Andy responded. "At the staff meeting, almost half of our team said they'll be forced out in three months. They will either retire early or lose part of their retirement pension. In either case, they will suffer financial ruin or degrees of poverty in retirement. We have nothing to lose anymore. The company has put us in a position where there are no good options.

"While Henry cannot leave because he needs his medical insurance, he'll windup forfeiting twenty-five percent of the pension he would have earned. The older members of the team will also face new burdens in retirement, paying for medical insurance, when they were promised retiree medical benefits. In the past several years, few of them have gotten pay raises or bonuses. Do you think anyone cares that Giulia had a heart attack over this? No one cares anymore. The loss of jobs in our group will continue, especially if the rumors are true about the company moving our headquarters out of New York.

Andy paused holding out his hand, "Is it raining yet?" he asked. He looked behind to see if anyone was walking near them. He grabbed Reggie's shirt sleeve, "Look, I'm being more rationale about this than you may give me credit for. What we're seeing is a war of attrition going on, where few of the folks at the top are hurt but frontline staff like those in Vault Operations are being upended. The social contract I've lived with for 37 years is dead. I am sorry, but I no longer have faith that doing the right thing matters."

"Ok, Andy," Reggie responded. "I agree with what you're saying about the company, but can we really pull something like this off? You know the security protocol at the company better than anyone. You helped set up these procedures. How do you take securities out of the vault without the cameras catching the action? Won't we all get caught? Are we all going to spend our retirement in prison?"

"Reggie, let me put this in perspective. Giulia could have died today. Her daughter would have lost a mother. Giana would have lost a grandmother. Most importantly, they would suffer the loss of financial support that Mia and Giana so desperately need. And what about Henry and Mei? He's facing a life of diminished income and uncertainty at a point in life when he deserves so much more.

"If I didn't believe this could be done, I wouldn't suggest it. But I will think on this some more and work through the fine details. You'll also have to decide if you're joining me. I'll have to talk to each person on the team to see if we have consensus. This won't work if the group is divided. My takeaway from this crisis is that we must do for ourselves from now on."

Over the next several weeks, the lights in Andy's kitchen were on well past midnight. More than a dozen legal pads were used to document timelines and questions that needed to be addressed. He kept his promise, spending long nights and weekends. He was committed to plotting out even the smallest details on how the theft of bearer bonds could be executed.

But mid-way through the exercise, Andy realized the most critical step in the process was finding someone to fence the bonds. It had to be someone skilled at laundering and someone he could trust. Several weeks would slip by. He went through the rolodex in his head of family members, distant relatives – and people who know people.

Andy could not ask his uncle Lou, who had retired from the financial industry. Over the years, he had heard Lou had connections in his old Brooklyn neighborhood to "made guys". However, Lou was an honest guy who made a fortune and now lived quietly on the west coast of Florida, near Naples. The thought of Lou prompted Andy to begin looking through family photo albums one weekend.

He had an epiphany, after seeing a picture of Gino's Café near the old neighborhood. This was a meeting place for guys who were "connected." He took a day off from work the next week to see if anyone from that period was still around. Was Gino's Café still there? As he walked the block in Brooklyn, Andy could see two tables out front of the café. It was like walking back in time. There sat Vinnie Santorelli now in his eighties, with a newspaper and sipping his expresso.

"Vinnie, it's Andy Russo," he said sticking out his hand. Vinnie paused for a minute, taking off his glasses. He didn't recognize the face, but he recognized the Russo name. It had been decades. "I think I knew your father." Vinnie said. "It was Jimmy Russo, yes? He was a good man. He was a barrel-chested man who worked with his hands. Didn't he run the grocery store down the street here? As I recall, he was a guy who never got in trouble. The boys at my table here, they never messed with Jimmy …and he stayed away from our business." Slowly, he reached up to shake Andy's hand. "So, why are you coming to me now?"

"Look," Andy responded, "I need some advice to help a friend of a friend who got mixed up in something. He's trying to get rid of securities." Vinnie waived his hand. He didn't need to know more. He didn't want to know more.

"Tell your friend to call my grandnephew, Joseph Testa. Joey works on Wall Street. He helps folks clean up stuff, if you get my drift. We call him 'the Banker.' He is very good. He doesn't talk about what he does or who he does it with. What I'm trying to say is that he's someone your friend can trust."

"That's great Vinnie. I don't know how to thank you. After all these years, I wasn't certain I'd find anyone from the old days," Andy told him.

"Wait a second, is this name for you – or for a friend?" Vinnie asked. "I'm an old man now. I don't want your father coming down here after me. He never did nothing wrong, from what I remember. It's not right if I'm getting his kid into trouble now."

Andy put his head down. It wasn't clear to Vinnie if Andy was being sheepish or wasn't ready to tell him that his dad had passed away more than a decade ago.

"I'm sorry Andy. I liked your dad. But just the same, you better not get into any trouble. Each of us has a legacy that's handed down. Yours is to honor your dad by always doing the right thing."

"Vinnie, thank you. I will remember that. I have been doing the right thing my whole life. I'm not going to change now."

Andy sat with Vinnie for an hour and drank espresso. The visit brought back so many good memories of his years in Brooklyn. As a kid, he wondered if his small stature disappointed his old man. But their bond always remained strong. His dad came to admire that he had, in his words, this "brainy son" who worked on Wall Street. These memories brought a huge smile of satisfaction to Andy's face.

By mid-June, Andy had finalized his plan. He needed to reach out to Joey Testa to ensure the bonds could be sold, but this hurdle could not be resolved before he had the support of his team. The risk was too great, if he didn't have a consensus. He began a series of clandestine meetings to gauge support and answer questions. Everyone had to come to this decision on their own. Once he put it to the entire group, he would consider this a binding endorsement. Only then could he approach Testa.

"Stella," Andy buzzed her on the phone Monday morning. "Can you join me? I want to discuss a plan I've put together."

Andy's plan to field test his pitch to the vault staff was shelved as soon as Stella entered his office.

She had experienced another physical attack by Nico. "What the hell happened? he asked. Her right eye was swollen shut. Her lip was split, as if someone slapped her repeatedly or punched her face.

Andy came around the desk and put his hands on her shoulders. He guided her to a seat.

Stella's voice cracked with emotion. "After receiving word from her lawyers that the court had upheld his petition granting joint custody of their son, Nico showed up at her apartment. He such a vengeful, spiteful person. I was so hurt and angry that there didn't seem to be any escape from this man. I lost it. I screamed at him. I called him every name I could think of. But he didn't really need an excuse. Once he started to beat me, his only goal was to exert control and use his son as an excuse."

Andy's reaction to this news took Stella by surprise. He spent twenty-minutes calming her down.

"Stella, the abuse you've experienced is not unlike what everyone talked about at our recent staff meeting. The company's actions are both psychologically abusive, and they threaten our physical well-being. I can't sit by and watch my vault family suffer. The plan I came up with is radical. It's dramatic. And it's not without risk – and our success depends on everyone. But if our team agrees, you may never have to worry about Nico again."

"Andy, I can't live my life if Nico is in it. If he has joint custody, Sam and I will never be free. So, if your plan offers me an exit route, I am ready to take the risk. I am that desperate. I'm putting my trust in you. I know you will not fail us."

"Well, we will see this week if everyone agrees to the plan. If we go forward, I'd like you to consider moving with Sam to a villa I'm planning to buy in Tuscany near the city of Florence. My aim is for you to have resources of your own and never see Nico again."

CHAPTER 16
REACHING A DECISION: LIVING A LIFE OF VALUE

No one listening to Andy discuss a theft from the largest depository in the world would believe that with all the technology, security procedures, cameras – and history at Americlear, a theft of this size and magnitude could be possible. But those who worked in the vault knew better. Experience over decades empowered them to exceed expectations, even if their actions would now cross the line between what was legal and illegal. For them, it had come down to a decision of accepting loss and suffering versus retribution and redemption.

The meeting in Andy Russo's office began at 8 a.m. There weren't enough chairs for everyone to sit down. Andy thought this would ensure meetings in his office never lasted too long. Reggie offered once again to stand in the back. This was his way of letting the older women who worked in Vault operations sit. It also ensured Reggie had the advantage of guarding the door if anyone showed up unexpectedly.

"Ok," Andy began, as he sat back on the top of his desk,

"Let's settle down and see if we can reach a decision. Like many of you sitting here, we've spent a good chunk of our lives protecting and maintaining the Vault. When you look around the room, there are members of our family that are no longer here. Each time we have faced a threat to the integrity of the Vault or the firm's reputation for safety, you have sacrificed. But that sacrifice has never been followed with recognition and rewards. Instead, we've seen a steady pattern of layoffs, staff cutbacks, and the elimination of raises, benefits and bonuses.

"I confess," Andy continued, lowering his head for a minute in reflection. The silence in the room made him realize he had to speak. "While you have stood by me as your leader, I have failed to protect you. For much of my career, I was a 'company man.' I repeated the party line from senior management, even when I knew in my heart it wasn't always true. While I cared about all of you, I rationalized that my career and salary was not affected. I was not asked to share in your sacrifice. In truth, until Nancy died, I didn't know real loss. This wake-up call was once again reinforced last month when Giulia almost died from the stress of her job and the actions being taken by management. Yes, you will hear emotion in my voice today. I led with calm all these years; I now want to lead with chaos.

"I've met with each of you one-on-one outlining a plan to take back control of our destiny. This proposal is not without significant risk – a risk to win or lose everything. I won't sugar coat what's at stake, because it could mean our freedom. However, this time I'm not standing on the sidelines. I'm promising to take the lead and see the plan through. I've already made the decision. I stand here today ready to give up everything I have gained in life. I want to finally be worthy of your trust – and your love."

Andy stood up and began to pace in front of his desk. The drama of the moment began to build. Everyone had heard this pitch already. Many were excited to take action. Some were still uncertain. But no one felt, in the heart, their grievances were unjustified.

"Together, we're going to steal $100 million in bearer bonds from the vault. That's the proposal. Stealing negotiable securities from the vault has never been done before. A discussion of this nature, if discovered, by itself would put us all in jail, or at least have us fired. This goal cannot be accomplished without everyone in the Vault being on board and pulling together. I'm not asking you to put all your trust in me. I'm asking you to put your trust in each other. I realize it will be no easy task – and a yes vote means you too are willing to risk everything."

The room stayed silent as Andy went on to explain his plan in detail. He plotted a five-month timeline during which each staff member would be responsible for removing ten bearer bonds. The summer months were slow, and the annual audit of the Vault was normally conducted in January, leaving the group plenty of time to escape.

While he was uncertain about their likelihood of success, he was determined to leverage his experience and expertise to avoid detection. Like Andy, this groups' sense of doing the right thing had been eroded over the years. A long serving, poorly treated and aging employee population will do that. Each staff member sitting in the room felt betrayed. The longstanding social contract they learned in life had disappeared. The threat to them and their families was palpable.

No one wondered about the right and wrong of their desperation. Each had already spent long hours contemplating a future without hope. Their only hesitation was the impact a failed theft might have on their loved ones.

It is a strange thing about the human condition. By the time someone must decide whether to cross the line and commit a crime, they no longer hear the cricket sitting on their shoulder cautioning them on the outcome. It blurs the line between reason and irrational behavior.

"Now, I've met with each of you. There seems to be a consensus about what's going on at the company. Yet are we angry enough to go down this road of no return. Some have said to me that it isn't just about the money. We have all seen too many of our colleagues who have lost jobs – (or their lives) – over the past decade. Many of you have expressed fears never talked about before."

"The hell with this place," Bea injected, "The decision by management to end the pension program and retiree medical benefits will significantly impact employees who have been with the company the longest.

"I told my husband this situation is a Catch 22. If I retire early, I can keep the current full value of my pension, but I'd lose working another five years. No one will hire me. On the other hand, if I stay working, I'll lose money on the conversion of my pension to the company sponsored non-contributing 401k plan. There is no question in my mind, but this management decision is trying to force out older employees from the company. It's horrible and unfair."

"Yes, it's clear to me as well," Edith added, "Our loyalty for nearly three decades means nothing to the current leaders of this company. We're expendable. And without the retiree medical benefits we were promised, our survival will become a balancing act of expenses. If anyone we love becomes sick, we will lose any cushion to safeguard us from paying our rent or covering medical bills.

"The stress this situation is causing all of us is just enormous. Look at what happened to Giulia. She's still in the hospital. Who's next? That could be anyone of us. And if we get sick, will the company take care of us? No, they will not. I have tried to be a good citizen since I came to this country, but the world around me no longer believes in these values."

"Giulia is my 'mammacita'," Jose spoke up. "Since I came to this job, she has looked out for me. She had guided me when I made mistakes filing securities. She has coached me about my job and about my life decisions. I can see how worried she is about her grandchild. I don't know how she might feel about us robbing securities. I would like to know her opinion. Maybe I shouldn't give mine since I'm so young. I have years ahead of me to make up any loss in the new 401k plan. However, you've all taken me in. You are my family. I want to support whatever the group decides."

The phone ringing in Andy's office abruptly stopped the meeting. Stella left to intercept the call. While the conversation continued, she soon returned and motioned to her boss. "I'm sorry," she told Andy, "But Giulia just got home yesterday. She is calling in to join our meeting. She asked to be put on speaker phone."

"I'm sorry not to be with you in person," Giulia began. "I came home last night from the hospital. The doctors have ordered me to rest. However, I told Andy I could not be absent from this discussion. Like many of you, I fear what lies ahead for my family.

"I have tried to set a personal standard to be gentle and soft spoken. I don't look for conflict, even if it looks for me. But I feel attacked by these recent decisions. Maybe we've worked too hard all these years and perhaps we have all stayed too long. I've been thinking about the circumstance since collapsing in the Vault. My fears have almost cost me my life. And I wonder now what would have happened to my family – and those who are extended family at work.

"So, I won't hide at home. I have not lost my moral compass. I do feel, however, that my company no longer reciprocates. I cannot be silent. I feel we're being targeted. And I'll speak plainly. I believe we're being targeted because we're immigrants, who work in the basement. No one thinks about us or cares about us. I support the plan Andy has shared with you. And I am anxious to return to work and help execute this plan. I realize the danger in this decision. Each of you must find peace with it. I am at peace with mine."

A long silence hung over the room after Giulia spoke. She stood apart from the group as a voice of reason. If anyone had reservations, her voice could make them disappear.

"Ok, it's 9 am," Andy said to the group. "We'll need to adjourn before the phone calls from the Operations group begin." No formal vote was taken.

Even younger members like Jennie Li and Reggie were in sync with Andy. Being younger, these folks didn't face the same financial impacts. They had the time in their careers to recover. But how would anyone in this environment know what the future would force upon them? When would it become their turn?

If they shared one common experience it centered on the unpredictable nature of life itself. If you have traveled a path that began with nothing, perhaps you are less afraid when the unknown threatens you.

CHAPTER 17
THE BANKER SIGNS ON

Andy finally called Joey Testa on the phone number Vinnie gave him. His plan was meaningless without someone to launder the bearer bonds. After several rings, a gravelly voice answered. "Yes. Who is this? Who? Did you say Vinnie gave you my number? Are you from Brooklyn? Ok, I'll meet you, but no promises."

He was not surprised by Testa's initially cautious and non-committal response. Testa pushed for a meeting date that allowed him time to checkout Andy. He had asked Andy a series of questions. But there wasn't much to find on Russo. His online presence pretty much confirmed what he did and where he worked without anything unusual popping up.

The office address for Testa was in the MetLife building in midtown Manhattan. Vinnie had instructed Andy to refer to Joey as his banker. Andy's memories of the fixers in his neighborhood were dated, and he had clearly seen too many movies over the years. He was nervous meeting Joey. In Brooklyn, a "made man" was always in the company of six to eight burly guys. They all carried guns and wouldn't hesitate to use them.

Andy needed backup. He asked Reggie and Stella to join him, but he gave them explicit instructions. Andy felt first impressions were important with someone like Joey Testa. He wanted Joey to know he had his own crew, ready to step in if needed.

They arrived on the 42nd floor of the MetLife building and began looking for suite 122. Andy wore a black suit, black shirt, white suspenders and a red tie. He also had a black fedora hat with a white ribbon banding the hat, which was pulled down over his glasses. Reggie followed his boss' instructions wearing a black shirt, pants and tight-fitting vest that made his chest and arms bulge. Reggie's presence was intended to send a clear signal. Andy had muscle if he needed it. On the flip side of that equation, he asked Stella to wear something red and seductive. He realized she might have a limited wardrobe, but Stella was resourceful. She found the perfect red tube dress at a consignment store uptown. She still owned a pair of black high heels from her wedding. Stella was tall to begin with. In four-inch black heels, she was both imposing and distracting. Andy was hopeful she could charm this young thug from the old neighborhood.

It was hysterical how out-of-place they all seemed in this modern office building. The group looked like something out of a 1940s mob movie cast. Andy didn't understand why the security staff downstairs asked him so many questions about where he was going.

Joey's executive assistant greeted Andy and his crew as they entered Suite 122's narrow foyer. "Hi, I'm Sandy. May I help you?" she asked.

Sandy was nothing like someone might imagine as an assistant to a mob guy. She was tall, thin and naturally blond. Andy initially guessed she might be Swedish, with her large blue eyes. However, he realized the first impression was wrong. She clearly had a British accent.

"We have a meeting with Joseph Testa at 10 a.m.," Andy responded. "I'm Andy Russo. These are my associates."

Sandy invited Andy to have a seat. She explained Mr. Testa was on an overseas call. "He'll be with you in a few minutes."

The office lobby had several couches and three curved barrel chairs in brown leather. Andy walked around the chairs twice before sitting in the middle chair. Reggie and Stella waited, taking cues from their boss. Once settled, Andy's partners in crime sat opposite on the grey couch.

The artwork on the walls got Andy's attention. He had studied Art History in college. Across from his chair, he immediately recognized a Jackson Pollack painting with colorful drippings of blue, black and red. He walked over to take a closer look. On the far wall, there was a Morris Louis painting. Louis was known for painting wide vertical stripes of bold colors. As he studied the paintings, Andy was shocked when he realized these were original works of art. This did not fit with his childhood memories of mob guys. It felt more like he was sitting in the senior executive office at a bank on Wall Street. They waited fifteen minutes, looking and feeling very uncomfortable. On the coffee table sat copies of the *Financial Times*, *The NY Times* and several financial trade journals, including Bloomberg magazine.

From the side of the reception desk, a middle-aged man soon appeared. He had to be six foot tall, with salt and pepper shortly cropped hair. The shirt was tailor made and trim across his arms and chest. Andy guessed maybe he was near mid-40s but in good physical shape. He seemed very relaxed, almost casual as he approached his guests.

"Hi, I'm Joey Testa. Welcome. Do you want to follow me back to my office so we can talk?"

Reggie and Stella both stood up and towered over Andy. They followed their host into his office. They stood next to their boss, turning down Joey's offer to sit on the nearby couch.

"Mr. Testa," Andy started the conversation, "our goal here today is to find out if you can sell $100 million in bearer bonds."

Joey Testa was taken back not by the question but Andy's directness. He sat back in his chair, looking at the three people dressed like old-school mobsters. A smile quickly crossed his face. Their outfits were comical. Yet, he realized by their earnestness that they were not joking.

"Yes, we can do that," he replied. "Our fee for handling a transaction like this is usually fifteen percent or about $15 million in this instance. Please keep in mind this fee reflects the risk we are taking and the anonymity we offer. We don't just go to the market in one fell swoop. We can unload these securities in the public market or through private arrangements over a period of days. How we execute these sales will remain confidential."

"Well, our plan is to deliver the securities in increments rather than all at once," Andy stated. "It might be easier for us to package up the bonds in smaller amounts, perhaps $10 to $15 million per delivery."

"Yes, we can manage this arrangement," Testa responded.

Andy Russo knew he was at a point of no return. He had doubts whether they would succeed in stealing the bonds. But he had now crossed the finish line finding someone who could fence the financial instruments. He sat quietly for several minutes trying to assess the situation. Both he and Joey had been so direct and candid, he wondered if this moment was too good to be true. He was guarded that Joey might take the securities and never pay him. What recourse would he have, if his banker didn't follow through with payment?

Testa sat patiently waiting for Andy to respond. A million questions ran through his brain. Where were these bonds coming from? How did this ragtag group get $100 million in bearer bonds? And did he really care where they got the bonds?

In Testa's line of work, the less you knew, the better off you were. His job, like those who came before him, was to simply fence the goods; get the best price possible and move on. There was a huge secondary market for bearer bonds, from folks who did not want banking regulators to track their movement of money. The market included foreign business leaders, government officials and organizations mostly engaged in illegal activities. He estimated he could get a twenty-five to thirty percent profit by reselling the bonds.

"So, here's my offer," Andy began. "We'll pay you twenty-two percent or $22 million to launder the bonds. We may have to increase our target and steal $122 million in bonds to cover this expense, but I'm assuming that won't be a problem."

"Wait," Testa stopped him. "I only asked for fifteen percent. I'm not worried. I'll make money on the other side of this transaction as well."

"Yes, I know," Andy replied. "But aside from a banker, I also need a travel agent. I need new foreign passports and new identities for twelve of my closest associates. Some of them may also have a spouse or children. It's key for me to have two private jets waiting at Teterboro airport ready to whisk my people away to a country without extradition to the U.S. I'm figuring one plane can be headed to South America, maybe Ecuador or Venezuela. The other flight might take them to Switzerland or Asia.

"We will pay you $7 million to have this travel plan firmly in place. We're asking you to commit resources to help gather these folks, if needed, and get them to the planes. I realize no plan is failsafe, but this strategy comes closest to that aim."

"That's a lot of money for a backup plan – and a good deal of trust that we'll keep our word at my end," Testa said. "It will only cost me a $1 million for the identities and the planes."

"Wait, there's more," Andy responded. "We will give you the bonds in increments, which can then be sold. As my banker, you'll establish bank accounts for these new identities and then wire transfer funds to my people in the country where they relocate. This approach allows us to be certain you and your associates are keeping their end of the deal with payments. We'll hold back the last increment of bonds until the end of our relationship. If the backup, fast exit strategy is not required, we'll hand over the last $7 million batch of bonds– and you can keep that as our bonus payment."

"Wow," Testa remarked, "You've really thought this through, haven't you? So, I assume this is a one-shot deal? Or are you planning to make this a regular transaction of selling bearer bonds?"

"No," Andy answered. "This is a one-time transaction, but I'm trying to make it as attractive to you as possible."

"Well, you've succeeded," Joey commented. "I'm comfortable with everything you've requested. I believe my folks can accommodate your requirements. I'm also appreciative that you've sweetened the deal. You've been more than fair. I know my colleagues will be motivated to make this work. But before I give you a final response, I'll need a few weeks to complete our due diligence and check you out."

Andy and Testa spent another fifteen minutes discussing details and exchanging how contact between them would be managed. Stella would handle the passing of phone messages. Andy insisted on personally delivering the envelopes filled with bearer bonds. Testa identified Rick Soto on his staff to serve as the point person getting the new passports, identities, bank accounts and travel prepared. Rick would coordinate with Stella to get photos and details. Soto would source local addresses in key countries overseas that could be used as home addresses for banking accounts and wire transferring funds. The key was to avoid any tracing of wire transfers to a U.S. bank account or home address.

The meeting was over in an hour. Both Andy and Testa remained businesslike and focused.

On the subway ride back downtown, Andy, Reggie and Stella sat quietly. They had cleared a major hurdle, but no one was ready to celebrate a great victory. Their plan could never move forward without a way to liquidate the assets, but pulling this off would require support from the entire vault team. And if they pulled this off, where would they go?

Andy wanted to have a backup plan. It was clear most of the older employees would be forced to accept early retirement, except for Henry. But if most of the vault team was gone, how would a theft be tied back to them? Henry was likely to stay working. Ironically, he could be part of the theft and yet he could hide in plain sight.

The bearer bonds were kept in folders by the name of the financial institutions. Each bond represented about $1 million, some more and some less. They only needed to take 100-120 bonds or pieces of paper, spread out across the 700,000 bonds held in files. An audit in January would take several months to complete. A new crew of younger employees in the vault might overlook missing bonds. If there ever was a time to take their revenge, the stars were aligned.

In the coming weeks, Andy met privately with each member of his team. The door to his office was revolving nonstop. There would be no pressure tactics used during these discussions. Everyone had to choose for themselves whether they joined him or not. His only request was that they do no harm by talking to each other or with friends outside of the office.

He was surprised to find the staff felt as angry and resigned as he did. Their greatest strength – and the greatest threat to the company was in their calm -- and their clarity.

Each staff member feared the risk of being captured. They shared feelings of regret and shame with Andy, as if violating a valued friendship. However, notwithstanding their inner conflicts, each felt their life options had been narrowed. They were resolved to finally do what was best for themselves and their families.

CHAPTER 18
BUSINESS AS USUAL CAN BE UNPREDICTABLE

Almost from the outset of removing securities from the vault, mistakes would be made. This was not an experienced group of criminals. The employees agreed everyone should have a target number of five to ten bearer bonds they'd steal from the vault. These numbers could change as the opportunity to take bonds presented themselves. But the small numbers gave staff members confidence they could pull off their part of the action. All agreed that only one bond should be taken at a time to help avoid discovery. A single bond found out of place could easily be explained as a staff clerical or filing error. They also agreed to limit the number of bonds taken from a single financial institution.

Since bearer bonds were not issued from one central bank or single source, there was no sequential numbers or registered owner listed on these financial instruments. They were completely liquid. Bonds in years past, going back to the 1800s, could be issued by a country, a state, a company, etc., but only the person physically holding the bond could claim ownership. Due to the risk of losing these bonds, most banks eventually housed their portfolios of bearer bonds at Americlear's central location. The computers were used to keep track of how many bonds were being held for each financial company, though the physical paper was required for proof of ownership and cash value.

Elvin Adisa was not a household name at Americlear. He worked for a cleaning service company that was hired by building management to twice daily pick up the trash and clean up the restrooms. Elvin's job covered the floors below street level, including the area outside of the vault. Under normal circumstances, he had little contact or connection with vault employees. He had come with his family from West Africa. It wasn't hard to recognize Elvin. The cleaning staff were required to wear these yellow vest jackets which made them appear ridiculous. Elvin didn't care. He had a job.

Reggie would see Elvin each day on the floor. He always made a point of getting up from his desk, walking down the hall and going over to say hello. At first, Elvin was taken aback by this tree trunk of a man. After a few minutes his neck would start to hurt straining to look up at him. Elvin was no more than five feet four inches tall. Eventually, he figured out it was best to take two steps backward when his new friend came over to chit chat. He enjoyed these short conversations, though Reggie would smother him with questions about his homeland.

Elvin never understood when Reggie tried to tell stories about his former football days. In his country of Nigeria, football was soccer. He was so confused trying to imagine this monster of a man running down a soccer field, at twice the size of any competitor. Nevertheless, these two very different souls found common ground and their friendship broke up the daily routine for both.

It was a Thursday morning. Reggie was preoccupied with a report he was putting together for Andy. Suddenly Elvin appeared at his desk. "Excuse me, Mr. Reggie, but I needed to ask you something. Normally, I am told to report these things to my supervisor upstairs. I was cleaning in the men's room and found this piece of paper on the floor in one of the bathroom stalls."

The green color and large dark type immediately caught Reggie's attention. His eyes opened as wide as they could, in shock and disbelief. His good-natured friend had found a bearer bond on the floor in the bathroom. How was this possible? Reggie immediately stood up from his desk. He gently took the paper from Elvin and calmly assured him that he had done the right thing.

"Elvin, this paper should not be in the men's room. My boss down the hall," he said pointing toward Andy's office, "will be very happy that you found this. I will go speak to him right away. Are you almost finished for the morning down on our floor? I'll let you know what my boss says later today, but I'm certain he will be very grateful. Thank you, my friend."

By the time Reggie reached Andy's office with the bearer bond in his hand, he was sweating nervously. He knew immediately who made this mistake. Edith had spoken often about young Jose having a can-do attitude and hardworking commitment, but at times he could misplace or make errors filing securities. Edith and Giulia were like a fairy god mothers to Jose, looking after him and fixing an error if it occurred.

Reggie was reluctant to jump to conclusions, yet the stakes could not be greater at this very moment. If Elvin had reported what happened to his supervisor, the situation would be in Lincoln Smith's office within the hour. The plan Andy and his team put in motion would unravel quickly. No one would have thought such a thing could happen. Perhaps it was the natural order, Reggie said to himself that the unpredictable was predictable.

Andy sat in his chair, shaking his head in disbelief. Jose had no idea why he was called down to the office. At first, he didn't even remember taking the bond. How is that possible, Andy asked himself? Jose, however, was quick to accept responsibility when questioned. He left the vault that morning. By 10 a.m., he was ready for his usual morning constitutional in the men's room. The bond was held against his leg by a pair of high knee socks. He couldn't recall and fully retrace his steps. When he left the bathroom, he totally forgot about the bond.

After several deep breaths, Andy said, "Jose, you must tape the paper to your leg before you pull up your socks. Do you understand? If anyone other than Elvin had found this bond, we would all be in jail. Do you truly understand the risk here – and how important this is to all of us? We are relying on you to be extra careful from this point forward. If there's any problem, you must tell Reggie or me immediately. Now, nothing said here today should be shared or repeated with anyone at work or at home. Are we good?"

Jose sheepishly nodded in agreement. He was beyond grateful that Andy did not get angry and chew him out. He knew he deserved it. Up to this point, he had not fully thought about or understood the danger of being caught. Instead of dwelling on the incident, he embraced Andy's coaching to do better. It was one of Andy's rare gifts that he really worked at knowing his people and giving them the encouragement they needed to succeed.

"Reggie, I spoke to Jose. I didn't think yelling or shaming him would make Jose be more careful, but I did challenge him to do better. I tried to reinforce he was responsible to the rest of the team. Thank you for stepping up with Elvin."

Andy then took a long walk outside to clear his head. It would take several hours for him to calm his nerves. Had he miscalculated his team could see this theft through without discovery or capture? He kept asking himself, what other details have I overlooked?

The most unsettling moment came a week later when Lincoln Smith from Security stopped down to see Andy. Lincoln had a long career in the military police and intelligence before starting a second career at Americlear. For all his expertise and experience, Lincoln was not an intense person. He was affable and friendly with folks. However, he could turn relentless if his suspicions were raised.

Andy had cautioned the staff. The greatest danger were the cameras in the vault. He never trusted the urban legend stuff about the floor areas of the vault marked X, Y and Z. He had no reason to test these stories. Had Jose's indiscretion already sandbagged the operation?

"Lincoln is on the floor," Edith signaled to her colleagues in the vault. She returned from the Vault entrance. However, he did not enter through the turnstiles. He was headed to Andy's office.

It was understood that Lincoln never needed an appointment or had to be announced when he stopped down to see Andy. Stella greeted him with a big smile. She asked if he wanted coffee. He thanked her but declined. He was carrying a laptop under his arm. She waved him to go right in Andy's office.

Her boss paused from the management report he was writing, typing in the latest vault statistics. Summertime was best for organizing information that would be required for the fall submissions of next year's budget request.

"Sorry to intrude Andy," Lincoln began. "I wasn't anxious to raise this issue with you, but it does concern what's going on in the vault."

Andy froze. He coughed several times to clear his throat. His breathing became more labored. He grabbed his coffee mug to make believe he was drinking, which he hoped hid his facial expressions. Could Lincoln have uncovered their plan this quickly? If he figured it out, Andy knew it was unlikely the code of silence could be maintained. All Security needed was one employee to spill the beans and they'd all fall like dominoes.

Andy invited Lincoln to sit down. Nervously, he waited what seemed like an eternity for the next shoe to drop. "I've been looking at security footage," Lincoln said as he opened his laptop screen. "I think you can see for yourself, what I found going on in vault is quite interesting."

Lincoln slowly turned the laptop so Andy could see the screen. His eyes darted toward the door, though he knew he'd never get there before Lincoln would have him twisted up on the floor in handcuffs. He sat back relaxed and took a deep breath. "Ok, Lincoln, what do we have here?" he asked.

Andy first heard noises, which he did not recognize. The video was a little dark and grainy, but he could make out two people near the break room. He took off his glasses and wiped them clean with a tissue. Lincoln tried to adjust the light on the laptop. Again, Andy could hear muffled sounds. It was like someone was moaning. "What is that?" Andy asked, scratching his head. Lincoln was not about to lead the conversation. He wanted him to figure it out on his own.

In a few minutes, Andy could make out a woman's face. She was Asian. Her head kept tilting backward. Try as he would, it was too dark to see the table she was sitting on. Several more minutes would pass. Suddenly, he could see a man's head bobbing up and down. Eventually, the man stood up. His back was toward the camera, but Andy could guess who it was. Quickly, the man dropped his pants and closed the distance with the woman. More moaning could be heard, and the table was banging against the wall.

A big smile came to Andy. Relieved, he shook his head. Andy knew that Lincoln's video was no laughing matter, but he couldn't help himself. He chuckled for a minute staring back at the video. He was relieved the plot to steal bonds had not been discovered.

"What's your take?" Lincoln inquired.

"Well, I believe the nonsense we've heard all these years about the floor areas X, Y and Z not being in camera view needs some revision," Andy told him.

Lincoln responded with laughter.

"It's the area marked X that is out of camera range. The other places marked on the floor were perhaps, at one time, someone's idea of a joke," Lincoln replied.

"I wonder what Jenni Li and Richard would say about this?" Andy said out loud. Now, both men stopped, looked at each and started to laugh. These two veterans had known each other and worked closely together for more than a decade. It was clear Lincoln had never seen anything like this before at Americlear.

The vault had been violated, in a very strange way. Lincoln seemed more amused than angry.

"Do you want me to call them in?" Andy asked. "I suspect something like this will cost them their jobs, once the HR folks get a hold of this. If the corporate HR folks don't drum them out of town, I'm guessing the rumor mill will certainly end their careers."

"What I propose Andy is that we keep this between us."

Andy couldn't believe what he was hearing. Lincoln was not an intense guy, but he certainly was no softy either. Why was he willing to look the other way? These young people were clearly unprofessional and out of control.

"I'll ask you to caution them. They can take this private stuff to a place where they have more room and won't be filmed," Lincoln said with a big grin.

"Boy, I don't know what to say Lincoln. I can't condone what these folks have done. In 40 years, I've never seen something like this. They really don't know how lucky they are. I'll keep my mouth shut about this and just thank you, on Jennie Li and Richard's behalf."

"It's ok, I was a kid myself once. I may not remember since it was so long ago," Lincoln remarked, "but it's easy to see how they could get carried away.

"Also, Andy, I haven't told anyone yet, but I'm taking the early retirement package. I guess I'm looking at things a little differently now that there's a light at the end of my tunnel.

"Like everyone else, I can't accept that I must lose so much of my pension when they convert to the privatized 401k plan. I didn't expect my career would be over this soon. I know it's not worth the energy to try and fight it. I'm a little more relaxed at this point about security issues at the firm."

"Your leaving will be a tremendous loss for the company," Andy confided. "Since we're sharing today, I should tell you that I'm likely to follow your lead. I hate it, Lincoln. I hate what they're doing to us...and the people who work for us. I don't know if senior management will regret this decision. From my perspective, it is dangerous to lose the institutional memory, considering the growing complexity of finance and securities transactions."

"I agree," Lincoln responded. "Maybe Richard and Jennie Li have the right idea. The new generation is living in the moment. It's not that they don't trust the future. They just live like they don't want to worry about it."

"What will you do?"

"Margie and I bought a small house in Maine a three years ago. We're not crazy about the winters, but seeing the trees change colors in the fall is amazing. Almost every September or October, we go hiking up Cadillac Mountain in Acadia. I have more than two hundred unused sick days left. I figure I'll leave Americlear before the October early retirement deadline. I trust we'll kickback and eat lobster every day to celebrate our newfound freedom," Lincoln concluded with a wry smile on his face.

"Sounds like a plan. It's been hard on me, not having Nancy here to share the next stages of my life. Maybe I'll come visit you in Maine," Andy said. "I haven't quite decided my next steps. Perhaps I'll take a vacation in Italy. Nancy and I often stayed in Tuscany. I want to get far away from this place. In the meantime, however, I will speak to Jennie Li and Richard. They need to find a new lovers' venue. Thank you, Lincoln. You've been a terrific friend over the years."

After this visit, Andy gained a greater appreciation for his colleague's balanced approach and compassion. He could have nailed these young people, but his reaction tried to make peace with current events.

Jennie Li was unflappable when Andy told her of the video Lincoln showed him. She regretted getting caught, but she was so pleased to be with Richard. Jennie Li understood, however, the timing and circumstances had now changed. The priority was the plan to remove bonds. She needed to use more discretion. Rather than cause more embarrassment, Andy asked Jennie Li to talk to Richard. He felt confident that hearing what Lincoln saw would be shocking enough to get their compliance. No more night encounters in the vault.

The silver lining in Lincoln's visit was that even Andy had not been one hundred percent certain where the cameras could capture employees in the vault. Unwittingly, Lincoln had signaled the only safe haven was the floor area marked with an X. Andy believed this information was an unexpected blessing in disguise. The area X was rather small compared to Y and Z, but it was only a short distance from the shelves where bearer bonds were kept.

Over the next several weeks, the staff in the vault had become quite creative in hiding a single piece of paper. Bea was rather large breasted, so she'd just pull her blouse open and tuck the bond under her bra. Edith was more reserved. She began wearing loose fitting sweaters and taping a bond to the back or front of her shirt. It was odd to see sweaters in July and August, but the air conditioning was indeed chilly. Luckily, no one was paying attention to these details.

Jose followed Andy's advice and started taping a $1 million bearer bond to his leg, while wearing his knee-high compression socks. He'd bend down between the rows of files like he was going to tie his shoe. The sock would be pulled down. He could stand back up without attracting any attention, or so he thought.

Andy knew over the course of his long career how resourceful employees could be when it was needed. Even Jennie Li who reached Hong Kong, and later America, hiding in the bottom of a skiff across Kowloon Bay from communist China, was ready to risk it all once again. For her, it seemed easier to tuck a bearer bond inside the back of her high-waisted black thong underwear. This highly independent woman thought it was sexy to keep these valuables so close to her body. She began wearing tops and slacks with lots of spandex, to hold onto the bonds.

Giulia finally returned from her medical leave. Luckily, she did not suffer any permanent damage from the heart attack. The doctors recommended a longer recovery period of rest and no stress, but Giulia's work ethic wouldn't allow her to sit home and do nothing. Her medical team insisted on surgically installing a pacemaker to help regulate her heart.

After nearly two months, she was not bitter about what happened. But like so many of her colleagues, she felt it was time "not to get angry, but to get even." Andy had been a regular visitor at the hospital. He also continued seeing Giulia when she went home. He'd bring flowers and order meals delivered to her home. He was keen to help Giulia, her daughter Mia and little Giana. The granddaughter was excited to greet him when he visited on weekends.

"Amo miozio, Andy."

The plan was now well underway. At first, Andy was reluctant to have Giulia participate. He felt she had been through enough and worried about the stress. Regardless of whether she joined her colleagues in the theft, he was determined to include her in sharing the rewards. Giulia had become his sounding board. He trusted her. They would spend hours going over the details and progress of removing bonds. She also proved quite perceptive about issues that needed caution and careful thought, like not trusting the cameras in the vault. Her decision to support the theft came naturally. She fully understood the risks, but there would be no other option to secure her family's future. She encouraged Andy to use her years of experience and the respect of colleagues to guide the plan from within the vault. Andy concluded her reserved nature would help protect and ensure their success.

The breakroom was filled with balloons and a chocolate cake, to welcome and surprise Giulia on her first day back on the job. Everyone was thrilled to see her.

She specialized working in the section of files where the bearer bonds were kept. Her return gave colleagues an excuse to visit and congregate in this area. Giulia could easily walk a few steps from the floor area marked with an X. The employees' hugs and kisses became a convenient way for her to stuff a bond in the back of their blouses or inside Reggie's unbuttoned shirt. He wore an XXL blue shirt. Giulia would joke with her boss, "A person could hide a file cabinet of papers inside that man's shirt without notice."

Andy walked around with anxiety. While Lincoln told him the cameras were not filming area X, he kept this information to himself. He figured it would force his team to be extra careful. And if area "X" did expose them, they'd know soon enough. Andy kept remembering the grainy pictures of Jennie Li and Richard in his head. Since they were videoed at night, the cameras only caught blurry images. In that scenario, however, it was still enough to make out the people in the security video. To remove securities, most of the action had to occur during daytime hours when all the lights in the vault were turned on.

The staff was constantly finding new ways to remove the bearer bonds from the files. Henry asked his wife, Mei, to sew a new pocket in his khaki chinos. He would stop by to see Giulia and roll the paper like a tightly woven scroll. Then he'd slide the security down the original pocket to the extended pocket that almost reached his knee. Henry was calm and deliberate in his movements. Others referred to it as Henry's sleight of hand.

Giulia would also periodically pull color coded files and send them over to Henry for copying. Henry would shuffle through the corporate bonds in the files. He'd pull the one bearer bond out of the file. He'd copy and throw the documents into a garbage can at his workstation, as if they were being discarded. Once or twice a day, he would then take the garbage to be emptied at the paper shredder. Away from the mainstream of activity (and cameras), it was easier to put the bearer bond aside and place it in a new file. Henry was able to leave these files with Reggie or drop them off at Stella's desk.

No one laughed at the private joke they all shared. Well, maybe an occasional smile with a nod, as they passed each other in the Vault. But for the most part, it was business as usual. Removing bonds was not an hourly task. It was slow, steady and spread over several weeks.

Until the proper handoffs were completed, no one felt at ease. From beyond the vault, no one was likely to detect anything on these pokerfaced employees. On a few minor occasions, a second bond was mistakenly taken from the file of a bank. Andy would get wind of this through Giulia and signal for it to be returned. The strategy, whether right or wrong, was to minimize the number of bonds from any one bank or institution. During an audit, folks unfamiliar with the vault might be quicker to conclude a counting error with only one missing bond. Experience reinforced the need to avoid anything that might lead someone to suspect a pattern.

By the end of August into early September, Andy had made four envelope deliveries to Joey Testa. During his visits uptown, Joey would invite Andy in for an espresso or cup of coffee. He could not get over what a calm, cool character Andy seemed to be. Perhaps it was Joey's turn to make incorrect assumptions and project his world onto Andy's team. Early on, he figured Andy was a master criminal at work. But if that weren't true, he certainly came across more relaxed than anyone he had ever dealt with before.

For his part, Andy never let a detail slip. He quizzed Joey on the progress of the escape backup plan they initially discussed. He was pleased to find out the new identities and passports had been completed. Joey agreed to hold onto the legal documents, which he could make available to Andy on short notice. "Andy, you don't have to worry. It's safer that these documents are not found in your home in a crisis. I do not have any travel planned before our transaction is completed. I personally promise to deliver these documents to you at the airport if the situation starts to go south. The jets will be there. Your people will be out of the country before anyone comes knocking on the door. Consider that a promise among thieves. I hope Vinnie told you I can be trusted."

The most important test for Andy, however, was whether he could see money being wire transferred into new bank accounts for his team. He rejected the idea of payments at the end of their deal, fearing the bonds could be sold and his people not paid. Having the deal unfold in stages, fencing the bonds and dividing the proceeds would reassure both parties of their good faith. The insurance on their deal was the $7 million bonus Andy agreed to pay for the passports and travel agent support. This payment would be made with the final delivery of bearer bonds.

The banker provided Andy with regular updates with a list of deposits in various bank accounts. Andy let out a sigh, when he saw the accounts. The knot in his gut lessoned. Joey can be trusted, Andy whispered to himself.

For his part, Joey began to show a rare emotional attachment to his client. He figured out this man he was dealing with was just a regular guy, an honest guy. Joey rarely asked clients about their motivation. Andy would not be an exception. However, he grew to genuinely liked this guy. On his fourth or fifth visit, Joey told him, "Look, I want you to know that beyond this deal, I'm here for you, Andy. I rarely ever tell that to a client. Once a deal is over, we part our ways. But I've really enjoyed getting to know you. The folks you are protecting seem special and they must truly value you.

"I have lots of resources at my disposal. If you ever get in a jam or need my help, I don't want you to hesitate to call me. I'm not – and I won't – ask for anything in return."

"Thank you, Joey," Andy responded. "I must admit I didn't know what to expect when we started this venture. In the old neighborhood, the folks in Vinnie's line of business could be quite rough. Maybe things have changed. You've been a perfect gentleman."

"Yes, it has changed, Andy. A new generation has refined the nature of our business activities and how we conduct ourselves. But let me assure you that we haven't completely lost some of our past resources. Being tough is not our first choice. We certainly can rise to the occasion, if necessary."

Joey finished his remarks with a smile on his face. It reminded Andy of when his own daughters were young and seemed on the edge of getting into trouble. He would tell his wife Nancy the girls were acting mischievously. He felt relieved that Joey seemed to be on his side. Whether as a client or as a friend, Andy knew this was the better place to be.

By September, it became clear that CEO Connolly was getting her wish with older employees filing papers for early retirement. However, what she didn't expect was the race for the exits. At the management committee meeting, Don Franks, the new head of Human Resources, reported that more employees were filing early retirement papers for October than anticipated. "We may be in a talent bind," Don informed his colleagues. "Seems to me we have a crisis brewing," he reported. "At the current projections, we will experience shortages especially in key leadership positions critical to the firm's operations."

Connolly turned to Alice Feingold, the new General Counsel and asked if the company could force certain senior staff members to delay their retirement or limit them from exercising their rights following the announcement last spring. The CEO, who was rather cavalier about this issue when the program was announced, now had misgivings. Perhaps her plan should have been phased in. She would not admit it at the meeting, but Connolly realized she should have followed HR's recommendation to interview staff slowly to assess their reaction and intentions on early retirement.

"Daeva, I don't believe we can restrict employees from acting on this employee retirement program once we set the rules on this," Alice replied. "We likely made an error not conditioning this offer on management's approving their request. Our only option now is to behind the scenes solicit key personnel to stay and possibly offer incentives to do so."

Everyone sitting around the table could see Connolly was not pleased. Her face grew red, and she had trouble sitting still. The group recalled how resistant she was to advice offered before the plan was announced. But Senior officers were reluctant to tell her what she needed to hear versus what they thought she wanted to hear. The new CEO did not welcome dissent on a strategy she advanced. If the plan failed, it was almost expected that blame would be assigned to forces beyond their control. For a company whose reputation revolved around minimizing risk, this may not have been the ideal leadership style.

The next day, Don was summoned to the CEO's office. "What the hell was that about," she asked Franks. "Why would you raise this issue? Why would you embarrass me in front of the management committee?"

"I'm sorry, Daeva. That was not my intention. I thought reporting on whether employees were taking the early retirement option was a timely issue, since we're so close to the deadline we set."

Connolly began slamming the desk with her hand. By the third stroke hitting the desk, Don thought for certain other employees would hear the noise outside of the office. "Ok, OK," Connolly screamed at Franks. "I fucked up. I FUCKED UP. There, I said it. Are you happy now?"

Franks wasn't certain if he could say anything to calm his boss. He sat with his head looking down in his lap, embarrassed by their exchange. The silence hung in the air like flapping wet laundry. Again, Don told his CEO, "Look, I'm sorry. Maybe I should have held that information for a private discussion. This is all my fault, not yours."

Franks felt threatened for the first time in his career at Americlear. He had never angered any of the CEOs he worked with. This was new territory. To lower the temperature, Don pulled out a list of the top ten senior level managers who had signaled they were leaving. He handed it to Connolly across the desk. "If we agree these folks are critical to keep onboard," Don suggested, "I believe your personal outreach might convince them to stay."

Connolly distracted herself for several minutes looking at her email on the computer. This was a ritual all senior staff experienced with Connolly. Franks believed it was her way of dismissing advice or people she didn't respect. That list was quite long. He wondered if she overreacted since no one had commented about the management committee discussion. Sometimes leaders wrestle with their own insecurities, which bounce around in their head. Franks was not about to litigate blame. He knew better than to share these opinions in the town square or speak plainly with the new CEO.

She eventually took the list from Franks and began to look at the names. Andy Russo, in charge of Vault Operations was followed by R. Lincoln Smith, head of Americlear Security. Further down the list were key folks in IT, Risk and Settlement. The top of the list won her attention. From their past interactions on employee layoffs, Connolly wasn't certain she liked Russo. But she considered him an easy target. Everyone referred to him a "company man," which she felt gave her an advantage. She asked Franks to set up meetings over the next several days. She also wanted talking points on why they should stay onboard for another six months to a year. She wanted a list of incentives that could be offered to make extending their tenure attractive.

Franks left as quickly as he could. It would take the rest of the day to shake off the confrontation with his CEO. He asked himself what he could have done to avoid this experience. He was left without answers. He also wondered if this incident might come back at him down the road or shorten his own tenure. Once damaged, it was never easy to win back the trust and confidence from this CEO. In his heart, he knew she rushed the plan the prior spring. Both HR and Legal had lobbied to slow the rollout. The situation was not of his making, but Franks could see there was an expectation that he had to accept responsibility.

CHAPTER 19
MAKING A BREAK WITH THE PAST

Andy was the first person Franks scheduled with the CEO. He did not think Vault Operations was a more critical area than Corporate Security or the Risk Department but figured it might get him off the hook if Connolly scored an early victory. Andy was known as a team player, affable and good natured. If there was anyone Connolly could convince to stay beyond the early retirement date, it would be Andy.

Nevertheless, Don spoke several times to Andy in advance of the meeting to assess his reaction and try to sell him on the importance of his role at Americlear. But for the first time in his career, Andy was keeping his feelings close to the vest.

"Don, thanks for stopping down to chat. I'm not ready to give you my decision. I'll think about it. Seems like Connolly may have some regrets at this point."

"Andy, she has raised with me the prospect of incentives for senior officers who agreed to remain on board. The subject is likely to come up when you sit down to talk."

Andy and Connolly had interacted many times in the year before she became CEO. He was not a fan. The years Andy spent at Americlear had been devoid of politics. The company's culture had prided itself on teamwork and collaboration. Senior officers might disagree at times, but no one tried to kill their opponents. From the moment she arrived, the atmosphere changed. The roll out of the early retirement program and the elimination of retiree medical benefits was a clear signal the future was about winners and losers. The writing was on the wall, regardless of Connolly's immediate challenge to delay his departure.

"Good morning, Andy. I think you know why I asked you to join me this morning," Connolly began the meeting. Clearly, our HR group did not consider all the impacts that an early retirement program could have. I'm sorry if their mistakes upset you or others on your team. I'm trying to clean up after the elephants and get this company back on track. We've identified 10 critical areas of the company where leaders are still needed to keep our safety and continuity of operations. You're one of those leaders Andy."

The silence between the two lasted several minutes. Andy was in no rush to respond. Daeva was twisting in the wind. She turned to her computer, as if she was waiting or looking for some important message. Connolly didn't see how disrespectful it was to turn her back on him. Andy knew his CEO wanted him to react, but he refused to answer the back of Connolly's chair. He held his ground until she turned toward him, and he had her full attention.

"Thank you, Daeva," Andy began. "This has been a difficult time, after more than thirty years at the company, and for members of my team who have been with me almost from the beginning.

“I don’t believe you ever met my wife Nancy,” Andy began. His opening comments were meant to be a dig. Connolly, along with other senior executives, knew how sick his wife had been the past two years before she died. Connolly never cared to show any concern, until or unless it served her agenda.

“Well, a year ago after my wife Nancy passed away, I considered stepping down. I struggled with my purpose here at Americlear – and in life generally.”

Connolly began to squirm in her chair. She wasn’t certain where the conversation was going. She didn’t regularly feel comfortable when discussions touched on family or required some understanding of personal feelings.

“Then I worried about how isolated I might feel going into retirement without the person I expected to grow old with,” he continued. “Nancy, in her quiet, was my inspiration. She gave me the support and encouragement to succeed and be good at my job. In the months following her death, I struggled. However, I eventually found a new purpose looking after the employees who had also been so much a part of my life.”

Andy now leaned forward in his chair; his hands clasped. “I believe you know I vocally expressed reservations about the early retirement plan and the elimination of retiree medical benefits. The folks down in the vault are truly on the front lines of this organization. They have committed themselves whenever the company faced a crisis, to long hours or whatever else was needed to keep our standards of excellence and to protect the industry. But the decisions made last spring were like a slap in the face to their loyalty. These staff members have already endured numerous staff cuts, reduced raises, and the elimination of bonuses. None of them ever saw the Street’s upside in pay, and yet they were asked to sacrifice when the down cycle came.”

Connolly couldn't sit idle any longer. She cut him off. "Look Andy, we can't relitigate the past," Connolly said. "I've tried to explain the rationale for these decisions at our Managing Director meetings each month."

Now, it was Andy's turn. He interrupted Connolly and looking at her with disdain responded,

"Daeva, maybe that's it. You've been CEO for almost a year. You ran several major businesses for a year before that, but you've never walked down to the vault. You don't, as a rule, talk to any of our employees on the front lines.

"Did you know that Giulia Samartino, our senior vault supervisor, had a heart attack a few months ago? She was so stressed and worried about the impact of your new policies on her daughter and a grandchild with special needs, if she's forced to retire early. Or Henry Wong, who will lose money when his pension is converted to the 401k? Henry can't leave the company, because his wife, Mei, needs health insurance to cover her upcoming heart surgery."

"I'm sorry I don't know these employees. Not everyone has faced what these staff members are dealing with," Connolly told him.

"How would you know?" Andy asked.

Andy had some things to get off his chest. He sat for several minutes gathering his thoughts. He also wanted to see if Connolly would step up and fill the void. This was a last chance for the CEO to say her mea culpas and prove to her subordinate she really cared. But she would not step up. Andy was one senior manager that was not afraid to speak truth to power.

"Look," Andy began, sitting upright and poking his arm in the air, "for decades, immigrants have been kept in the basement of this building much like the cotton fields of an earlier generation. After Jameson became CEO, these practices changed, and things were getting better and more diverse. But I see us backsliding. No one seems to care about the impact policy changes are having on employees who have dedicated themselves to this firm. I am not playing ball anymore. I've been the loyal soldier repeatedly. The only way I know to make a personal statement to you is to stick to my plans and retire early. This won't change anyone's reality here. It won't save my staff from the heartache they will face. But I can't condone or look away from the harm folks are experiencing. Please accept that my decision is final."

He stood and started toward the door. He knew Connolly wasn't finished talking, but he was done listening. She could have tried to acknowledge what he was telling her. He wanted to hear Connolly make the smallest effort to sound human, as if she cared about the people who worked at the company. As he reached the door, he could hear Connolly's last-ditch effort to change his mind. Yet, she misjudged thinking money could buy loyalty.

"Andy, we didn't get to discuss the incentives we'd offer you. I hope you won't completely close the door. We still have a few weeks to go before your decision is made," she said standing up as he left.

The meeting with Connolly lasted only twenty minutes. The CEO listened, but didn't really have a clue who or what Russo was talking about. She had never heard those employee names before. What Franks in HR thought might be an easy victory was a complete disaster. The CEO was not happy. After Andy left her office, she called Franks and told him "That was a waste of my fucking time." She hung up before he could respond.

In the afternoon, Connolly was scheduled to meet with R. Lincoln Smith. He had expressed concern about the elimination of retiree medical benefits coverage, but Connolly saw victory in Smith's decision to extend his tenure six to eight months beyond the early retirement deadline. Connolly sweetened the decision by offering a bonus to help cover the retiree medical insurance co-payments for three years. Connolly concluded Andy was a malcontent, rather than a thoughtful and caring manager. Franks didn't try to persuade her otherwise. He was simply relieved the second meeting got him out of the doghouse.

By the end of the week, Franks had coached and helped Connolly keep five of the ten senior officers. These included a long time IT executive specializing in legacy computer systems, the head of Security, and the top Risk Management officer. Each signed documents extending their early retirement rights and included confidentially agreements regarding the incentives they were guaranteed at year end.

It wasn't immediately clear what motivated Connelly, but she seemed concerned about negative word of mouth building at the company as the decision deadline approached. She was keenly aware when the retirement program and benefits changes were announced in the spring, there were several instances of sabotage. These included IT programming bugs that surfaced, errors in settlement statements and funds wired to financial firms. Ironically, the only operational area not experiencing any push-back or sabotage was Vault Operations.

Connolly was not taking anything for granted. Her instincts were to get aggressive with employees and preempt any further negative reaction. She brought together the Senior Risk Officer, head of Corporate Security, the Chief Information Officer (CIO) and the senior Auditor to propose a sweeping review and audit of all operating areas of the company. She was always more comfortable using force to communicate with employees. She insisted the review include a thorough audit of the vault, even though it was the only area of the company where no errors had surfaced. The annual audit of the vault in January would be moved up to begin in October, as soon as a team was assembled.

Andy, true to his word, filed his early retirement papers on October 1, 2012. He was not aware Connolly had decided to move up the annual vault audit. He found out after he submitted his decision to HR, when Lincoln stopped down to wish him good luck. Whatever Andy might try at this point to delay his departure, it was too late.

There was one final envelope delivery to make with stolen bearer bonds. The bonds used to pay Joey Testa a bonus of $7 million for travel services had been held back. Andy wanted to make certain he could confirm all wire transfers of cash landed in individual bank accounts for his team. Following a detailed strategy and schedule, he never thought the backup plan of new passports, new identities and jet transportation might be needed. After Lincoln's report, Andy was almost certain the team might have to make a run for it. The employees were extremely careful to only take one bond from a bank's file or portfolio. However, if the audit uncovered or concluded bearer bonds were missing, the jig was up.

A review of IT programming initiatives and settlement recordkeeping had already been launched. It would take ten days for the audit of the vault to get underway. Andy could no longer steer the ship out of danger. He would rely on Stella, Reggie, and other team members to keep him abreast of efforts and coach them on steps they could take.

After thirty-plus years, Andy had his going away party at 2:30 pm on the first Friday in October. The gathering included 20 long time middle management employees and his vault staff.

Many senior officers would follow Connolly's decision not to attend. At 4 p.m., the party ended. An assistant director in the HR department helped Andy gather his last box of personal effects, walk him to the Water Street entrance, took his company ID card and said goodbye. In this instance, regardless of his service to Americlear, there would be no long embraces.

On the following Tuesday morning, a call from Ben took him by surprise.

"Andy," Ben's voice sounded startled. "I'm at Montefiore Medical Center in the Bronx. Stella was brought in here last night by her parents. She's been beaten badly. I thought you'd want to know."

"Wait, I didn't hear you," Andy told Ben, "Where are you, again? How bad is it?

I'm on my way. Is she conscious?"

"She's been going in and out of sleep. The doctors tell me she has a concussion and a few broken ribs," Ben replied.

Andy responded. "Ok, I'll be there straight away. I'm coming."

Andy's hands were shaking. He was beside himself. He had only been gone from Americlear a week. It wasn't complicated to figure out. He knew Stella had lost the custody fight with her ex-husband.

When he arrived in the Bronx, Ben was sitting by Stella's bed. Andy noticed he was holding her hand. She was fast asleep. The pain killers were clearly doing their job. Ben stood up and walked outside her room.

"Ok, let me tell you what I know," Ben began. "Stella's parents brought her to the hospital near midnight. She managed to call them. They found her on the kitchen floor in a pool of her own blood. Nico beat her badly and then fled the scene. What's sad is they found Sam hiding in a closet in the bedroom. He heard the arguing and then the screams. Stella had schooled him to hide rather than try to reason with his father.

"I got the call around 5 a.m. this morning. After talking with her parents, I sent them home to get some rest. They were here the whole night. I don't know what they'll do, both have work today. I guess I should tell you, Andy, that Stella and I have been seeing each other."

"When did this start?" Andy asked. "Stella never mentioned it to me."

"Well, it was innocent at first. Just a friendship. Both of us agreed to hold off getting too serious. Then she had the custody fight going on in court. I certainly didn't want to complicate that. I also had a full plate with the new CEO taking over. If it was meant to be, we thought it could wait to tell others. Her parents were told in August, when we both took vacation and spent a week at my brother's bungalow in Cape Cod. I got to spend time and bond with Sam during that trip. I know that was important.

"Andy, you need to know, this is more than just an office romance. I wouldn't do anything to harm her career. I believe this is the real deal. I'm hoping it's the real deal."

Andy smiled. "You know I think the world of you. Stella is making better decisions now. And I realize neither one of you is a kid anymore. Maybe life is rewarding you both at this point. I don't know if she told you. I asked Stella to go with me to Italy for six months. At this point, she's like a third daughter to me."

"No, she didn't tell me. But I'm certain she had her reasons. I'm not going to second guess her. She's got enough on her plate."

The two men sat by Stella's bed for several hours. She woke up close to 11 a.m.

"Did my parents leave?" she whispered.

"Yes," Ben responded. "I was here early. I encouraged them to rest up and come back later this afternoon. Your mom was going to see if she could cancel her appointments today. I'm glad you had them call me."

Stella smiled.

Andy got up from his chair and walked to the bed. He leaned down and kissed Stella's forehead. "You really gave me a scare," he told her.

Right after lunch, Andy excused himself to run an errand. He promised Ben he'd return by dinner time. Andy was not a vindictive person, but he had had enough. It was time to stop Nico from hurting this beautiful and loving young woman. He stopped in the lobby to make a phone call. "Yes, I can be at your office in about twenty-five minutes. Does that work for you?"

The meeting with Testa was unscheduled. He waited fifteen minutes for him to finish a call. His assistant then ushered Andy into his office. "I'm sorry to barge in like this," Andy began. His eyes began to fill up with tears. He wiped his face with the back of his left hand.

"You told me if I ever needed a favor, I should ask. Well, I'm here to see if you can help me."

Andy proceeded to tell Testa about the young woman who wore the famous red dress months ago. The banker did not take kindly to the details of her being beaten by an ex-husband. For this new generation mobster, hurting women was off limits.

"I'll handle it, Andy. You want him dead? I can arrange that. We needn't ever discuss this subject again. Just give my assistant an address."

"No. Not dead," Andy pleaded. "Can you tell me what you will do?"

"Let's not discuss it," Testa answered. "But rest assured, he won't bother Stella Jones again."

Before leaving, Andy updated Testa and asked if the backup plan would be ready in two weeks. He wanted the airplanes to fly his team before the end of October. If anything changed, he would call him. Testa was not alarmed. All the bearer bonds had been moved and sold, already. He had made a handsome profit reselling these instruments to clients in the U.S, South America, and some Asian clients who wanted anonymity. No one at this point could trace any evidence of the transactions. He asked Andy to make the final $7 million bonus payment by October 22, if plan B was being implemented. He assumed Andy trusted him at this point to keep his word.

The subway ride back to the Bronx was quiet. Andy thought about the villa he was going to buy in Tuscany. He had rented a small apartment in the town of Imprunetta years before. At that time, he couldn't afford staying at a villa, but he promised Nancy, "someday, this will be our dream." Villa Di Cali was a twenty-minute drive from Florence.

From the Villa, you could see the Duomo in Florence against the skyline. For more than four centuries the Duomo was the largest dome in the world. Filippo Brunelleschi in the 1420s, as an expression of his own faith, sought to build this architectural miracle, which used the latest theories and techniques known at the time to hold the dome's weight. It was the first church to use self-reinforcing walls to support its size. At night, Andy imagined his daughters and grandchildren standing outside of the villa and hearing the bell tower ringing.

With Nancy gone and his children busy with their own families and careers, Andy planned his escape to Tuscany. Stella had agreed to help Andy get settled in his new home. Her son, Sam, would take a break from school. Perhaps she'd sign him up for the American school in Florence in the new year. If Andy's plan worked, she would finally have resources. She might never again have to worry about working to support her son. But Stella had ambivalence about living in Italy permanently. She wanted to see her parents in New York, so Sam could stay close in their lives. And then there was Ben.

Andy realized he had Nico Farentino's address in his phone's database before leaving Testa's office. He left the information with Testa's assistant before heading back to Montefiore Medical Center.

Ben left the hospital before Andy returned. Andy divided his time in the afternoon between the hospital cafeteria and sitting next to Stella's bed. The nurses came in periodically to encourage Andy to let her rest. There was no place Andy really needed to be, as his time at Americlear had ended. He decided to wait until Stella's parents returned. His spirits were lifted when they arrived with Stella's son, Sam. She was so invested in this child. Nothing brought a smile to her face faster than this child.

Downtown, a knock-on Nico's door came several hours before the police followed up on the spousal abuse complaint filed by Stella's parents. Nico had no idea of what was coming. When he opened his apartment door, he could see the men wearing what appeared to be utility worker uniforms.

"Hi, we're working on an electrical problem in the building. We need to check your apartment to see if you've been impacted by the power station that was damaged."

Nico opened the door wide to let them in. He was somewhat surprised that three men entered the apartment, but he was easily distracted when the first man asked where the electrical box was located. As the third man entered, the door closed, and he slid the security chain across to keep anyone from going in or out.

Little time was wasted once inside. Nico had turned from pointing to the other room when the first man sucker punched him. He went down, his head hit the floor. The other two men joined in kicking Nico. "C'mon fellas, let's soften him up." Nico laid on the floor trying to catch his breath and absorb the pain. However, he was mistaken if he thought a robbery was underway and he could wait until the men left the apartment.

The three men towered in size over Nico. Two lifted him off the floor, while the third man they called Charlie punched his midsection several times. Nico's body heaved and spit fell from his mouth. The men straightened up his body so Charlie could break his nose with one roundhouse punch to the face. At that point, blood flowed freely. A cut could be seen across the bridge of his nose. Nico tried to stand up and regain some sort of composure. Again, Charlie hit him with a left hook. His body jerked backward. It seemed he had lost consciousness. "No, that's not happening," Charlie said. "We're just getting started."

Nico's body was allowed to drop on the floor. Two of the men found an upright chair in the dining area of the apartment. They tied Nico to the chair. His chest was held tightly by rope from the utility bags the men brought. Initially, his feet were free. A sturdy block of wood was found. While weak and in pain, Nico's foot was lifted onto the wood. Charlie stuck a kitchen dish cloth deep into Nico's mouth. At this point, one of the men handed Charlie the hammer. He hit Nico's foot with such force that his body ricocheted backward in response to the horrific pain. Nico's eyes rolled up toward the ceiling. Again, Charlie struck Nico's foot. His associates then insisted on putting the wood under his other foot. The extreme beating would continue.

It was clear and purposeful that several toes on each foot now looked mashed and broken. They paused to give themselves – and Nico a short break.

The rag was pulled from Nico's mouth. He was crying. "Why? Why are you doing this?" he kept trying to ask.

"We hear you like to beat up women," Charlie replied. "You know, my mother is a woman. Now, why would you want to beat my mother?"

Before Nico could respond, one of the men stuffed the cloth back into his mouth again. As Charlie finished talking, he grabbed Nico's hand and broke three fingers. Even with the rag deep in his throat, screams escaped. Charlie was both forceful and deliberate. He took one finger at a time. He bent it backward until he heard the crack – and then he pushed it further.

By this point Nico was struggling to breath. The trauma and pain were unbearable. He began hyperventilating. The men walked away from Nico to talk in the kitchen. "No, no, no," Nico could hear the men saying to each other. One of the men returned with a cold damp rag and wiped Nico's face. Nico would have given anything to drink some water.

"So, here's the problem Nico," Charlie told him. "I've seen a picture of your wife. What's her name? Stella? I think Stella's a mighty fine-looking woman. Wouldn't you agree?"

Charlie had barely finished his sentence when he reached for Nico's left hand. Nico's body shook back and forth. He knew what was coming. He tried to stand up, before the two men forced him back into the chair. It was time for Charlie to repeat the punishment on the other hand. Nico started to sound like a man who was literally going berserk.

His pinky finger now pointed to the left at a forty-five-degree angle. “Does that hurt?” Charlie asked, as he tapped the broken digit. Again, Nico’s body thrashed.

“You see we have rules, Nico. I’m not certain you understand.” Charlie explained. The two men let go of Nico’s shoulders. They walked over to a bag and reached inside. Nico head was bowed over. He was moaning. He had no idea if the beating was over, but he understood there was a connection between Stella and the most severe beating he had ever experienced.

“I fear you haven’t truly gotten our message,” Charlie said out loud. As Nico lifted his head, his eyes widened beyond his sockets. One of the men pulled the cord. The small electric chain saw failed to start on the first pull. After two more attempts, it sounded like it was ready to do the job. The other man pulled on Nico’s arm. Nico fought with all his remaining energy to get away. He was making the most God-awful sounds, screaming in fear and crying uncontrollably.

Suddenly, Charlie waved the two men off Nico. The chain saw shut down. He stood close to Nico’s head. “I’m going to give you this one opportunity of a lifetime,” Charlie said softly. “We want you out of town today. You are never to speak or contact your wife Stella again. If you fail to follow what we’re telling you, we will be back – and we will cut off pieces of you until you get the message. Do you understand?”

Nico was delirious. He couldn’t stop crying uncontrollably. He watched as the guy walked around with the chain saw. The three men made believe they were still arguing about whether they should use the chain saw. Nico was still crying and shaking his head. The teenager who grew up being cruel and tough with everyone, especially with women, no longer wanted to confront anyone. Life teaches you there is always someone stronger, tougher and meaner than you. The punishment seemed excessive even for guys who did what these guys did for a living. They enjoyed beating and torturing him. Nico realized that whoever sent these guys was dead serious.

After twenty minutes, Charlie called Nico's brother, Frankie. "Listen, this is Charlie. Your brother Nico has had a rough day. He needs to leave town by tonight. You better come over here now and help him. We don't want to come back tomorrow. You understand what I'm telling you?"

At first, Frankie thought this was a joke. But as Charlie talked, Frankie knew better. He could hear Nico crying in the background. Frankie said to himself, whatever Nico did was coming back to haunt him.

"I'll be there soon," Frankie answered. "I'll make certain he's gone." The voice at the other end said, "We don't want to see his face no more. Ever. You got it?"

They left Nico tied in the chair. His feet and hands were mangled. Blood trickled down his face and onto his shirt. He was afraid to move. He waited for his brother. Frankie insisted Nico get medical treatment, but his brother begged him to just pack his bags. He would stop at a hospital once he was safely gone from the city. He was done with New York. And he knew he never wanted to see or speak with Stella again.

A police unit arrived at Nico's apartment three hours later. A complaint by Stella's parents of domestic abuse were no longer a priority. They found the door to the apartment slightly ajar. With their weapons drawn, the police searched the small one-bedroom home in the East Bronx. The closets had been cleaned out. Items were strewn on the bed and floor. The kitchen was still intact with dishes, pots and glassware in the cabinets. Whoever lived here, they concluded had skipped town quickly.

They knocked on several neighbor doors. A few reported

hearing noises, but other residents claim they saw Nico and his brother leave the building long before police arrived. Finding blood on a chair and the living room floor, the cops knew they would have to return and assess if a serious crime had been committed. The follow up visits to the building and the police outreach to the landlord would end in a few days. The question of what happened to Nico would remain a mystery. No one saw him again. He had vanished.

Andy would never learn the back story. Testa had given his word and that was good enough. His anger had dissipated. Did Testa "make him dead," he asked himself. He was afraid to ask. Andy didn't want to know. It was different for Stella. Andy couldn't tell her. Once she got out of the hospital, she feared for weeks that Nico might reappear. But Nico never called or showed up at her door again. Somehow, he had disappeared from her life. She wasn't certain how that happened. However, she was grateful and never questioned her good fortune.

CHAPTER 20
MAKING A RUN FOR IT

Fear of the unknown was catching up to Connolly as she worried the company would crumble if key senior employees retired early and fled. And the ones that stayed might create havoc. She began hammering away at all the details she had let slide in the past.

The audit of key areas of the company in early October would once again give her a false sense of control. While a CEO has wide authority from the Board and full control internally, Connolly feared being undermined by possible employee sabotage.

At their first meeting, the Senior Risk Officer (SRO) for Americlear asked his fellow committee members if tackling an across-the-board review of all operating areas at the same time might be spreading themselves too thinly. Connolly did not attend the meeting. His colleagues, the Chief Information Officer (CIO), Senior Auditor and Lincoln Smith all agreed that some pecking order was needed to prioritize this review. Smith went so far as to recommend the audit of the vault be delayed until a new leader was installed. He shared with the group that Andy Russo had taken his package and was now gone.

The feedback from the committee to the CEO was not well received. Connolly called the SRO and directed him to commence the review of the various departments immediately. Connolly wanted a show of force, so employees knew she was serious. If someone was going to rebel and try to undermine the company, she would find and fire them. She asked Smith to assign someone from his team to temporarily oversee the vault audit, until a replacement was chosen for Andy. The CEO chose to ignore the reaction her decision would create. Half of the major departments in the company were under review within a week. However, this move also distracted employees who gathered in larger numbers chatting at the coffee station or lingering in the employee cafeteria. Slow to get back to their routines, many walked around shaking their heads. In their minds, the company was under siege from within even if no one understood why.

Smith could not afford to assign Sal Perez, his deputy chief of Security to lead the audit team in the vault. Instead, Perez recommended their department's "pit-bull" be put in charge. He hoped this might placate the CEO's strong feelings about Andy and the vault. Boris Romanov trained as a cop in Russia. He was six foot two inches with broad muscular shoulders. His family fled to the U.S. when he was twenty-five, looking for a new start. Romanov brought a healthy skepticism to his job, not truly trusting anyone he worked with or any assignment he supervised.

Smith met with Romanov and Perez before launching the audit in the basement. "Boris, in my twenty years at the company, I've never heard of any issues suggesting the vault operations and recordkeeping had been compromised. Andy Russo enjoyed a terrific reputation, and he managed one of the best employee teams I've ever seen. Please hear what I'm saying. I did not believe this audit was needed, especially since no issues had surfaced down there. But the CEO asked us to complete this task, so we're giving you the lead role on this project. However, I'm asking you to avoid getting too invested in this assignment. These are good people. They deserve our respect. Do you understand?"

Boris listened to what he later described as his boss' long-winded caution. However, he was determined to reach his own conclusions on these employees. No stone would be left unturned. He felt his ultimate success would come from finding violations of procedures, mistakes in recordkeeping or missing documents. Boris requested Perez assign two colleagues from the security department and one junior staff member from the Auditor's department.

Smith came down to address a staff meeting of Andy's employees in Vault Operations the first week in October. He tried to reassure the staff that the audit would be painless and completed in four to six weeks. Boris was introduced as the person who would lead the review. Smith asked for their cooperation.

"Andy always talked about this team as a group of consummate professionals and committed to excellence. The company has a review going on in half a dozen operating areas. This is all just part of what a new routine over the next six months may be. Instead of doing a vault audit in January, our CEO asked various senior managers to complete these reviews before year-end."

It came as a surprise to the vault staff that Smith was not informed that Edith Colon, one of the senior clerks, had also accepted the early retirement package. She was leaving the company at the end of week. Smith was then taken aback to hear that Giulia Samartino had taken a second medical leave, following her recent heart attack. He knew about the heart condition from his last discussion with Andy, but he suddenly realized Boris was not going to have two of the most senior vault staff members to help him complete the audit.

There's always an assumption at companies that employees don't know what's going on at a senior management level. However, a firm with a mature or aging staff has the benefit of their own back channels. While many of the rumors shared across this network may turn out to be untrue, these employees are better informed when it comes to policy decisions, especially those which may impact their lives. Younger employees at companies are handicapped, since they don't seem to have the spy networks created over decades. At Americlear, this network for long tenured staff reached every critical department impacting their well-being, including Human Resources.

Smith spent an extra half hour with the vault employees trying to figure out what would be needed to complete the audit. After he left, Boris spent the better part of the next hour quizzing everyone in the room. He was determined to understand Who's Who and how he could work around the missing senior vault staff. Boris zeroed in on Jennie Li. Because of her responsibilities overseeing the transfer of ownership records online, Boris figured she had the best insights on daily procedures in the vault. This assumption was not completely true, but Boris needed to find a way forward.

He then contacted the firm's Envelope Services Unit to borrow extra staff support. This area was slowly disappearing from the days when thousands of runners in the 1970s and 1980s delivered and picked up stock certificates at financial firms. The group suffered regular staff cuts, so the best Boris could find were two people who had a limited understanding of the vault but could recognize various financial instruments.

The first week for Boris was frustrating trying to assemble a team and develop a strategy to pull and examine files in the vault. Andy's staff signaled their cooperation with Boris but weren't fully vested in the success of the project.

Their own self-interest…to avoid prison…would dominate their actions. However, seeing the lack of expertise on Boris' newly assembled team, they began to feel more confident that these audit people weren't certain what they were looking for. Jennie Li was able to persuade Boris they should start and prioritize physical stock certificate files before turning to more complex instruments like money market instruments, corporate bonds and bearer bonds. Her assertiveness and straight talk appealed to Boris. He felt she understood and supported the job he was given. His growing trust in her opinion was visible to the entire vault team.

In the meantime, Andy was taking no chances. He had learned of the vault audit underway, led by Boris. While he was relieved to hear Jennie Li was guiding the process, Andy knew Boris was impulsive and often veered off course from a game plan. He was not a guy who followed his boss' direction.

Andy was not about to take any chances with the freedom of his former employees. By mid-October, he contacted Joey Testa to put in motion the "exit strategy." They set Sunday, October 28 for the group to gather at Teterboro Airport. One flight would head south to Latin America, the other flight would land in Boston and connect with a flight headed to Switzerland. The escape plan would have staff arrive in countries that did not have extradition treaties with the U.S. or did not enforce extradition agreements.

Once they arrived overseas, Joey would direct folks to countries and people he had on the ground to help them get settled and access their money in foreign banks. Both Joey and Andy did not want to take any chances. These bearer bond instruments were hard to trace, and they were already gone from the vault. How do you know something is missing, if no one is certain if it was there in the first place? The computers kept a tally of bonds by financial institution, but each instrument was hard to identify. Unlike equities, there were no central registry and bearer bonds did not have uniform identifying numbers on the paper.

They both knew the greatest threat was from someone on the team being detained by law enforcement and giving up the details. While this might seem remote, Andy was cautious. He briefed each employee. While some were not keen to leave the country, he convinced some of them, like Henry Wong, that this trip would be a short visit. If their ruse was not discovered, each staff member could enjoy the vacation and return home. Some members of the team were set to move overseas with the resources they might gain from the bearer bonds. It wasn't unusual for some immigrants to return to their home countries in retirement, especially if their U.S. pensions were stronger than the local currencies. Half the group agreed to leave, but ultimately some wanted to return and retire in the U.S.

Andy's goal was to keep them safe and give them the freedom to choose their next stages in life.

The vault team busied themselves over the weekend packing suitcases for their trip south or east. Each was sworn to secrecy. They agreed to tell friends they were taking a vacation, but no one could say where or for how long.

Andy's team started to arrive at the airport at 6 a.m.

"Edith, where are you going?" Bea asked. "

"We're traveling to Brazil, where I'm told the weather is between 70-85 degrees. The hotel had its own swimming pool and ocean temperatures at this time of year are quite warm."

"What about you?" Edith responded, as she put down her suitcase.

"Oh, we decided on Switzerland and then we're traveling by train to see a cousin in Belgium. It's so amazing to get away like this," Bea said laughing at her good fortune.

"I understand Jennie Li is headed to Lucerne with Richard Gordon," Edith told her. "I guess after dating six months, Richard has finally earned his place at her side. I kidded with Jennie Li that her travel was truly a vacation for lovers."

The vault team completed a regular workday on Friday, as they tried to keep up the appearance of normalcy. They described their last day as a bit chaotic. Boris, followed by several staff members on his investigative team were running from one set of shelves to another holding securities up to the light and asking repetitive questions. If Andy's team members had their doubts, they were soon convinced Boris' team was clueless on what they were doing and how to verify the instruments they began examining.

Jennie Li was certain Boris would be frustrated and very angry that no one showed up the following week. She thought it would also feed his paranoia. But the news of storm Sandy traveling up the east coast provided some cover for the group. Once it hit the New York region, many companies might face some disruption and staff members not showing up for work.

Teterboro is a small regional airport in northern New Jersey. Mostly, the airport is used by private jet traffic. Over decades, it became increasingly popular with company executives, because you could get in and out of the airport rather quickly. There would be hundreds of flights in and out of Teterboro each day, but the terminals were small and there was little traffic in the area. The airport became more widely known to the public when Sully Sullenberger's U.S. Airway's flight 1549 was hit by birds in 2009. The New York Air Traffic Control Center desperately searched for an immediate place for the plane to land. They directed Sullenberger to a cleared runway at Teterboro airport only a few miles away. However, with both engines disabled, the plane could not glide the distance to Teterboro and landed miraculously in the Hudson River.

By 6 a.m., Andy's team had gathered by Gate 5. As his staff stood with some immediate family members in tow, suitcases were set down near several rows of chairs. Much to Andy's surprise, Joey Testa made a personal appearance to ensure the planes left on time. Joey didn't mind the hands-on service. These folks had made him more than $22 million in profits from bond buyers, without a lot of effort required on his part.

Andy and Joey stood talking near the terminal exit doors, when the General Manager at Teterboro approached. The weather is overcast with a rain coming from the storm headed up the east coast.

"Mr. Testa, you've been a terrific customer of ours. I hate to be the bearer of bad news, but I don't think your guests will be flying out of here today."

"What's going on?" Joey asked. "As far I can tell, it's just a little rain. I don't even see much wind blowing outside, so why would you cancel us?"

"Sir, it's Sandy," he replied. "The storm is headed our way. Sandy has already cut across the Western Caribbean and hit

Jamaica. The National Weather Service predicts it is now a category three storm and gaining strength. They have issued weather alerts, and they started cancelling flights. We expect they'll be more than 1,300 flights cancelled across the country today and tomorrow that number will triple. I regret your colleagues here may have to wait a few days for the storm to pass us by. We're told the storm will be felt by tomorrow in both New Jersey and New York."

Joey returned to Andy, "Our flights are being cancelled. I know you wanted to be out of here. The New York and New Jersey airports are grounding all flights because of Hurricane Sandy, the storm headed our way. I'm afraid we'll have to postpone the trip a few days. Do you want to tell your folks?"

Andy spoke to Joey for several minutes. He was firing questions at him. Nothing seemed to persuade Joey that he – or the vault employees – had any options but to wait out the storm. Almost everyone with them in the terminal had seen the TV monitors and heard about the storm. However, everyone hoped they could get out of town before it reached New York. The airport management explained flying over the storm or around the storm was simply not an option. Everyone in the airline business heard this storm was getting stronger day-by-day.

Over the next hour, the group of employees stood silently by the window near Gate 5 and wondered what was next. They were now prisoners of nature. There would be no bold escape to places unknown. No celebrations from the long years of labor and sacrifice. And likely there would be no payback for poor treatment they received from their employer in response to loyalty and service. Their momentary glee was slowly succumbing to the reality. What does doom look like?

Well, Andy could tell, as he watched his staff members

staring into the overcast day and the rain. No one was talking. After the long silence, one by one they would quietly withdraw and drag their suitcases to a waiting car service. Once home, they were left to their own imaginations and fears. Tomorrow, some would show up at work to try and slow Boris down or steer him away from the green shelves that held bearer bonds.

"Good morning, Andy." It was Stella voice he heard on the phone, while drinking his first cup of coffee. "They stopped the audit."

"What? The audit? Why?"

Stella had showed up for work, like on any other normal day. But it wasn't normal. And nothing would be normal he thought until the vault team was rounded up and sent to prison. Or they finally managed to escape the country as they had planned.

"Andy, you're not focusing. I'm sorry if I sound loud, but I need you to hear what I'm trying to tell you. Lincoln Smith called Boris on Friday and told him to postpone the audit of the vault."

"Stella, do you have any idea what's going on?" he asked.

"Hold on. I'm going down to get Reggie. I'll have him call you back in five minutes from your office."

The waiting seemed endless, an eternity. Where the heck was Reggie, Andy asked himself?

Once again, the phone rang. Andy was still holding the receiver in his hand. "Yea, I'm here. What's going on Reggie?" he asked.

He could hear Reggie laughing, almost in disbelief. "The word came went out on Friday, late in the day," Reggie began. "The CEO has ordered the companywide review of operations and IT to be put on hold. It appears everyone is worried about that storm. I hear seventy people died in the Caribbean. The weather reports say it will reach the east coast shoreline, then New Jersey and New York over the next three days."

"I saw last night when we got home," Andy said. "Is this a real concern or is our senior management just getting panicky?"

Reggie told his former boss, "We are in the crosshairs of what is now predicted to be a Category 1 storm when it hits New York," Reggie explained. "The scuttlebutt is that management may have waited too long to organize and execute an emergency plan. Friday was the first crisis meeting on the storm. That guy, Boris, has been returned to his security detail. Lincoln asked Jennie Li to sit in on the crisis meeting, somewhere in the back to hear what management is planning."

"This sounds serious," Andy responded.

"When they heard the TV reports about the growing crisis, both Edith and Giulia showed up at the crack of dawn. You know our folks. With all that has transpired and with the exposure we all face right now, they still showed up to see how they could help mitigate the risk from this weather event. Giulia recommended that securities be moved from the vault to a new and safe location. It's not clear whether they will act on this suggestion and find an appropriate alternative vault before the storm gets here. I'm hearing the current bias is to try and batten down the hatches and weather the storm."

Andy's first instinct, like those of his staff, was to return to Americlear and help the firm manage through another period of uncertainty. Setting aside the theft of securities, he and his team remained committed to the overall integrity of financial markets in the U.S. He would not be an apologist for actions taken in response to management's treatment. However, as twisted it might seem to someone outside the company, the vault staff never lost sight of their mission to protect the industry.

Feeling somewhat guilty sitting on the sidelines, Andy put in some phone calls to the COO. He offered to come back to help the company relocate physical securities if they were going to make that decision. The calls were very friendly. But it seemed the CEO had already decided on Friday not to move vault documents. She thought the task would be too time consuming and might not be completed before the storm arrived.

Over the coming days, the entire team of employees in Vault Operations team worked to prepare as best they could. The stacks of files which normally might sit waiting for Henry to feed into the digital copying machine were tackled quickly. Jose was assigned to help Henry. If they couldn't get these physical certificates in the digital data base, Jose would use the backup equipment to ensure recent stock certificates were copied and stored in an area designated for duplicate record keeping. Jennie Li asked to keep two of the staff members Boris recruited from the Audit department. These staff members could be trusted to help her speed the update of ownership records, which normally lagged three days after trades were completed at the stock exchanges.

Giulia cautioned the group that no paper should be left unrecorded in some form of backup procedures by Vault Operations, and no files should be left out on desks. "If we can't get into Manhattan for a few days or if the building suffers damage from the storm, we want to pick up the action without losing any time from work not completed in prior days."

The mood in the vault was focused and purposeful. This was once again one of those finest moments for Andy's team to tackle and do whatever was needed. However, they were not alone. Doing whatever is needed is something unique in the culture of Americlear.

The New York Stock Exchange (NYSE) led the industry

announcing closures on Monday, October 29 and Tuesday, October 30, anticipating the weather predictions of storm Sandy's one hundred plus mile an hour winds and rain. The last time a weather event closed the NYSE for two days was in 1888. No one expected a normal resumption of trading or transportation until Wednesday, October 31.

CHAPTER 21
BORIS QUESTIONS GIULIA AND SEES A CONSPIRACY

On Monday, late morning, Giulia Samartino was summoned to Andy Russo's old office. Stella greeted her at the door and encouraged her to stay calm.

Boris, who had stopped conducting the audit, was sitting at the desk looking at the screen on his laptop. Jennie Li was sitting next to him. Boris sat for nearly five minutes without saying a word.

"Mrs. Samartino," he began, "while the audit of this vault has been put on hold due to the storm, I've been spending time going back over the security cameras located near the floor area marked X." Boris slowly turned the laptop around to show Giulia standing near the shelves. She's suddenly surrounded by several employees who come up to greet and hug her.

"This incident seems highly unusual for the employees working inside and outside of the vault. Can you explain?"

Jennie Li leaned forward to interrupt, but Boris waved her off from speaking. "Ms. Zhou, I'll ask you to stay quiet and let Mrs. Samartino speak for herself."

As Giulia looked at the recording, she responded, "Well, I just returned from a medical leave. The month before this video, I had a heart attack in the vault. My colleagues came by to welcome me back to work and wish me well. I don't think there's anything nefarious going on."

"Do the employees always gather as a group inside the vault? Isn't that a violation of the rules? I know the male employees are not allowed to wear sports coats or suit jackets. Women are not supposed to have any handbags, etc."

"Yes, that's true," Giulia responded. "And generally speaking, we don't hold meetings or gather as a group while working in the vault, but that's not a rule. I'd say it's more a practice, which on some occasions is not followed."

"Ok, Mrs. Samartino," Boris said. "But I want you to look very closely at the young man in the corner of this video. Let me back it up on screen so you can see what I see." As Boris fiddles with the keyboard, Giulia looks over at Jennie Li who seemed surprised and rolled her eyes toward the ceiling. The video is grainy, but it's unmistakable that a young Jose Ramos is standing next to the group greeting Giulia. As two women try to hug her at the same time, the young man seems to set a file down on the shelf and kneel. His absence from the filming has clearly caught Boris' eye and roused his suspicions.

"What was that young man doing," Boris asks matter-of-factly? "Why did he kneel down? What was in the file he set down on the shelf? Why was this going on just as the other employees greeted you? Was this young man trying to take and hide something? Had he taken something off a shelf for reasons other than work?"

The questions from Boris kept coming. The man clearly concluded that a conspiracy was underway in the vault. Something criminal was going on. He just could not figure out if Jose was acting alone or if more employees were involved. "I've asked these same questions of Jennie Li before I called you in to discuss. She claims not to have been in the vault at the time this was taken. She also suggested I was wrong to think anything was going on, though she could not tell me why this person disappears from this group video shot."

"What do you see going on Mr. Romanov?" Giulia asked. "If my memory serves me correctly, Jose Ramos came over to join with others and greet me on my first day back to work. While everyone was taking turns giving me hugs, it looks like Mr. Ramos set his filing down to kneel and tie his shoe. I don't think anything else was going on at the time. You may be reading into the video something that simply is not there."

Giulia's soft-spoken approach and calm in a crisis had always served her well. She had been with Andy from the beginning of their working careers. He valued her because she never lost her control. Even when Bea Siegel had melted down numerous times in the vault after the death of Louise, Giulia would step in to coach the team on what to do. She would often kneel and hug Bea, if she collapsed into an emotional ball of regret.

Boris's suspicions were upended by Giulia's reserved response, but he wasn't quite ready to let go. He felt it was his mission to uncover unscrupulous and illegal activities, whether they were real or the product of his imagination. With great care, the employees on Andy's team had committed the perfect crime over a six month period. They feared the audit might uncover evidence that could lead to exhaustive interrogations, where someone might ultimately break down and confess the theft of bearer bonds. But no one suspected the cameras in the vault would expose them in this way. This time, Boris was not crazy. He had the tenacity and perhaps the hubris to think he could find a crime – and now he had achieved his aim.

"Look, I'm not a well person," Giulia said. "There's a storm coming and we're trying to get the vault ready, so we can avoid problems. I've been out on medical leave, but I'm only here to help our team deal with the storm. Everyone is leaving work early so we can get home safely. Our priority is the storm. I understand you're just doing your job, but if there's nothing more I'd like to go back to my work. I think I've answered all your questions."

Boris paused again. "Well, Mrs. Samartino, let me tell you what I think. I believe what we see here on this video is not innocent. Something was going on down here in the vault. I don't know if you were directly involved in this activity, but clearly this young man was trying to hide something, or so it would appear. I have a duty to report this video to my bosses upstairs. I'm assuming they'll want to follow up interviewing you and other staff members, once the storm has passed this week. I apologize if anything I've said today has upset you. But please think carefully about your answers the next time we sit down to discuss. Your responses could have consequences for you and these other employees."

Jennie Li stood up when Giulia got out of her chair. Boris remained seated behind Andy's desk. His eyes would dart back and forth to the computer screen as he scribbled notes on a yellow legal pad. Jennie Li did not escort her colleague back to the vault. She thought it looked better staying behind. She made small talk with Boris, but the security officer was tight lipped about his next steps.

The employees in Vault Operations put their fears aside. They could see the likelihood of their theft being discovered was not going away. And it was clear, nothing they did in a crisis like the storm would erase or mitigate their misdeeds.

Bea said it best during a lunch break in the vault, "Tomorrow is tomorrow. We may not know what's around the corner, but today we'll pull together as we've always done over the years. We've been taught and led by a good teacher. I just hope we can make a difference this week. Baruch Hashem. The rest is in God's hands."

Andy's call to Joey Testa was made soon after the interview Boris completed with Giulia. Andy was determined to ensure their escape plan did not fail. The storm would soon make landfall in New York. Joey tried to assure Andy that he would arrange for the two flights to be at Teterboro before the end of the week. This timeframe was given to Joey by his contacts in the airline business. Everyone was being cautious about when normal operations would resume after the storm Sandy swept through the region.

The Teterboro flights were rescheduled for Friday, November 2, to provide a scheduling cushion. All NY airports were expected to be packed, once travel resumed. Andy did his best to get the word out to his staff about the new flights. However, this time he encouraged the team not to plan a short trip. If the audit resumed or Boris convinced his bosses to start an investigation, they might never return to the U.S.

He spoke to each employee and warned them it might be better not to come back. Some took this news harder than others. Many still had relatives in the U.S. they didn't want to leave. The assumption had always been that after a period, no one would discover any missing securities and travel back to the states would be safe.

Andy green lighted the employees telling family they had vacation plans, but he swore them to secrecy on where they were going and when they'd return. "Now's the time to say your good-byes," he coached them, "but don't get dramatic. If you sound panicked, they'll wonder what's going on. This might complicate things down the road." Most of the team had their bags ready to go by their door. There was nothing more anyone could do but to wait out the storm.

In the coming days, the news was filled with the impact of rain and wind on the New Jersey coastline and the direct hit on New York City. Everyone globally watched as video captured the storm crashing across the coastline. The waves of water from Sandy poured over the sea walls and flooded streets in Lower Manhattan on both sides of the island. No one dared venture out in the extreme weather conditions. Most of the damage reports on the nightly news centered on the earlier reports as the storm reached the mid-Atlantic region. Locally, everyone was held hostage at home by the conditions and devastation outside. The news included reports of widespread power outages and the challenges being faced by emergency crews.

All New Yorkers and those along the New Jersey shoreline could do was to ride out the storm, hunkering down and saying an occasional prayer. Andy and his team would have little contact until the weather conditions started to improve.

The New York Times headline on October 31 said it all, "After the Devastation, a Daunting Recovery."

"Explosions and downed power lines left the lower part of Manhattan and 90 percent of Long Island in the dark…The New York City subway system — a lifeline for millions — was paralyzed by flooded tunnels and was expected to remain silent for days...if not weeks. Seven subway tunnels between Manhattan and Brooklyn were flooded."

"Airports also took a beating. More than 15,000 flights were canceled, and water poured onto the runways at Kennedy International Airport and La Guardia Airport, both in Queens. Officials made plans to reopen Kennedy, the larger of the two and a major departure point for international flights, on Wednesday."

Andy, like so many others, greeted the news reports with horror and shock. In his lifetime, he never heard of so much destruction being caused by one storm. He was grateful to find his children were safe in California on a trip. He sat by the TV for hours listening to the news, which was bad and then it became worse. In Long Branch, New Jersey, where Andy and Nancy frequently visited, the boardwalk was destroyed and many homes along the shoreline were lost. The very large windmill that sat above the roof of his favorite hot dog place had been blown off its perch and was scattered across a parking lot. The news included dramatic damage reports on coastline cities and lower Manhattan suffered a literal wall of water.

In his quiet moments reflecting on the destruction from the storm, Andy realized a window of opportunity had opened. He fought his own instincts to get to the office and help the industry he so loved. No, this would no longer be an option. His time had passed. It wasn't just that he had left Americlear. The company was direct in telling him he was not needed. Sad as that moment felt, Andy was resigned. He went to the kitchen for more coffee.

He sat at the laptop and sent emails to his team. He asked everyone to confirm they and their families were safe. He confessed feeling guilty at the challenges their company and

Wall Street might face after Sandy. Later in the day, he sent a follow up email confirming their flights to get out of town were still scheduled for Friday.

"It may take a few days for this whole situation to become normal again. Once that happens, Boris will be pushing to resume his investigation. This may be our only chance to escape as planned. Please don't assume there will be another one," Andy pleaded in the email. "You will fly using your current passport, so don't forget to put your documentation in your purse or coat."

On Friday, November 2, Testa arranged for his customers to meet privately at 4 p.m. in a room he rented at the back of O'Leary's Bar and Restaurant in Terminal 2 at Teterboro. The flights were not scheduled to leave before 6:30 p.m. While airlines had resumed much of their activity by Thursday, the airport was still busier than usual trying to catch up with flight cancellations. Testa did not identify himself to the team members, but he made a point of handing out envelopes holding their new passports, identity papers and bank statements. His assistant, Sandy, held onto the briefcase carrying these materials. Joey then introduced Jimmy Valenti, who would brief the travelers.

"Ok, if you listen up, I'll explain how this travel and your transition will work. My name is Jimmy Valenti. I will be your travel agent and your family concierge here in New York. If you open your envelopes, you'll find new identity papers, a bank statement, and further instructions. The flights today will head to two destinations; one to Switzerland and the other one will fly to Brazil. Some of you will then take a second flight to your destination.

"Your U.S. Passport will be used for security here in NY, but once you land overseas, you'll start using your new Passport identity. Your instructions will provide you with a bank address and details for your new senior private bank account manager. This contact, while a bank employee, will be helping you with both your financial needs, as well as your personal support in the country where you'll stay. Initially, these employees have arranged a hotel for you and family members. Most of them have already secured either a rental property or possible homes to purchase in the new location. You will have plenty of time to consider your options and they will take care of executing your decisions.

"As both your banker and your local concierge, these individuals will work overtime to address whatever needs you may have. For example, they are expert in helping you move money from your new bank back into the U.S. if needed. They know all the requirements and banking laws to avoid scrutiny by IRS and banking regulators. If at some point you decide to return to the U.S., they can handle the transfer of funds, the sale of property and the travel arrangements. We offer you a one-stop safe and secure service. They can also provide investment advice and arrange for legal support of wills and estates, whether you require that support in your country of residence or back in the U.S.

"If you're wondering how this is all paid for, you can relax. Andy has arranged an annuity with our company; essentially a sum of money that will earn interest and cover the expenses for this specialized and tailored service to each of you. This annuity should cover all of you for the next 20 years and beyond. Your bank statements reflect the sum of your own assets for retirement. Nothing further will be charged to your accounts, except your own personal travel returning to the U.S. or other destinations. Questions?"

"If we decide to remain overseas," Reggie Seawright asked, "where will our children go to school?"

"Your private banking officer will assist you with all transition issues, including finding programs for Americans living abroad. Our company has dealt with these issues before, so we have the expertise, whether it's related to schools, doctors, medical facilities, wiring money home, transportation, or whatever else you may need," said Valenti.

"What if we decide in a year to return home, will you help us come back?" Giulia wanted to know.

"Our goal is to support you, now, and down the road. So, the answer is yes. We will help you move back to the states if you decide that's what you want. How we do this may get a little complicated. If your legal status is compromised in the U.S., we may recommend you return using your new identity papers and foreign passport. However, if the situation is different, you could return with your U.S. identity. Whatever is required, we will help you with that transition as well."

"How will I communicate with relatives back home? The whole point is that no one really knows my new identity and location, yes?" Jennie Li asked.

"Good question," Valenti responded. "Your local concierge will help you facilitate this type of communication. Depending on your destination, we can use a variety of methods for you to freely contact family. You won't tell them your address overseas, but you will be able to communicate without anyone's knowledge or tracking your whereabouts."

Valenti fielded another dozen questions before the group was done. He told Testa he had never faced folks that asked so many tough and detailed questions before. "Most people just want to know if they got their money," he commented. "Whatever this group did for a living, they were extremely detailed and cautious." Testa smiled in response.

Stella had told her son, Sam, and her parents that they were going on a vacation to Italy. But at the airport, her son figured out he might not be returning anytime soon. Since Valenti never mentioned the theft of bearer bonds, Sam had no idea why he was leaving town. Stella would soon get her own surprise. Her vacation and short term stay with Andy would soon become a more permanent option.

Andy had months before finalizing the purchase of his Villa in Tuscany. He saw the property years ago. While the company, Tuscany Now and More rented villas, Andy paid them to broker a deal with the owner. This was a dream come true for Andy. He figured his grown children would come to visit during school breaks or for vacations. He wanted to look out over the landscape from the villa at the trees and vineyards below. Nancy was no longer alive, but this was a dream they talked about often.

The escape plan was quickly executed. Andy and his team left the U.S. on Friday, November 2, 2012. As he sat quietly on the airplane flight, he reflected on his long years working at Americlear. Life presents unpredictable challenges. Andy gave up trying to figure out what was right or wrong with the decisions he made. His moral compass may have been broken. He might be found out and vilified the rest of his days. But he closed his eyes to pray, thankful that nothing he did had harmed those he cared about. His last thought before drifting off to sleep was wondering if, after the storm, their deeds in the vault would eventually be discovered. It was always hard for Andy to sleep on a plane, but not tonight. He would be out for several hours.

CHAPTER 22
NEW BEGINNINGS AND RESTLESSNESS

Two weeks would pass after Andy reached his villa outside of Florence. There was little news he could find online regarding Americlear in the aftermath of the storm. Andy had asked friends at the company to text him, once there was any news. It was time to let go and stop looking over his shoulder. He had gotten confirmation that his team had all reached their destinations safely. It was now time to focus on settling himself, Stella, and Sam in their new home. No more looking back, though a lingering angst he had not anticipated remained.

The villa could accommodate at least fifteen guests, with a second building next door that was being restored to house more company. The swimming pool, off the kitchen area of the home, was huge. It was also not heated, so Andy was in no rush to join Sam doing what kids do. Andy needed a small car. Finding a vehicle that was an automatic rather than a manual transmission was quite a task. But Testa's local contacts were strong in Italy. They convinced a rental car company in Florence to sell Andy a new Fiat 500 hatchback. He would share the car with Stella, which they could use traveling to small fruit and vegetable markets in neighboring towns. Once a week, Andy made a point of driving his extended family into Florence (Firenze) for touring and dinner together. In the first month, Sam visited the Uffizi Museum three times. But he never complained, since Stella kept her promise to visit the best gelato store in town on their visits.

Stella was mindful of the Limited Traffic Zones (LTZs) which restrict driving in the city of Florence. Only taxi drivers or residents were allowed in the historic center of town. Others faced getting ticketed by police. Florence had truly become a haven for tourists, with a more relaxed feel than almost any other location in the country. Visitors could park on the outskirts of town and walk across one of the multiple bridges. Sam and Stella could reach many points of interest in fifteen minutes. The November weather was cool, between forty-five and sixty degrees. Sam was pleased to wear the new brown leather coat his mom bought him.

As they became acclimated, Andy would on occasion join in their walks around the city. Andy encouraged them to attend church services before going out to dinner. The exposure to religion was new for Sam. Andy first visited Santa Maria del Fiore, the Duomo, one of the largest churches in the world. The beauty of the church was undeniable and breathtaking.

If Sam wasn't interested in the church's history or bible stories, at least he could be mesmerized by the sheer size and beauty of the building. Over the course of their first month in Italy, Stella made certain Sam had visited each of the five largest, well-known churches in Florence. He could see and hopefully begin to appreciate the unique structure of the churches, Santa Maria Novella, the Basilica of San Lorenzo, Santa Croce, and others. Stella also tried to sow the seeds of Sam's connection to Italy, with talk of her mom Bianca's ancestral home near Sienna just south of Florence.

With Andy's help, they also navigated the streets of Florence to find the Great Synagogue, which dated back to the 1800s. The building was a unique combination of Italian architecture and large, unusually shaped windows which reflected the influence of the Moors. Sam was not so keen to hear stories on religion, preferring to simply enjoy having a chance to sit down during their walking tours. For this young man, God became synonymous with a building where you could rest.

For Stella, the visit to the Great Synagogue brought back her thoughts of Ben Klein. The custody issues with her former husband were now behind her. Ben represented a new beginning, she hoped. Stella was no longer a twenty-something. She had endured several very rough years. She wanted a chance at a different type of life, with someone who would love and value her. She wondered when and if she'd see him again.

Stella initially struggled to choose between the danger she and Sam might face joining the theft of bonds and the financial freedom it offered her. But she knew losing the custody battle with her ex-husband was an existential threat. The words of her colleague, Jennie Li, would haunt her, "A woman should never rely on a man in life. She needed to stand on her own two feet, to rely only on her own wits and resources." Stella had come to a realization reluctantly. She had to escape her prior life. She embraced her decision out of fear and with determination to change her circumstance. She would go it alone, without Ben, if necessary.

Sitting in church reminded Stella that as a child she would go with her mother on Sundays and pray. Bianca would try to teach her daughter about the importance of God's presence in her life. She reflected on how hard her mom and dad worked to give her a different life, perhaps a better life. Stella had now matured. Stella found new purpose trying to define and shape the road ahead. She had grown to appreciate those memories of solitude and watching her mom deep in her thoughts.

Jennie Li had unknowingly become her patron saint. Her toughness and compassion helped Stella find clarity. After the hospital stay and the last beating from Nico, Jennie Li visited her at home. "Look, Stella, fear is never the answer. Fear paralyzes us from doing…and being…learning…and growing. Don't set your standards in life by the ugliness you've experienced. It will drag you down. Rise up. Take no prisoners.

"Yes, it's ok to love a man, if he respects who you are as a person. He must be willing to embrace and celebrate your flaws, just as you accept his. None of us ever finds a perfect person to be our partner in life. Instead, we should simply look for someone who can inspire us to be our best selves."

Stella spent her time in church thinking she now had resources to do more for Sam. She also wanted to lessen the burden her parents faced, as they struggled to keep up with their jobs. And then there was Ben. Would he be the guy Jennie Li described?

As a rental property, no one really cared if guests had regular access to the Internet. The idea of vacationing in Italy gave folks an excuse for not being tethered to an employer. The villa could offer periodic connection, especially in the early morning or very late at night. However, for the most part, guests were happy to blame the technology if they didn't regularly check-in with their bosses or staffs back home in the states.

It would take Andy considerable effort to find a vendor near the villa who had the right WIFI and technology expertise. Then he focused on finding someone who would reliably show up when they agreed to come. The villa had a long winding driveway connecting the main house and the parking lot. Several other villas shared the use of this driveway. The former owner had resided at the villa as a child back in the 1950s. While the realtor and Andy knew a rehab of the property was needed, the upside was the villa's twenty-minute proximity to Florence.

The small town of Imprunetta was one mile away, and offered a few stores, a weekly farmer's market and Tre Pini, a terrific restaurant where Andy would take Stella and Sam regularly. A four-inch-thick aged Porterhouse, named Steak Florentine, and a bottle of Marchesi Antinori Chianti Classico wine became Andy's celebration dinner of choice. During the week, Andy had hired a local woman to food shop and prepare modest meals for his guests. But on Friday nights, if the group didn't travel to La Giostra in Florence for their amazing homemade pastas (e.g., fettuccini with white boar ragu), their local haunt provided an equally special meal.

Several of the stores and restaurants in Imprunetta offered their own WIFI, which strangely seemed to work better or stronger than what Andy's new family found at the villa. Traveling into town became sort of a refuge to email friends/family and search the net for what was going on in the world. Regrettably, the news from home on storm Sandy's impact sounded devastating.

From Florida and up the coast to New Jersey and New York, more than 200 people had perished. Stories kept appearing on the Internet highlighting the damage in multiple cities. The TV news suggested the damage assessment would easily exceed $80 billion. However, this was simply a guess on the part of officials, who still could not fully inspect and quantify the impacts in different States, among energy suppliers and the thousands of small business owners. Islands in the Caribbean hit by the storm still lacked any power almost three weeks later.

Andy received a half dozen emails from relatives. The Jersey shoreline had been devastated, with hundreds of homes simply washed away or damaged beyond repair. Long Branch and Point Pleasant had lost significant chunks of their boardwalk. The storm tore the wood from their pilings as easily as you might rip a piece of paper. New York City downtown was so overcome by flooding in the streets, local businesses, and transportation areas, many employees were unable to leave in their apartments or return to work. Strangely, little information that was being reported mentioned Americlear.

By the third week of November, the new WIFI equipment was installed. New cables were run from the villa down the driveway to the main road, Via Ponte a Jozzi. Andy began regular outreach to his industry contacts back home. And stronger access to the internet allowed him to read the New York Times every night.

The first story mentioning Americlear indicated that the building experienced four feet of water in the lobby after the storm. Few people would understand the significance of this information. For Andy, it felt like a lightning bolt cursing through his body. If water filled the lobby, it meant that the vault several floors below the street was flooded. Something like this had never happened in the thirty-eight-year history of the company. By the third week of November, the company still did not have access to the vault.

Bonnie Davis, a spokesperson for Americlear, was quoted in the news story saying that no one could get into the vault to fully assess the damage. "Our headquarters remains inaccessible. Americlear's workers have still not returned. We are still operating our computers from regional and out-of-region data centers to support the settlement of trading on financial markets." Andy sat shaking his head. He realized the catastrophic nature of that statement, nearly three weeks after the storm was over. He wondered why the first comment from Americlear was coming from Bonnie, rather than Ben Klein.

He emailed Ben a few days later, asking him if everything was ok. He did not get a reply. Andy wrote again. This time, he invited Ben to come visit Stella and Sam. He explained that both his children and their families were joining him in December for their first holiday in Italy. Andy decided to splurge, hiring a local chef and support staff to serve their guests. Stella's parents were also coming for the holiday. It was the first time either one of them had left the U.S. Again, he did not hear back from Ben.

The call from Lincoln Smith came the following Monday.

"Andy, sorry to bother you. I heard you were on an extended and well-deserved vacation in Italy. Good for you! I don't know if you read about Sandy's impact on us. What happened here is a complete nightmare. It's taken nearly three weeks just to drain the water from the vault. As you can imagine, all the financial instruments we had in the vault floated up to the ceiling. Since the certificates just sat in files on the shelves, there was nothing to hold back the force of water. It was like an ocean wave rolling through and destroying the system your team had created over several decades.

"Our senior team asked me to reach out to you. The water damage has created a unique set of issues operationally and from a security point of view. In addition, we also need to quantify the financial losses we may have experienced, so we can file insurance claims."

"I wondered if that happened," Andy responded. "I just got a new WIFI setup here and read what I could find on Americlear. How can I help?"

"Well, after weeks of near chaos, we hired a company called Drymate International. They have finally gotten the water pumped out of the vault. Their specialty, if you can believe this, is they can take the soaked physical certificates and freeze dry them. Once we audit what was damaged, it will be possible to replace those documents. What they're calling a restoration process could take six to eight months. The good news, as you know, is that we can fall back on the electronic records to continue our support of the financial markets' record keeping.

"While Drymate may help us salvage and reconcile what was in the vault, the firm's existing location has suffered significant damage. It's clear that the operation of the vault will have to be moved to a new location. There's no way we can just fix this.

"Andy, I can share with you that most of the senior management team regrets not taking your advice years ago to decentralize Vault Operations. I've been asked to see if you'd participate as a consultant in a series of conference calls with a cross-functional senior team at Americlear to provide advice over the coming month. Suddenly, everyone has pulled out the modernization plan you wrote back years ago. Of course, Americlear will compensate you for your participation."

Andy sat scratching his head. He didn't need the money. But after months of fearing his escape with bearer bonds might soon be discovered, it appears the company had bigger issues to resolve.

Once the company dried out all the documents, would they

find financial instruments were missing? Andy couldn't be certain. But he figured it was better staying close to the action so he could signal his team if they were in danger.

"It looks like these huge clumps of wet paper are all balled up throughout the vault," Lincoln remarked. While our spokesperson has told the press, and the financial industry, that we have a robust backup electronic file of ownership records, we simply don't know if that's true. A readable physical document is needed to audit and confirm any losses. The freeze-drying effort is just a short-term solution so we can account for documents in our possession. Our Audit and Legal departments believe we could be facing significant losses.

"Lincoln, did Ben signoff on the press statement claiming Americlear did not experience any losses from the storm and there would not be any financial impact on the markets or clients?" Andy asked.

"I'm not certain how to tell you this. Ben is no longer at Americlear. He and the CEO butted heads on our media statement. He refused to go along with a public comment saying there would be no financial losses, since no one at the firm believes that will be true. Strikes me the CEO was more concerned with appearances. She was clearly responding to the politics and posturing in the moment. Ben wanted her to just say we were uncertain about losses and could not comment until Drymate finished their work.

"I'll be honest. It got ugly, the back and forth between Ben and Connolly. Alice Feingold, as General Counsel, tried to weigh in on Ben's behalf. She also thought a more modest noncommittal statement was the safer way to go. But Connolly was not having it.

She remained concerned about appearances – or I should say,

preoccupied with her own image. Ben resigned rather than tell the press something he knew to be untrue.

"Wow, I'm really disappointed to hear that," Andy responded. "Yet, I'm not surprised.

"Will the news about Ben change your decision, Andy?"

"Lincoln, I'm still going to help. I think what happened to Ben sucks. I have my own feelings about the CEO, but the priority right now is getting the ship righted and on the correct course.

"Andy, thank you! I will ask you to keep our conversation confidential. My agreement to stick around on the job six months must now be extended, because of this work on the vault relocation. I'm trying to keep my head down and not lose sight of this goal. Someone else will have to tackle the politics. Or at least I hope they will. If you'll send me an email address, I'll follow up with the schedule for our conference calls."

Drinking coffee in the study located down the hallway from the kitchen, Andy sat by the beautiful French doors opening onto the patio. He wondered about his friend, Ben. It took courage to stand up to a CEO. Ben had survived, working with two CEOs. No one believed Ben would compromise his values – or his reputation, just to keep his job. The third CEO, Connolly didn't truly understand how important it was to have someone the press respected. Financial journalists had worked with Ben for twenty plus years. His personal assurances could stop a negative news story, because reporters trusted him. If they found out that Connolly purposefully mislead them about the impacts from storm Sandy, the press would be relentless in criticizing her leadership of the most trusted organization on Wall Street.

Andy began to second guess himself. He couldn't be certain if helping Americlear during this crisis was a smart move. On the one hand, it gave him access and insight on the efforts underway to restore physical certificates damaged by the storm. But what would he do if the audit of documents recovered by Drymate found a discrepancy in the records of bearer bonds? Yes, he might gain an early warning of danger the audit posed in discovering the theft. However, his involvement with Americlear would also provide detailed information on how and where to find him. Had he unwittingly given up his chance of escape?

Weeks passed by. Still, there was no word from Ben. Periodically, he'd ask Stella if she heard from him. He did not share the news that he had left Americlear. As time passed, he sensed Stella was starting to doubt whether she would ever see him again. The idea that the two of them could ride into the sunset together seemed more unlikely.

How naïve she concluded. Just because you have money does not mean it will bring stability, certainty and love. Andy worried she would sink into depression, if she learned Ben quit the job and didn't immediately come to her in Italy. He convinced himself that he should not get in the middle. If he defended Ben's lack of communication, Andy worried he might jeopardize her trust.

Andy resisted the invite during conference calls from senior executives for him to return to New York and see the progress being made by Drymate. "It's truly amazing," Jake Toporek, head of Risk Management commented. "We visited the warehouse downtown where Drymate has been working with the waterlogged securities. The process is very slow. Clearly, many of these documents will eventually be replaced, but the technique to freeze-dry the paper has allowed us to read enough detail to complete our audit."

The news of Drymate's success sent a chilling reminder to

Andy that the perfect crime no longer seemed perfect. Maybe it never was to begin with. At this juncture, his team members remained at undisclosed locations and a safe distance from a pursuit by law enforcement. But a few members of his team wanted to return to New York. Henry Wong had to bring his wife, Mei, for her scheduled heart surgery at Weill Cornell Medical Center in December.

Reggie had been asked to return and help with the transfer of restored and newly generated certificates to the vault locations outside the New York metro region. While Reggie wanted to leave Americlear after the heist, he and his wife wanted their children to finish the school year in 2013. He would return to the company to help, as long as he did not pick up information or find suspicion that a crime may have been committed. If anything started to surface, Reggie as one of the security professionals would be the first to know.

Andy had never fully considered what was often characterized as the "long arm of the law." If discovered, he had no doubt that the industry would be unforgiving …and the federal government would chase these criminals to the end of the world.

He came to believe and accept his shortsightedness. If he thought longer and harder about the relentless pursuit that might follow him and others, he likely would have concluded the crime did not pay. This lifelong affable guy had allowed his anger to get the better of him. Perhaps fueled by the loss of his wife, he became an advocate fighting against injustice. No, he wasn't going to blame Nancy. She had done everything right in life. She certainly didn't deserve in death to be an excuse for this turn of events. Could he really stand up in a court of law and claim his crime was motivated by his wife's passing?

"Wasn't it enough?" Andy thought that he was righting the

many wrongs he found with his employer. How often along his nearly 40-year career had he seen and stood by while his staff suffered clear discrimination and mistreatment? Why hadn't he stood up sooner? Why hadn't he sacrificed as Ben did, quitting the job before he compromised his values? Would it have made a difference? Likely not, he told himself. But he had been a "company" man for so long, he almost lost sight of what really mattered. The company had given him success and rewards to provide for his family. While he empathized with his employees, he wasn't ready to go beyond periodic and modest protests.

However, Louise Taylor's death in the vault shook Andy's tolerance. Her death was a step too far. He worked hard at putting this shocking event behind him. He struggled, like so many of the people who worked with him – and trusted him. For the first time, Andy started to feel more responsible for these employees than he reasonably should have. Was he making up time for the guilt he felt from earlier waves of employees let go during the economic downturns in 2002/2003 (after 9/11), and the financial crisis in 2008?

Andy's positive, can-do nature had always gotten him back on track. In time, he attributed his anger and guilt over Louise's death to circumstances beyond his control. The searing pain of the event would surface occasionally, as it did for Bea and others, but then be suppressed it again. Life was about moving forward, not dwelling on the past.

No, Nancy's heart disease diagnosis and death was not the cause of his anger at the company. It's just that it wasn't the same without her, Andy had lost his clarity about why he was still here. Her loss left him with so many unanswered questions. Her happiness had been his purpose in life, above all other things. Yes, he loved his children. But Nancy saw something in him that strengthened his resolve and inspired him when he lost his way. Without her, he didn't have a purpose. The members of his team lifted him up during his darkest period. How could he reconcile what he saw going on at the company, while ignoring the love that literally saved him.

"Maybe Ben is right," Andy wondered. "If you can't stand up for your values and what you believe regardless of the consequences, who are you…and who will you become?

"No, I can't right all the wrongs of the past. No, I'm not Robinhood, sticking it to the man. I am late to the game of feeling noble or fighting for some greater good. I'm just a flawed person finally trying to get it right for someone else."

While he used the conference calls with former senior colleagues to gauge the level of danger his team might face, Andy continued to find excuses for not returning to New York. His home in Tuscany was under renovation and he expected family to visit over the Christmas holidays. Everyone on the calls were buoyant now that the damage from storm Sandy was better understood. Drymate's work was reducing the size of losses feared, though the discussions of vault contents got less specific when they reached the subject of bearer bonds. No one seemed to have answers. Andy did his best to probe the discussions, cautious not to invite scrutiny or suspicion.

The modernization plan Andy wrote in the '90s provided an effective blueprint for implementing a series of new, smaller decentralized vaults, where paper ownership records could be held. These smaller vaults would still offer excess capacity in the event of a crisis like 9/11 or another catastrophic storm. Locations of these vaults would be secret, but they had to be near major transportation routes. Redundancy requirements for a vault location were defined by the working group on several levels, including alternate methods of transporting financial instruments and access to trained personnel.

After 9/11, the company had established a robust, fail-safe data security network, with the ability to capture electronic data simultaneously at distances of more than one-thousand miles from New York. The breakthroughs in technology after 2005 expanded the bandwidth of fiber optic cable used in telecom by a factor of ten. This essentially changed the security equation. Instead of one file or packet of data being sent over a fiber cable in sequential order, the breakthrough now allowed ten packets to be sent simultaneously. Both the volume of data packets and the size of simultaneous transmissions dramatically redefined security safeguards for Americlear and for the industry. In addition, Americlear was given priority on the national telecom grid, which allowed them to send massive amounts of data across huge distances, without any potential of loss or failure to reach its destination. If the file hit a slow spot on the telecom network, it would automatically reroute itself without human intervention.

Andy envisioned something similar for physical instruments looking ahead to the future. The industry needed a highly flexible infrastructure that allowed the movement of instruments in electronic form and assured the safety/security mirroring the firm's data security. Clearly, over time the use and reliance on paper securities would be eliminated. However, it took the industry nearly forty years to reach a point when only one to two percent of all financial records were paper based. That said, Andy was quick to point out this percent of paper still translated into millions of securities certificates.

The original plan Andy had submitted after 9/11 required updating. The task force on Vault Operations refined the goals and specific requirements based on changing industry trends.

Yet, nothing in the new plans would help reduce the burden for his team in the New York vault. Quite the opposite. Once implemented, the plan called for one of the vaults to be moved to New Jersey, which would double the length and time of commuting for employees. For front line employees who didn't have access to public transportation – and didn't own a car, it might be extremely difficult to reach their job.

Sandy had forever redefined where companies operated. Many financial firms seized on the storm's impact to move sizable numbers of staff to New Jersey, for flexibility, reduced expenses and lower taxes. A smaller number of firms relocated to upstate New York and Connecticut. Some firms opened or expanded offices in the south or southwest of the U.S., where a new hiring effort got underway paying lower salaries than required in New York. The losers in this new post-storm environment were New York employees. The biggest losers were lower-level front line staff, who found themselves without options to commute or keep their jobs.

The lack of information about the effort to recondition and recover waterlogged bearer bonds continued to increase Andy's anxiety. He desperately tried to keep his emotions in check, but slow steady progress by Drymate could mean it was only a matter of time before someone discovered bonds were missing. He had not stayed in touch with anyone on staff, since arriving in Italy. Andy felt it was a mistake not to have regularly kept tabs on his team. He knew Henry would return to New York for Mei's medical care. However, the news of Reggie's returning took him by surprise.

At this point, he was home free, but Andy could not let go. He had to follow through on his promise to protect the team once they committed themselves to the theft of bonds.

His first call in almost a month was to Jimmy Valenti, the point person Testa had assigned to support the vault staff. Valenti was surprised to hear from Andy, but he understood once he was given a briefing on the situation. Valenti was one of Joey's most trusted lieutenants and the only person other than his boss who knew the full details of the bond heist.

Andy asked Valenti to canvass and report back how members of his team were coping in their new locations. It was important to know whether other team members were getting itchy to return to New York. With their overseas bank accounts flush with cash, Andy expected his former employees to be calm and to start planning the next phase of their lives.

But family members back in the U.S. could be a powerful draw. The cash could falsely give folks a feeling of invincibility. Life could be bent to their will versus the other way around. The vault team members still feared repercussions from their actions. But their confidence would only grow as they learned about the flood damage from Sandy. Few of them knew about Drymate and the progress this firm was making. Salvaging even a third of the bearer bond portfolio might lead to a conclusion that instruments were missing and something untoward must have happened.

Anyone returning to New York could open the door to rigorous interviews by the Security folks at the company. He imagined that Boris was simply waiting patiently with his video of Jose in the vault. He wasn't wrong. Boris tried on several occasions to give his boss, Smith, a briefing on the work he had done before the storm. Nothing short of jumping up and down or screaming down the hallways was likely to get his boss' attention while Drymate's efforts were underway.

Valenti worked to get answers for Andy within a week after

hearing from him. He would not trust or rely on email. He plotted a schedule of telephone calls, after signaling to team members that he needed to touch base with them. Valenti was careful with his questions not to spook anyone that there might be a new level of danger. A few members had heard of the Drymate's efforts from former colleagues. They did not share much with Valenti about their communication with friends back home. Valenti did his best to dissuade them from this contact, so they wouldn't compromise their location.

Even in countries without an extradition treaty, he tried to educate Andy's team on the resourcefulness of U.S. authorities to find and seize criminals. "Excuse me, but you hired us for our expertise in avoiding capture by the police. Please trust that we're giving you the best advice to protect you, your family, and the loved ones you may have back home. You have gotten this far without any jeopardy. Don't push your luck."

For the most part, everyone followed the instructions given at Teterboro airport. They limited their communication with other members of their vault team, and they avoided contact with friends and family back home. Jennie Li and Richard were two who regularly spoke with other employees at the company. While apologizing for breaking protocol, they were doing their own research to determine if they could go back to the U.S. to see families without the authorities knowing. Valenti gave them an update on Drymate's progress, encouraging them to wait until the new year.

"I don't know if they truly heard me," he told Andy, "But I did my best to scare them shitless. I'll have our folks monitor their movements the next two weeks. If I get a sense they are making travel plans, I'll alert you. I did not find them rebellious in any way, so perhaps they heard me."

“Jimmy,” he replied, “thank you for the time you put in on this. I’ll circle back to you in ten days. If any of these folks do return, I’ll ask Testa to keep a plane ready to help them escape again. They may not deserve our efforts to protect their freedom, but we can’t let anyone get discovered or caught. Our fates are inextricably linked one to the other. Please give my regards to your boss.”

CHAPTER 23

THE HOLIDAY SPIRIT TAKES HOLD AND BORIS ATTACKS

The taxi could be seen for nearly a mile away as it drove along the winding country roads leading to the Villa driveway. No one really took note of the car. The local staff Andy hired to cook and take care of the Villa were all busy preparing breakfast on the large patio overlooking the Tuscan landscape. Stella and Sam were getting washed up and dressed to meet Andy downstairs. Their bedrooms faced the rear of the Villa and shared the view of the back patio. Looking down from the windows they could see the staff below setting the table.

Andy loved to have music keep him company. He was on his second cup of coffee. He stared out from the patio as Tony Bennett played on his modest iPod and portable speaker. No one meant as much to him musically as Bennett. He often told his wife Nancy that he favored him over the other guy -- Frank Sinatra.

One of his favorite songs was "When Love Was All We Had." The song was written by two Argentinians, Jorge

Calandrelli as composer and the jazz pianist, Sergio Mihanovich, who wrote the lyrics. He'd played this song so often, Nancy knew the lyrics by heart,

"We started out as children on a carousel
Leaving all those fairy tales we knew so well
...
And everything was possible when love was all we
had."

He would often tell Nancy that Tony Bennett could tell a story in a song, with such feeling and inflection in his voice. "It's like he was singing this for me," he'd explain. "And I can't help but think of you whenever this music comes on the radio, or when I play it on my iPod."

Andy always had these small ways of keeping his memories of her alive. He now sat on the patio of a Villa he and Nancy dreamed of. He couldn't help but want to feel her presence. If only she were here, so he could grab her arm to dance.

By the time Stella and Sam reached the breakfast table, Andy had finished his private moment thinking about Nancy while listening to Tony Bennett. The music had clearly lifted his spirits. The day would be off to a fresh start. "Never waste a moment," he'd counsel his new family members.

"Plan for what you may not anticipate, but at the same time you have to live in the moment; value what you have; allow yourself the chance to linger with an emotion that inspires you."

Sam listened but didn't really get it. Stella smiled sitting down next to her boss.

They were halfway through the meal when the staff heard the knocking at the front door.

"Good morning," the rich baritone voice at the door replied, "I'm here to see Andy."

The staff all spoke broken English. They had not been told someone was coming to see them. "Please wait," Alma asked the visitor. She closed the front door and walked to the rear of the home.

"Were you having something delivered today?" Alma asked as she stepped onto the patio. Andy shook his head and finally got up from the table. "Why don't you stay here," he told Stella and pointed at Sam.

As he opened the front door, a big smile stretched across his face. "I was wondering when we might hear from you," Andy asked. He stuck out his hand and then pulled the man into a quick embrace.

"Ben, it's so good to see you. I'm happy you came. And I believe there's someone here who will be even happier."

"I'm sorry it's taken me so long to answer your emails. After resigning, I had to figure out some things. I spent some time visiting family in New Jersey. I wasn't certain if this trip to Italy would be a short or longer trip. So, is she here? Have I completely burned my bridges?"

"I don't think you need to worry about that," Andy replied. "I do believe she started to doubt if she'd ever see you again. I suspect you two will need some time alone."

Stella had been talking to Sam when she looked up. She was frozen for a minute, uncertain if she doubted what she saw or if she had forgotten all the things she wanted to tell him.

She jumped from the chair but slowed her pace as she got closer to Ben. Gently, she pulled him into her arms. It may be the nature of great love that whatever comes between a couple, the small things disappear quickly. What you remember most is how you felt in someone's arms. You remember the person you wanted to become, not because someone imposed demands. It's just that you become the person this great love inspired. You realize how much springs from inside when you touch their skin, smell their body next to your own, and then there's the kiss. How could anyone truly understand the power of two lovers kissing for the first time or for the last time. In that moment, much of what we know of the physical world around us fades, as we reach beyond to that magical place.

Ben and Stella made their way back to the patio. No one commented. Their private reunion restored energy and hope. They held hands as they walked back to the breakfast table. Andy engaged Sam in small talk to distract him, but this 11-year-old was not having it. He could see how happy his mom was whenever Ben was around. Unlike his father, Ben was a calm influence and someone Sam felt he could trust.

Ben shared stories during breakfast about the impact of storm Sandy on New York City and nearby in New Jersey. Only six or seven weeks had passed, but he felt certain the damage would take years to overcome. This was certainly true of both the repair and replacement of homes and buildings, but it also included the sense of loss felt by people who lived there.

"Right now, our employees are still scattered to the winds. Only a few have returned to the building. Eventually, some will relocate to two new buildings in New Jersey. I've heard the vault could not be restored due to the water damage. Andy, you may have new information on that. All in all, the damage assessment is not complete. Yes, the data centers far from New York are handling the resumption of trading at the stock exchanges. But there's high anxiety at the company and uncertainty about what comes next."

Andy replied, "Ben, I hope you'll stay with us. We have plenty of room here in the villa. My children will be joining us soon for the Christmas holidays. Stella has been guiding the renovations in the building next door. We agreed she should have her own space on the property for her and Sam. I don't know if it will be completed by the holiday, but the main building has a third floor. We could probably host the entire vault team here."

Laughter filled the table. Stella would eventually excuse herself. She and Sam would take the car into town for the farmer's market on Thursday. Her absence would give Ben some privacy to talk with Andy about Americlear.

"How bad did it get?" Andy asked.

"Well, I tried to ignore the signs early on," Ben responded. "Connolly was never easy to talk to. There's an edge to her, as if she's waiting for you to say something that pisses her off. I could see at the start; she wasn't looking for advice from folks who may have experience. She is a true example of a tops down executive. She simply wanted folks to follow her direction, and there was little room for dissent.

"We were not on good terms for months before Sandy devastated New York.

There were a few instances at senior staff meetings where I might urge caution or try to guide our public statements. But I had already been removed as a regular attendee at these meetings. I was asked to show up only when the group had to discuss the legal and PR strategy. Andy, you know this isn't my first rodeo.

"You'd be shocked. Alice Feingold interrupted the management discussions to say she agreed with my media recommendations. How often does a General Counsel ever support talking to the press? I was speechless.

"Alice told Connelly, 'Ben is right to suggest we fill in the blanks, so the press doesn't write negative stories. And his idea to avoid statements saying we had no losses, at a time when we just don't know, is the right balance to protect us.'

"However, our CEO was not about to acknowledge the company may have been harmed by the storm. She told Alice the press could not be trusted. They would say there were losses from Sandy, unless the firm denied it upfront. She eventually turned and was shouting at me in the meeting, when I got up and simply walked out.

"I can't put my finger on it, Andy, but something larger is going on. I don't believe it's just Americlear. I talk with my PR colleagues, and they all feel there's been a decline in company values like transparency and a commitment to the well-being of employees. There's so much focus on the bottom line. In response employees are abandoning their loyalty to the firm's reputation and success.

"At this point, I won't complain. The severance package HR offered me included a year of compensation and pro-rated bonus, based on my tenure at the company. In a way, I now have time to figure out what I want to do with my life. Whatever that is, I would like it to include Stella and Sam."

Andy wanted to give his friend a break. He could see leaving his job was still a trauma. He suggested a guided tour of the villa and the building next door. He told Ben to leave his suitcase in an empty bedroom on the second floor. This bedroom had its own bathroom. It was down a hallway from Stella. Sam had his own room, closest to the stairs heading to the first floor. Andy's room was downstairs and located near the front, with two large doors that opened and looked out across the Tuscan hillside view. "The home is simply magnificent," Ben told him. Andy explained how the prior owners had redone the villa, since the year when he and Nancy had first visited.

A handful of workers were constructing new walls and two more bathrooms, next door. After a lengthy inspection of the second home shaping up next door, Andy casually asked, "Do you have a plan? What's next?"

"Well, most important to me right now is being with Stella. I neglected this relationship, putting the job as the higher priority. You can see how that turned out. Why do we do that? Is any job worth more than finding and valuing someone to love. I never expected to feel this way about someone. The past month, all I thought about was not losing her. I told my mom I found someone that I wanted to marry, if I didn't already ruin the relationship being absent from it for so long.

"Beyond that, I've seriously thought about taking a break for a year and trying to write a book. Now, I don't know if I have the skill or the discipline, but this is my opportunity in life to take some risk. I wrote several articles about my dad and mom a decade ago that were published in local newspapers on Father's Day and Mother's Day. I didn't expect much. It was really a cathartic exercise to pay tribute to them. The reaction from readers, however, convinced me that my story resonated. People wanted to read something life affirming and perhaps be reminded of their own families."

Andy spent time giving Ben the background on his periodic conference calls with the post-Sandy task force back at Americlear. He was pleased the company embraced his decade old plan to decentralize vault operations. However, Andy was cautious not to mention anything about the heist of bearer bonds. He realized at some point either he or Stella might tell Ben what happened. Andy wasn't certain if he should tell him or wait for

Stella to find the right moment. But he did not feel there was any rush to involve his honorable friend.

Stella arrived back at the villa several hours later. Her mood could best be described at giddy. Sam could not believe how happy she was. It had been a long time since he heard his mom singing on the car ride home. She brought the regular mix of vegetables, fresh bread, and home-made pasta. In addition, she asked Mr. Gambisi at the Wine store for two bottles of his favorite Chianti Classico wines. Mr. Gambisi offered wine from three different wineries. Stella recognized the Marchesi Antinori red chianti, which they drank their first week in Italy. She was anxious to share her newfound taste for wine with Ben.

Unexpectedly, she arrived at the villa only to find Ben had gone to sleep off some of his jet lag. Once again, Stella was left to wait for him. This time, however, she had confidence that they would enjoy a great celebration dinner and reunion. She rarely doubted her instincts once she studied a situation. She knew Ben had come for one thing – and it was the one thing she wanted as well. Yes, he was the one she had hoped might change the course of her life. Stella was mindful of Jennie Li's sisterly advice, "Never rely on a man. Have and keep your own money. Don't judge your value through the eyes of a man." She dwelled on this advice before Ben showed up. But he had come all this way just for her. She knew a compromise was needed with Jennie's cautions.

"Hello, is this Mrs. Ramos," the voice asked? "This is Boris Romanov with Publishers Clearinghouse. It looks like Jose may have won a contest he entered worth $10,000."

"I'm sorry," Mrs. Ramos replied. "I do not speak very good English. My son does not live at home any longer. He has his own apartment here in Brooklyn. However, I believe he is traveling."

"Oh, so Jose is not home now? Do you know where he is? I'm sorry but our contest deadline requires that I speak with him before the new year of 2023."

"I believe he is in Puerto Rico right now," Mrs. Ramos told him.

"No problem. Do you have a phone number and address so I can contact him when he returns?"

Mrs. Ramos gave Boris her son's address, believing he might win a sum of money. It didn't take more than a day for Boris to then show up at Jose Ramos' home in Brooklyn. No one answered the buzzer downstairs. Boris decided to stake out the apartment, waiting across the street. An hour passed quickly. Boris stood up when he saw someone, he thought might be Jose. The young man was wearing a red hoodie perhaps a half block away.

Boris crossed the street, but his path down the sidewalk was suddenly cut off by four young men who began pushing him. First, in Spanish, they started yelling at Boris, "What are you doing here man? You don't belong in this neighborhood."

By the third push, Boris tripped and fell to the ground. The men started to kick him. As he lay on the sidewalk, one of the men leaned down and put a knife to Boris' throat. In perfect English, he whispered, "Homie, you don't belong in our neighborhood. Go home Gringo. If we catch you here again, we will cut you."

After his last caution, the young man lightly stabbed Boris in his arm. It was just enough to prove he was serious. Again, he told him, "Go home Gringo."

Boris covered his head with his hands, expecting more pain. He stayed in his fetal position until he was certain they had left.

The men ran down the street in the direction of the red hoodie. They dragged Jose Ramos into a nearby alley and pinned him against the wall. “What are you doing here,” they asked. The knife wielder in the group held his blade up as if to slash Jose. “Aren’t you supposed to be in Puerto Rico?”

Reggie had cautioned Andy that Jose could be a loose cannon and undermine their plan. Testa promised to have his folks keep an eye on him. They were not wrong to do so. Jose explained he came back early to surprise his mom. Testa’s security detail escorted Jose to see his family. Afterward, they explained how stupid he had been to return to the states without telling anyone.

“Jose, we will keep an eye on your family,” they told him. “But if you sneak back here again, we’ll break your legs. Got it? There are too many people at risk. Do you understand?”

Jose understood they were not kidding. He arrived back at his apartment, packed a bag, and was led by Testa’s men to hail a cab. At the airport, he begged the airline reservation clerk for a ticket out tonight. The clerk was initially unsuccessful, but Testa’s team intervened. A wad of cash was discreetly pushed across the counter. Jose nervously looked in all directions to see if anyone was watching. With a boarding pass and his passport in hand, his newly minted friends escorted him to the security entrance. “Have a good trip, Jose.” He nodded in agreement and left the country.

This was the second attempt by Boris to track down team members from vault operations. The phone rang off the hook at Henry Wong’s residence. No one was there to answer, and the Wong’s did not have an answering machine. Boris knew he could be in big trouble, if his boss found out he was calling Americlear employees at home. While he had been unsuccessful in meeting with him about his suspicions, he remained obsessed with finding a smoking gun. If he could simply track down and question some of these employees, he was confident he'd get the information he needed to launch a full investigation.

Boris was like a rabid animal when he was in attack mode. Often, his superiors overlooked the way he broke the rules to get answers. In the past, his odd methods had helped to uncover issues or helped prevent violations of security protocols. But somehow it was different this time. He had lost any perspective about the larger picture. No one was really worried about missing stock certificates. Flooding from storm Sandy had rendered the vault useless. While Drymate was making some headway with their freeze-drying efforts, the vault still contained large clumps of soaked documents.

Often it was hard to tell what instruments were in these wet piles of securities. The goal remained to simply identify the name or number on certificates, so they could be verified with electronic records. Once verified, the physical certificate could be recreated, if needed by the financial institution. If the transition to only electronic records was adequate, the damaged paper securities could be discarded.

No one knew Boris had started tracking down employees who worked in the vault. The only evidence he had was a grainy video of Jose bending down, when a group of employees were welcoming Giulia back from her medical leave.

By his third attempt to reach Edith, he became even more convinced that something suspicious had occurred in the vault. Once again, his calls over three days went unanswered. If everyone is missing, then they must have a reason for leaving town. Boris overlooked in the aftermath of the storm; employees could not return to work for several weeks. Some were sent to temporary locations not impacted by the storm. However, the vault employees were stuck waiting for senior management to assess the damage and decide where these functions would be housed in the future. The idea to decentralize any part of the vault had not been made until the month after Sandy.

Left on his own, without supervision, Boris was ready to hunt down the employees he believed had committed crimes. He compiled a list of home addresses for Andy's vault team members. After several phone call attempts, he decided to visit and interview these employees at home. He did not clear this effort with anyone at the office. Boris was just being Boris.

When he reached Giulia's home in Brooklyn, Boris could see a stack of mail piled up by the door. He had called several times, but no one answered, and her voice mail box was full. Looking at the mail, she must have been gone a few weeks. A normal person likely would have left at this point, but not Boris. He buzzed various apartments in the building.

"Hello," a voice finally came over the intercom system.

"Is this Eddie Nelson?" Boris asked.

"Yes, can I help you?"

"Well, sir, I'm with the Security Department at Giulia's company. We were just concerned that she has not been at work, and we have been unable to reach her by phone."

"I believe Giulia, her daughter and grandchild are traveling. They left right after Sandy passed."

"Do you have any idea where they went or if they'll be home soon?"

"I'm sorry, who did you say you were?"

"Mr. Nelson, my name is Boris Romanov, from the Americlear Security Department."

"Boris, I can't really tell you where they were headed. I live down the hall, but Giulia didn't say when they would return. Do you want me to have them call you?"

"Thank you, Mr. Nelson. If you could tell her I came by, I would appreciate it."

Boris left at that point, but his suspicions only continued to grow. It seemed like the entire vault staff was traveling. He hadn't confirmed this fact, but he leapt to this conclusion based on his unsuccessful effort to reach folks. While he knew many employees could not return to the building, he still wanted answers.

By the second week of his search for Andy's staff, Boris got more than he bargained for. He had called Jennie Li's phone twice. Like the others on his list, he targeted her for a surprise visit. The apartment was in the east village's alphabet city at 190 East 7th Street, between B and C Avenues. The building was a newly minted brick six-floor complex that ran half the block. He found Jennie Li Zhou on the outdoor buzzer, apartment 313. As Boris went to ring the buzzer, two six-foot blonde models were exiting the front door. Politely, they held the door open for Boris. He seized the moment to enter and take the elevator to the third floor.

He arrived on the floor. The hallways were wide though dimly lit. He started to his left, but quickly figured out he was headed in the wrong direction. He turned back looking at the doors numbered 307, 309, 311. He was surprised to find the door open at number 313. He went to knock but decided to enter the apartment instead. Once again, Boris was getting ahead of himself. As he walked into the apartment, he did not call out or announce he was there. He discovered quickly this was a huge mistake, when an elbow hit him square in the face.

The second blow hit him low on the side of his body near his kidney. The force of the blow caused him to double over. A knee to the face and he landed on his back in a daze. His nose was broken and bleeding profusely. At this point, a light went on in the kitchen where the attacker had come from. Jennie Li looked down at her assailant for a moment before recognizing her intruder.

"What the hell were you thinking," she yelled at her prey laying helpless on the floor. "What are you doing in my building? Why didn't you buzz from downstairs or knock on my door? Did you really think you could just walk in without announcing yourself?"

The questions from Jennie Li were coming fast and furious. She was clearly angry that anyone would enter her apartment. He didn't move, except to pull a handkerchief from his pocket and hold his bleeding nose. The bright lights from the hallway and kitchen kept him feeling disoriented. It had been a long time since he had taken such a beating. He realized at that moment he had exceeded even his own idea of what his bosses might consider normal. He had gone too far – and someone put a stop to it.

"I don't know why men assume a woman cannot defend herself," Jenny Li said as she turned on more lights in her apartment. She wrapped ice in a kitchen towel and handed it to him.

Boris gathered his wits. He propped himself up on one elbow and slowly sat up, his back to the wall. He had no defense for his actions. When Jennie Li was done ranting, he simply responded, "I'm sorry. I'm sorry for coming to your home without any notice or asking permission. I'm sorry I am so suspicious of you and your entire vault team. I know what I did today is likely going to cost me my job."

The last statement hit home with Jennie Li. She could not ignore that reporting him would indeed cost him his job.

"Are you still thinking that someone took securities from the vault? Is that why you keep calling and showing up on my doorstep?"

"I found a video of you in the vault," Boris responded, almost in a whisper. His head was pounding, as he held his nose. "You don't work in the vault. You work in an area outside where you enter changes in ownership."

Jennie Li froze in her tracks. Had her movements to take bearer bonds been caught on camera. Initially, she didn't want to acknowledge or answer Boris. Finally, she calmed herself.

"Boris, you're truly mistaken. I do go into the vault periodically to help members of our team. I also agree to work the night shift around holidays. I visit staff members in the breakroom. So, nothing you've seen or said is out of character for me."

Her comments seemed to make sense. Boris got up from the floor and sat on a nearby stool in Jennie Li's kitchen.

Boris, do you not understand the vault was flooded? There's no way any of us can return to work. I've been traveling with a new boyfriend on a vacation. I know they are struggling to recreate these documents, but it could be another month before there's any work for us. Why? Do you know why you have gone off the rails like this?

"We both fled communism, you in Russia and me in China. I get the part of this that teaches us not to trust people or institutions. But Boris, look at yourself. Will someone at Americlear give you a medal? At what point do you stop playing cop and just enjoy the life you have? If I report what happened today, you will lose everything you ever struggled to accomplish."

Jennie Li paused for several minutes. She was still angry, but she could see fear had filled his face. She walked to the kitchen sink and brought him a glass of water. He drank the water. He then sat silent, not exactly certain what to do next. She wanted the exchange with Boris to sink in.

She had made her point. She sat on a chair a few feet away.

"Boris, please go home now. I am sorry I hurt you. I think you've gone through enough for one day. I will not report what happened here. This stays between us. I don't know who else you have contacted or visited, but I do not want you to lose your job. I am giving you a chance to save yourself. Please, just go home."

He could not believe Jennie Li was forgiving him. Rather than push his luck, Boris said nothing as he stood up. He so miscalculated what he could get away with and now she was letting him off the hook. He could not bear making eye contact with her.

"I'm sorry for the trouble I've caused," he said before leaving the apartment.

True to her word, Jennie Li never told anyone of her confrontation with Boris. She and Richard had returned home to New York for the holidays and to see family. Once the New Year passed, they planned to travel for six months. They agreed exploring the world together might be a good test of their relationship before settling down. Richard wanted her family to have assurances that she had a fiancé now. Jennie Li was less worried. Her family would likely be surprised that she allowed a man to get that close to her.

CHAPTER 24
FINDING RESOLUTION

Jimmy Valenti had been keeping tabs on Andy's team members to determine if any or all of them might be returning to the US for the Christmas holidays. If he got word of travel arrangements, he'd reach out to the former employee. The first effort was to try and persuade them to wait until the New Year. Andy tried to keep tabs on Drymate's efforts to see if there were any discrepancies uncovered.

"Andy, I thought you'd want to hear about this right away," said Valenti. "I was calling through your team. Do you know some guy named Boris Romanov? Well, according to Edith Colon and Giulia Samartino, he's been calling their homes and leaving messages."

"What? He's doing what? You say he showed up at Henry Wong's apartment in Chinatown? I know his wife, Mei, has her surgery scheduled soon. Are you certain they said it was Boris?"

Andy was angry as he hung up the phone. Lincoln Smith had not mentioned anything about Boris calling anyone or continuing his investigation. Valenti had assured Andy that no one had spoken to Boris. Valenti had not reached Jennie Li Zhou but left a message asking her to let him know if Boris contacted her.

As he calmed down, Andy began to wonder if Lincoln knew this was going on. His only option was to call him in New York. He had to know what he was up against. Was the heist finally coming undone?

Andy waited until after his weekly conference call with Americlear seniors working on the new strategy for resuming normal vault operations. The group had made great progress on creating three new vault locations, with an optional fourth backup site. Negotiations were almost complete, and timelines were put in place to coincide with the work being done by Drymate. As physical documents could be verified, newly issued replacement certificates would be sent to the new vaults. A meeting in early December, before the holidays, was relaxed and folks were in a festive mood. Near the end, Andy told Lincoln he needed a word.

The follow up call came fifteen minutes later. "Lincoln, I got the strangest call the other day from a staff member who took the early retirement package. It seems Giulia Samartino has been getting phone calls on her answering machines from Boris Romanov. I couldn't really explain this, but I was certain if there were concerns, you'd be able to tell me."

"Wait. What are you saying? Someone is getting calls from Boris. I'm sorry, I just don't understand. Is it just Giulia who got a call or are there others? Wasn't Giulia the woman who had the heart attack?"

"I don't honestly know if there are others Lincoln. I haven't contacted any of the staff. I wasn't certain if this was something the company wanted me to know about?"

"Andy, I'm dumbfounded. I don't know what Boris is doing or why. I guess we're both in the same boat, but I'll follow up and have that conversation. Are your folks upset?"

"I've only heard from Giulia, so I don't know about the others. I didn't think, however, that Security would contact people at home without your authorization."

Andy didn't want to appear as if he knew too much. He got the answer he wanted on whether Lincoln had authorized these inquiries. He now tossed the ball over to his former colleague and friend. Near the end of the call, Lincoln sounded embarrassed and apologetic. He had been talking with Andy weekly and sometimes more often about the project to decentralize the vault. Hearing that his staff was calling "former employees" was unsettling. He worried that Andy might feel he was not being honest with him.

"Please give me a few days," Lincoln told him. "I'll find out what's going on here and let you know. I would have never authorized something like this Andy without telling you upfront. I value our relationship – and I very much appreciate the expertise you continue to contribute to the company."

When the call ended, Andy felt more at ease. If Boris was on to something or had any evidence of wrongdoing, he felt confident Lincoln would tell him straight away. For all the years they worked together, Lincoln never sugarcoated bad news.

It would be several days before Andy heard back. In the meantime, he had put in motion a plan to return to New York. He had promised Henry that he would be there when his wife, Mei, had her heart surgery. No one needed to know he was headed back. He spoke to Ben and Stella in detail about his trip. "Look, I keep my promises. Henry was there for me when Nancy died. I must do this," he told them. "This has been on my mind since we got here. I will not let him be alone."

Andy left from the Florence airport and connected on a flight from Rome. He did not plan to speak with anyone once in New York, except to call his children and confirm they were coming for the holidays in Italy. He had sweetened the deal, promising his daughters to pay for their family's travel and sightseeing tours. The children embraced this idea of a family gathering at Christmas as their mother's last wish.

Stella insisted on driving Andy early the next morning. The feelings he shared with her was like that of a third daughter. She looked after him and she never really asked him for anything. He made certain while Stella would benefit from the heist, her involvement would never be known. This was part of the personal request he made with Testa, as she recovered in the hospital. No matter what happened, he wanted Stella to be protected – and looked after.

As he got his small overnight bag from the rear of the car, Stella grabbed him for one last hug. "Please let us know you got there," she pleaded. "And email us your plans for the return flight. If Lincoln calls while you're gone, I'll contact you by phone and email."

Flight UA509 left Rome airport one hour late, but the pilot assured passengers that she could make up some of that time during the trip. Andy decided to fly business class so he could try to sleep. He would arrive late in the day at Newark Liberty International. A car service would be waiting to take him to a room he reserved at the Fitzpatrick Hotel on Lexington Avenue in mid-town Manhattan.

Andy arrived at Weill Cornell Medical Center by seven a.m.

He had been tipped off by Jennie Li that Henry Wong's wife was scheduled mid-morning for the repair of her heart valve.

"She's in room 408," the receptionist told Andy at the information desk downstairs. "Are you a member of the family?"

"Yes, I am," he replied with confidence. "I just flew in last night from overseas."

"Wow," the nurse responded. "I don't think I've had a family member travel that far for any of our patients. You can take the elevators across the lobby. Go up to the fourth floor and follow signs to Cardiac Surgery."

Andy got lost after reaching the fourth floor. He finally asked a hospital employee for directions, after wandering aimlessly. Luckily, he had not gone too far. Weill Cornell is a huge medical facility stretching more than a city block in New York. It ranks in the top 10 U.S. hospitals for cardiac surgery. Andy hoped and prayed on the journey that Mei's surgery would be successful.

Her room was halfway down the hall on the right. There were two patients in each room waiting their turn for a heart procedure. Andy knocked softly and walked in. Mei was sitting up in bed waiting to be taken down to the surgery room. Henry stood up from the chair next to her bed. He was speechless to see his boss.

"Andy, did you really travel all this way for Mei?" Henry asked. "I know you promised to be here, but I don't know what to say." Henry was a warm and friendly person, but he rarely showed emotion. As Andy walked around the bed, without any warning, he grabbed Andy's arms by the elbow and shook his hand several times. Then Henry began to cry. The two men hugged. They worked together more than two decades, but in this moment, Henry felt a bond no one could truly understand. The weight of the moment had lifted.

"Mei, how are you feeling?" Andy asked as he walked next to her in the bed. He leaned down slowly and kissed her hand.

"I am nervous," she responded. "But I am lucky. Both Henry and Lily are here."

Sitting on the far side of the bed, obscured by the open door, was one of Henry's daughters. Lily was quite tall, very trim and her jet-black hair stretched down her back.

"If I'm not mistaken," Andy asked, "Aren't you the oldest child? Henry always speaks so proudly about you. Didn't you finish college last spring? Did you find a job?" Andy's conversation was rapid fire questions. He was nervous about the surgery.

"Yes, I am working at Citibank downtown. I just finished their training program last month. I'm at the branch on Mott St. My goal is to work in private banking. I have a finance degree, and I speak both Mandarin and Cantonese, so the bank seems confident I could help increase support for wealthy Chinese who live or travel to the U.S."

"Well, I'm so happy to finally meet you. Isn't your sister also studying at college?"

"Chunying is also studying finance, but she is in Paris for one semester. I did not get to go overseas in college. I admit I'm jealous of my sister."

"Henry, I'll let you spend time with your family. I'll just go down and grab a cup of coffee. I came to be with you today, so don't worry, I'm not going anywhere. Mei, I'll be back before they take you downstairs."

Andy hoped being there for Henry would give him strength. He knew the toughest part of the day would be the long hours waiting for the surgery to end. As he headed to the cafeteria, he saw signs for the Chapel on the second floor. Somewhat spur of the moment, he decided to stop and pray for Mei. He really didn't care if it was a church, a chapel, a synagogue, or mosque. Andy always believed the presence of God was not a building but a feeling you carried with you inside.

Once the orderlies came to take Mei, Henry, Lily and Andy headed downstairs to the surgical waiting room. Before they wheeled her away Mei motioned for Andy and grabbed his hand. He leaned down to better hear her ask him to look after Henry. Andy knew that look in her eyes. Her tears welled-up and she grabbed Andy with both hands.

"Mei, you have my word. Don't worry. We want you to focus on getting through the surgery. Henry, Lily and Chunying need you. We'll be here waiting for you."

Mei shook her head acknowledging Andy. She then hugged and kissed her husband and daughter, in a rare display of emotions. Henry walked next to her hospital gurney until they reached the elevator. Mei and Henry had never been apart since they first met so many years ago. They would forever be bound together…by culture, custom, respect...and love.

The vigil downstairs lasted almost six hours. They did not have long conversations. Henry was deep in thought. Andy understood his job to support Henry's family would largely be carried out in silence. At times, he was frustrated having to hold back.

If this was a gathering of his Italian family, he imagined folks talking non-stop and arguing occasionally to help let go of the tension and uncertainty. He tried, at times, to ask Lily and Henry questions about their early years living in Chinatown. Their responses were short. He would not succeed in distracting them or having a long conversation without Mei being present.

Andy practiced his new role of being a silent, inward-looking relative. After the second hour of waiting, he began to scratch his arms. When the silence grew too difficult, he excused himself to do something – anything. He left for the cafeteria to bring snacks, tea and coffee. More than three hours into the surgery, the waiting room table was filled with refreshments no one would touch. Andy was not surprised by Henry's discipline staring stoically into space. However, he was matched by Lily, who only broke her silence on occasion to thank Andy for his kindness.

After four hours, a doctor in blue surgical clothes entered the waiting room and asked for the Wong family. Andy was immediately alarmed. He could see traces of blood on his clothing.

"Mr. Wong, I'm Dr. Gaston. I've been assisting Dr. Sinclair on your wife's operation. I wanted to give you an update. We're still working, but the surgery on your wife has proven more difficult than anticipated. We've run into some complications. Dr. Sinclair is still working to get this under control, but we thought you should be prepared if Mrs. Wong can't overcome the difficulties she is experiencing."

Henry's knees weakened. He grabbed Andy's arm to keep his balance. His face showed no emotion. It is not a Chinese custom to speak of death. Yes, inside he felt terror. What if Mei did not survive the operation? To acknowledge the possibility of death was to invite this outcome. No subject was more suppressed across one's lifetime than knowing our destiny -- but not the date.

However, while Lily respected customs she would not be bound by them. Strong and unyielding is the way Henry would describe it to Andy; stubborn is the way Mei would characterize their Americanized children.

She walked over as the men were still talking,

"Stop. Stop right now. Did you say your name was Gaston? Well, Doctor Gaston, my mother put her faith in you and Dr. Sinclair. None of us thought this operation would be easy. Life is not easy. But saving her life is what I want from you.

"You need to tell Dr. Sinclair, he better not quit on her. My mother came to this country to see her daughters grow up, get educated, marry, and have grandchildren. So, please, you tell him we're out here waiting for him to tell us he saved her…so she can see her dreams come true. Please, please tell him this life he must save."

Lily was not done. She followed Dr. Gaston out the room and halfway down the hallway. Her steely gaze could be felt on his back, until the doctor disappeared.

She found her father seated, when she returned. As generations have done before, Henry insisted on being alone. He would not bring shame to the family by any outward expression of feelings. He held his fear in check. This was how one honored those he loved.

Andy tried to reassure Lily, but she could not hold back her fears. She attacked. She willed in her mind and in her words for the doctors to perform earthly miracles. The mind functions rationally, but the soul transcends. In these unpredictable moments of uncertainty, the soul lifts us up to see beyond what can be measured. No one gets to choose. Death will find us in a crowded room or an empty subway. But Lily was telling the doctors, "Not today, not today."

In the next few hours, there was nothing left for Lilly to do but to follow her father's example. Growing up, Henry would teach his daughters that, "Silence is not the absence of words, but the presence of focus." It was time to focus on Mei, whatever fate may lie ahead.

There was nothing more Andy could do. He was overcome with a feeling of helplessness and despair. Once again, in his mind, he had returned to his bedroom only to find Nancy was gone. His grand gesture of coming back to support Henry might be for naught. The outcome was beyond his control. Andy suddenly felt weak and sick to his stomach. He left the waiting room desperate to get outside.

The cold air of December was like a slap in the face. Andy gasped for air. Tears he shed for Nancy had now returned. In this moment, he felt resignation that Mei might not survive. He dug into his pocket for the cell phone. Desperate for an escape, he called his daughter. The conversations were short. In truth, he just needed to hear her voice. "Dad, are you ok?" his daughter Anna asked.

"Yes, I'm at the hospital. Henry's wife is having heart surgery. You remember Henry from work? He's the fellow who brought that huge bouquet of white lilies and chrysanthemums to the wake, before mom's funeral."

"I think I remember. I believe Henry and his wife visited us at the house afterward. Am I right?"

"Yes, you're right. I couldn't get over those flowers. That bouquet was larger than any sent by the CEO or senior executives at my company."

"Is his wife going to make it?" Anna asked. At this point, Andy voice started to breakup.

"Dad, it's so good of you to come and support Henry. I know it shows him how much you care. But you're only one person and you don't get to decide this. Do you understand? I wish him and his wife good luck today. But please take care of yourself.

You are a very special person. Emily and I love you. And please call us before you fly back."

There is something godlike in the voice of a child. You love and nurture them unconditionally their whole life. And when you least expect it, they say or do something that rewards you in a way that cannot be put into words.

Andy was now ready to return and face the outcome. He had found his way back to his purpose – and the courage to achieve it.

He could see Henry and Lily standing by the door of the surgical waiting room. Their faces were expressionless. Andy prepared himself.

"Doctor Sinclair just left," Henry started to speak. "Today turned out to be a good day. Mei has pulled through the surgery. The doctors kept her chest open until they could be certain she was not leaking blood. The heart valve was replaced, and the patch of her major artery worked. She will be in recovery being monitored for several hours, just as a precaution. In an hour, they'll move her to the cardiac ICU."

Before Andy could respond, he saw a smile creep across Henry's face. Lily stood next her father holding his arm. Mei was saved. A family was saved. They were thankful without jumping up and down. Together, the group would head downstairs to the cafeteria. They could eat now; grateful the danger had passed. Lily excused herself to call her sister, Chunying. From a distance, Andy could recognize she was speaking Chinese. He had no clue what was being said, but her voice grew stronger and more ebullient.

No one would leave the hospital until late in the evening. Andy called Anna back to share the good news. She could tell a huge weight had been lifted from her father. It was hard for her to hear him speak about her mom, though she understood this was Andy's way of accepting the loss. Mei surviving her surgery gave Andy hope. Hope could not replace Nancy, but it gave her dad something more to hold onto in life.

Mei was awake before they left. She drifted in and out of consciousness. The doctors kept her medicated to control pain. Lily sat next to Mei's bed. When she opened her eyes, Lily would whisper in Chinese, "Jīntiān shì nǐ de xìngyùn rì" (today's your lucky day). Mei managed a slight smile before drifting off.

Andy filled Henry's head with thoughts about what was next in his life. It was not in Henry's nature to spend money he did not have. But Andy pointed out that Henry had been given a second chance with Mei. He now had resources, millions of dollars, in an offshore bank account. As she recovered, he would no longer be bound by worries about working, covering medical expense or taking a trip to visit Chunying in Paris. He invited his friend to visit him in Italy. Andy's mood was upbeat and "can do." In contrast, Henry, remained stoic even after Mei was sleeping peacefully in the bed.

By 10 p.m., Andy excused himself. He was exhausted by the long day. Lily made a point of thanking him for traveling all this way for her dad and for her mom. "Close friends are truly life's treasures," Lily told him, giving Andy a hug before he left.

"Is that one of your dad's Chinese proverbs?" he asked. Lily began to laugh. She knew her dad was fond of quoting Confucius. "No," she responded. "That's a quote from Vincent Van Gogh."

Andy asked her to work on her parents so they would travel and enjoy their second chance at life. He told Lily her family was always welcome to come visit him in Italy.

Henry was at a loss not knowing how to thank his former

boss. He had traveled so far, just to keep his promise. He shook his hand vigorously and agreed to update Andy on her progress. The night air was crisp, as he left the hospital. Andy felt energized by the cold and decided to walk the twenty blocks to his hotel.

CHAPTER 25

LISTEN: IT'S ABOUT APPEARANCES; IT'S NOT ABOUT THE TRUTH

Sal Perez, deputy head of Security, was sitting at the conference room table when Boris arrived. Sal motioned for Boris to sit across from where he was seated. There was silence for almost ten minutes before Lincoln Smith entered. Both Sal and Boris stood up until Lincoln took the seat at the head of the table.

"Boris, I called this meeting so you can tell me what the hell is going on. As far as I can tell, you've been freelancing for several weeks without the knowledge or approval of your immediate supervisor – or from me. To say I'm pissed, would be an understatement. Sal and I are ready to hear you out, but it's time to come clean."

The stage was set, and Boris felt certain he was going to be fired. He quickly launched his defense:

"While the storm interrupted the audit we started back in October, I had reason to believe there was video evidence of possible criminal activity. I tried to bring this evidence to you and Sal earlier, but I realized the circumstances after the flood in the vault took priority. Quietly, I continued to review security video footage, and I made efforts to interview members of Andy Russo's team. I thought it was quite odd that I couldn't reach any of these people. Since Mr. Russo had left the company, there wasn't any senior officer to talk with about my suspicions."

"Boris, for as long as you've worked at Americlear have you ever been involved in an investigation where someone started contacting employees at their home? Neither the Security department nor Human Resources have ever authorized this type of activity. When I got wind of this, just a few days ago, I asked Sal to canvass all our current and former vault employees. Under the best of circumstances, I might overlook this protocol breach, if it only involved current staff. But contacting employees who have retired and left the company is a new one and it puts the company in legal jeopardy. Do you have a fucking clue what I'm telling you?"

He knew there was nowhere to hide. Boris sat with his head down and hands folded in his lap.

"Did you really call Jose Ramos' family and pose as a representative of Publisher's Clearinghouse, telling his mother he won a prize in some contest? Is that what you consider to be our professional standards of conduct? Sal found a neighbor who said you were going through an employee's mail, when they didn't answer their door. I understand you missed Henry Wong at home, only because he had taken his wife to the hospital for heart surgery. But there were phone messages and written notes left telling him to urgently contact you. I believe the only person Sal spoke to that claims she didn't hear from you was Jennie Li Zhou. Now, I'd love to know why that didn't happen."

Boris lifted his head at the mention of Jennie Li's name. Had she really kept her vow of silence? No one had more of a right to nail his ass than Jennie. His invasion of her apartment was so egregious and desperate it even gave Boris pause, though he failed to listen to his own inner voice telling him, "Don't do this." If she told her story to his boss, he expected immediate dismissal. She would be the one bright spot on his misadventures. Her silence almost convinced him that his suspicions could not possibly be true. Jennie Li had proved her integrity – and her ability to beat him silly.

Sal detailed the repeated efforts Boris undertook to reach and interrogate employees from the vault. He had secured copies of voice mail messages left by Boris. Most sounded like he was misrepresenting the reasons for his call. These calls crossed the line, especially with employees who had already taken early retirement. Suggesting that retirement benefits could not start until certain matters were cleared up, was an abuse of his authority. Other messages created a sense of urgency based on damaged or destroyed certificates after storm Sandy.

When Sal finished with his documentation of events, Lincoln allowed several minutes to go by so the seriousness of Boris' actions would sink in.

Lincoln asked, "Ok so where's the evidence? I want to see what brought you to this point. Yes, I may have been distracted by damage from the storm. But I'd like to know what was motivating you to go off the rails like this?"

Boris reached for his laptop which sat on the chair next to him. He found the video he had of Jose in the vault. He turned the laptop around and hit play. Lincoln and Sal watched as three employees came over to greet Giulia, who had returned from medical leave.

"Now, I want you to watch the right side of my screen,"

Boris explained. "You'll see these employees coming over. You will then see Jose Ramos enter the camera frame. Soon he bends down and disappears for several minutes. I believe you'd agree, there are unwritten rules in the vault prohibiting employees from gathering in groups while they are working. I interviewed Giulia Samartino before we suspended the vault audit. Her best recollection was Jose bent down to tie his shoe. This violation of normal practices followed by Andy Russo's team convinces me that something was going on that warranted a more thorough investigation and grilling of staff."

"Ok, but this video is not evidence of a crime," Lincoln stated. "According to witnesses, this employee went to tie his shoe. Please tell me there's more to this story. Where is the evidence that something was removed from the vault?"

"Did you drop your video review of the vault after storm Sandy?" Sal asked.

"No, I continued to go through video for three weeks prior to the storm," Boris responded.

"And did you find more examples of suspicious behavior with Jose or other employees?" Sal asked again.

"Yes, there were two other instances I found on video where different employees were gathering with Giulia. These examples were within a day or two of the first group coming over to welcome her. My suspicions were heightened because Giulia was a senior clerk supervisor with 30+ years of experience. She should know better than to allow employees to congregate. She is also responsible for the filing of money market instruments and bearer bonds."

"Boris, you are raising something that could be considered very serious," Sal commented. "But I don't see any pattern here. And we're talking about an area of the company that has never seen any lapse of ethical behavior. Our annual audits have never found a single discrepancy in decades. Don't you think what you're suggesting would be quite remarkable considering the history here?"

"I understand," Lincoln added, "Giulia Samartino suffered a heart attack down in the vault two months prior to her return. Her personnel records are filled with written reviews and awards for exceptional service during her tenure. Andy Russo told me, at the time of the heart attack, she was under stress from the company decision to privatize the pension and eliminate medical retiree benefits. Everyone in the vault looked to Giulia as a role model. I can see where her return got folks excited. Do you understand?

"Were you aware Boris that Giulia returned early from her medical leave, once everyone heard Sandy would reach New York and threaten Americlear? Does that sound like someone involved in some inappropriate or criminal activity?"

Lincoln sat back, after sharing his perspective. Sal leaned forward, "Boris, Jose Ramos is a kid, maybe thirty years old. In the vault he is considered earnest, but forgetful and unorganized. He's been a project for Edith Colon, another senior vault clerk who manages him and tries to keep him on track. While I won't dispute what we saw on that video, you can't really judge this unless you know the people. We can't look at his actions in a vacuum. The point is you could have avoided the shit-show you caused by coming to me or Lincoln with your assessment. It looks to me like you were trying to be a hero, which is a dangerous position for anyone working here in Security. The whole Department could suffer a reputational blow if these employees and ex-employees pursued complaints with our Human Resources group. Do you truly understand the potential damage you've caused based on essentially a personal hunch?"

Boris couldn't help but try to save his job and reputation. He pressed on trying to assure his boss that he felt certain his investigation could uncover illegal activity.

"Well," Boris responded. "There's also a second video."

For several minutes, he fumbled with his computer screen. He was about to turn on the one person who had tried to protect him. Boris felt awful, but he also saw no other way forward. His professional life and reputation were on the line. At any moment, he fully expected his boss to dismiss and fire him.

"If you have something to show us, please get to it," said Sal. "We have to bring this matter to closure and move on."

His face grew red with embarrassment. Boris had reached a point of no return. He would never be able to face her again.

"It's Jennie Li Zhao in the vault," Boris pointed out as he turned his computer around to show his boss the video. "But her job is authorizing the change in ownership records, which is a process that is managed outside of the vault. When I questioned her, she told me it was not unusual for her to help her colleagues in the vault on the night shift near the holiday season. I didn't buy this explanation."

"I do know this employee," Lincoln responded, "and it sounds like a plausible explanation. Why do you think she is lying?"

"I tried to give her the benefit of the doubt. After the initial questioning, I let her explanation go. However, I went back in the video archive before the holiday season, I recently found another video of her using the facial recognition software we adopted three years ago."

Boris cued up the video on the screen. He turned the laptop around to face his boss. Sal moved his chair closer. Lincoln immediately recognized the first screen shot. He smiled as he looked across at his overly aggressive investigator,

"Did you see a guy in this video?" he asked.

"Yes, there is also a guy later on. I haven't had the time to study this second video. My intention was to go through it frame by frame to see if there is evidence, as I suspect of a crime being committed"

Lincoln Smith stood up to stretch his legs, "Boris, I'm sorry to tell you this but I've seen this second video before, and I discussed it with Andy more than a month ago. What you saw here is not evidence of a crime, but poor judgement by two young professionals meeting up in the vault to express their love.

Smith sat back down, still smiling as he looked over at Sal to move the discussion along.

Boris was too far gone. "I'm confident, if we could interrogate these employees, I could get one of them to confess."

Sal's eyeballs were rolling up to the ceiling now. He could not believe Boris didn't get it.

"Ok," Lincoln started. "Boris, I want you to listen to me very carefully. In almost forty years there has never been an incident in the vault where documents went missing. The turnover of employees is low, because the guy managing the vault all these years had put such an importance on loyalty and trustworthiness. What you're suggesting here goes against history. Why would this trusted team suddenly take such a risk?

"While you've gone off on your misadventure, the company asked their boss to help us following the storm damage to restore and decentralize the vault. We are lucky to have his expertise guiding this effort, which must be ready to go by mid-January. Our CEO has made this our highest priority.

"Bottom line: I don't believe you have uncovered anything

here to support your premise of possible illegal activity. The video tells us nothing. And I'm shocked you went down this road without more evidence. I could never condone the interrogation of employees on this flimsy speculation. But let me put this in a larger context.

"In order to prove your idea that a crime was committed, we would have to find that securities were missing. Yet we don't have proof that physical securities are missing.

"Drymate has been recovering water damaged documents so that we can compare and verify their existence with our electronic records. The Audit department has been all over this issue. If we can't audit and match the waterlogged securities with the electronic record, there's no way to prove anything was stolen. It may just be that documents were destroyed by the flood.

The issue of bearer bonds, which Giulia Samartino managed, is particularly difficult. The Drymate folks have not been successful in freeze-drying these instruments. They are not like other securities printed on special paper that can survive the seawater. Many of the bearer bonds are more than forty or fifty years old. What we found were huge clumps of wet paper. Separating and finding distinguishing marks has been a nightmare. And the ink written on the coupons attached to the bearer bonds have been erased by the seawater.

"Boris, are you following me so far?"

"Yes, I follow what you're saying," Boris said. "However, the employees don't know anything about the conditions of these bearer bonds. I could tell them as documents are being dried out, we're getting proof that some of these financial instruments are missing."

Lincoln paused, looking over to Sal, and shook his head in disbelief. After their detailed explanation, Boris still wanted to lie to employees in hopes someone might confess. But confess to what? Was he unredeemable?

"You don't seem to understand the larger context," Sal told him. "At this point, no one really cares if securities are missing. Don't look down Boris. We're trying to help you here. Look at me and listen very carefully.

"The company has filed an insurance claim for more than $600 million in losses tied to lost or damaged securities, including bearer bonds. The truth is we don't ever expect to complete the audit, because of the water damage. No one will ever be able to verify if the instruments were in the vault or not in the vault when Sandy hit us. This issue is simply a dead end."

Boris sat trying to absorb this news. He had always assumed an audit would eventually be completed.

"Let me share some added insight," Lincoln said, "but this is strictly confidential. Nothing I tell you now leaves this room. Got it?

"If the insurance company found out we were investigating the possible theft of securities, including bearer bonds, they would refuse to payout on our claim. We would be letting them off the hook. Currently, no one knows we've filed this claim for $600 million in losses.

Lincoln could not be certain Boris was listening, so he waited several minutes to continue his comments. When Boris looked up and sat back in his chair, his boss tried to hammer home the message.

"In the days after Sandy, our CEO refused to follow the advice of her senior team to issue non-committal statements to the press. Connolly wanted to come across as someone who protected the industry, both the financial markets and our customers. So, she claimed there were no losses. There were adequate electronic records of physical certificates. As a result, no firm, the industry or investors would experience any loss from Sandy.

"Two months later, it's clear Connolly made a mistake in her comments to the New York Times and global media. Bearer bonds and other instruments have been destroyed and the audit will fall short of verifying the vault's contents. She had no basis for saying otherwise. We believe her ego and preoccupation with her reputation got in the way of telling the truth. Having gone down that road making these statements, it would be too embarrassing for Connolly to recant.

"So, at this point, even if securities were stolen, we could never acknowledge that. None of us has the option now to change the narrative about Sandy. We are all at risk because of the CEO's worry about appearances.

"Our only hope is getting the insurance company to pay out our claim, so at least we can confirm to the world we did not suffer losses. Our reputation and our jobs depend now on the insurance covering the exposure. While our Board members, who work at major financial firms will be thoroughly briefed in the coming months, they have a shared interest in keeping this secret. Anything that undermines the industry's confidence in Americlear will harm the industry's reputation as a whole – and will increase regulatory oversight.

"Boris, I'm going to give you a chance to keep your job. You've made some horrible mistakes. The matter you have obsessed about the last month must end when you walk out of this conference room. This investigation of yours ends right now. Are we clear? Do we have your agreement? Can you accept that and say we're done with this."

While he was often pigheaded, stubborn, and mistrusting,

Boris now understood the landscape of issues his boss was navigating. He began to realize, even if he got confessions these could be recanted once employees found out no audit results or physical evidence existed.

"I accept," Boris responded. "I have made mistakes I wish I could take back. I am grateful you're offering me a second chance. I focused too narrowly on this matter, when I should have been talking with you and Sal from the beginning. I would like to take a few days off to clear my head. I got too close to this. I took it too personally. Nothing I did in this matter has helped you or the company. And I truly regret my behavior with these employees."

By this point in the conversation, it was clear Boris was visibly shaken and remorseful. He sat with his hands shaking. Lincoln and Sal let him sit for several minutes and calm down. They wanted the moment to truly sink in. Eventually, Sal stood up, followed by Boris. Lincoln still sat. Sal reached across to shake Boris's hand. "Thank you, Boris. Let's go back to how we worked before. There's a lot to get done."

Boris shook his head, acknowledging his boss' comments. Lincoln slowly got up but didn't shake hands. He wanted Boris to leave with a bit of uncertainty. He had kept his job. He had been forgiven. But it would take time and real effort for Boris to win back everyone's confidence and trust.

A day later, Lincoln scheduled a video call with Andy.

The story Lincoln shared about Boris was shocking to him. "He called the employees at home. What? He went to their homes. Lincoln, I had no idea any of this was going on. With all this effort, I don't understand why he didn't try to track me down? I'm not hiding."

"You have to believe," Lincoln told him. "If I knew about

this sooner, I would have immediately put a stop to it. I never did put the question to him about why he didn't call you? I'm guessing he doubted his own suspicions. He likely feared you'd poke holes in his theories, which would leave him without a conspiracy to solve."

Lincoln started to laugh, "I mean, can you imagine believing that a group of our employees would steal physical securities from the vault? The Americlear vault has been impervious to threats for decades. Until Sandy flooded the place, no one could conceive of a threat to the integrity of this citadel of safety and soundness.

"Connolly really screwed up. Her leadership style continues to unnerve folks," Lincoln continued. "Ben tried to warn her. Right now, she's so exposed having lied to the media. A story leaking out in the news claiming securities were lost or stolen would end her tenure. If the insurance claim of $600 million is not paid in full, our senior colleagues at the firm have discussed various contingencies to absorb losses."

"I give you all the credit in the world for not canning Boris," Andy said. "I guess he's done some good work over the years, though he will always need a tight leash."

"I don't think we're done with this matter," Lincoln responded. "Some of what he did is so over-the-top, your folks may still report him to HR. This would reopen a can of worms.

"You have every right to turn me down, but I must ask yet another favor of you? Could you to reach out to members of your team and let them know this matter is settled? Knowing Boris has been punished may help us avoid any further embarrassment. I'm only here for several more months on our vault project. I'd hate to finally retire with this blemish on my record and HR breathing down my neck."

Andy paused. What a strange juxtaposition he thought to himself. Boris had caught Jose and others on the team taking bearer bonds, though he didn't really understand what they were doing and why they were doing it. If he was a bit more sophisticated in his techniques investigating what he found, he would have uncovered the crime of the century.

Luckily, he hadn't gone back several months in his review of vault videos, which would show others bending down or putting documents in their clothing. What Lincoln had told him about zone X being out of camera range turned out not to be true. Andy never realized his friend had not confided in him. Lincoln was a dedicated security guy who would never compromise his advantage to ferret out wrongdoing.

Boris was true to his reputation of being a bull in a China shop. He blew his chance to pursue and uncover the truth, because he let his zealousness overcome his judgement. Andy could see how the storm's delay of his investigation and the staff disappearing out of town frustrated him to where he overreacted and lost control. It undercut his investigation -- and in the process lost his boss' trust.

Andy had let go of his moral compass. The years of seeing the downward spiral of how employees were treated gave him absolution. It was unlikely that he would have ever crossed the line, if Nancy were still alive. Yet, he would not second guess his decisions or dwell on something he could no longer change. He embraced his role as a protector of his team. These were good and decent people, who had more than paid their dues. He succeeded in shaping a new life for them – and their extended families.

"Lincoln, I will see if I can reach folks on my team over the next few days. You have my commitment to help contain this. I also want to thank you for your efforts to stop these wild accusations and behaviors which I know are inconsistent with the leadership you've provided. If I get feedback that can cause problems, I'll contact you immediately. Otherwise, I'll drop you an email when I'm done to confirm this matter is closed."

"You're a good guy, Andy. It's been an honor working with you all these years. But, most importantly, I'm proud to have you as a friend."

After the call ended, Andy sat in his study staring at the nearby wineries criss- crossing the landscape. He took long deep breaths. He had carried the danger of discovery for eight or nine months. If the plan had failed, he would be tortured by the penalties and shame his employees would experience.

The Christmas holidays in Tuscany were truly special. The renovations in the building next door to the villa were eighty percent done. Stella, Sam and Ben welcomed the opportunity to move in, since they would have greater privacy. The big surprise was the arrival of Stella's parents, Bianca and Kiko Jones. Andy had been calling them for almost a month. He volunteered to pay for their travel expenses, and he asked Jimmy Valenti to help them get passports in time for the trip. Stella ran outside when she saw her mom step out of the taxi. She screamed in delight seeing her parents and then she broke down in tears. Ben followed Stella and Sam. He was reintroduced though both her parents remembered Ben from her stay in the hospital. Ben motioned to Sam. They both gathered up the suitcases to bring them inside. Andy eventually walked over from what he started calling villa one and villa two. He greeted Kiko with a firm handshake and hugged Bianca.

The next day, Andy's daughters arrived with their spouses and children. Anna was married to Michael Falk, a commercial real estate lawyer in Boston. They had two children; Angela was eight and Richard was five years old. Anna had worked at an investment banking firm, before taking a break to raise her children.

Andy's younger daughter, Emily, arrived on a separate flight with her husband Jeff Barry. Emily taught elementary school in Robbinsville, New Jersey. Her husband, Jeff owned a book printing company. They had one child so far, Noah, who would soon turn six years old.

Suddenly, Sam had a small posse of kids to play with. He was the oldest. Stella tried to impress on her son that he had a big responsibility to watch over the younger children. It was ok to walk through the fields around the property, but he needed to be vigilant if the children wandered near the pool in the backyard. The role of leader came natural to Sam. He tried his best not to sound too bossy. He was excited to run around with them and to sit on the back patio drawing pictures to decorate the villa for the holidays.

Several additional staff members from Imprunetta were added to the villa payroll. Some would help with the cooking and serving of meals. Others would add to those making beds, changing linens and towels, or doing the growing bins of laundry. Andy made a point to pay every employee at the villa extra salary during the holiday season. The Chef and Sous Chef would get a weekly lump sum bonus. The remaining staff would find their hourly wages increased by five Euros, which thrilled them. An increase in take-home pay kept everyone in a festive mood.

The three days leading up to Christmas were filled with trips to Florence and surrounding towns. Through his growing list of local merchants in Imprunetta, Andy met and hired Santo Albizzi who ran a small family-owned tour company. Santo was in his fifties and managed trips for visiting tourists more than two decades. He had arranged with a local car service operator to take members of Andy's family to a choice of activities that he arranged in advance.

Santo split Andy's guests into two groups: one with Stella, her folks and Ben, and the second group with Andy's grown children. On the same day, one group was taken on a tour of Florence, which included the Duomo, the Uffizi Museum, and the best gelato shop near Ponte del Vecchio. The other group was driven out for retail therapy at the famous Firenze Outlet Mall, which consisted of sixty high-end stores. Andy handed out holiday gift cards the women could use to buy shoes or pocketbooks. The men were taken to the Florence Leather Factory, where they could find those buttery leather coats Italy is famous for.

Anna and Emily were sold on visiting a well-known ceramics factory, La Galleria Montelupo, about a half hour from the villa. The entire town of Montelupo Fiorentine is known for shops making beautiful Italian ceramic bowls, plates, vases and a wide assortment of clay ornaments for homes worldwide. However, Stella insisted Andy's children visit Matteo at La Galleria, where adults and children get a chance to work at the potter's wheel, shaping their own clay. Matteo is a third- generation member of his family…and a warm and wonderful host.

During Stella's visit, Matteo's father sat patiently with Sam coaching him how to shape the clay with his palms and his fingers. It was an odd, but magical feeling for this young boy to see his creation come alive. Matteo also insisted that Stella shape her own clay bowl. He would paint and put the bowls in a kiln several times before delivery to the villa or to her parents back to the U.S.

Andy knew exactly what he was doing arranging these days of touring for the family. The goal was clearly to incentivize them to visit him once a year.

He had made a big deal about attending church on Christmas Eve. Andy planned for his brood to attend mass at the Basilica di Santa Maria in the nearby town of Imprunetta. Santo made inquiries with the church and afterward Andy made a sizable contribution. Santa Maria dates back almost a century, though it required a major renovation after being bombed during WWII in 1944.

Christmas day at Andy's villa was dreamlike. Andy was up at the crack of dawn with the children downstairs. Sam snuck out from next door to join them. While the parents all slept-in, Andy used the drip coffee machine to make the kids hot chocolate. A contest was launched to see who could draw the best picture of Christmas in Italy. The villa staff were given the day off. While everyone was drawing pictures in the kitchen, chef Andy was busy making omelets and pancakes.

He worked hard at keeping the children focused on coloring their pictures – and away from opening presents until everyone was together. Within an hour, some of the adults started to show up. Anna and Emily had not seen their father make breakfast since they left for college. This was usually a routine he only performed on Mother's Day. His daughters started to join in and encouraged the grandchildren to help make toast and set the table.

Bianca and Kiko soon joined everyone in the kitchen. Ben and Stella were the last guests to show up. The couple relished having some time alone. The sheets rustled as morning hugs morphed into reckless, passionate love making. By the time it was over both were sweaty, their lips were swollen. Both sat back on the bed next to each other. Their breathing still racing. Stella put her head on the pillow and dozed off. Ben jumped in the shower. He woke her when it was her turn. Fresh and showered they walked down to the kitchen.

The house was filled with laughter. Screaming children raced through the downstairs. Everyone was hugging and expressing good wishes for the new year ahead. A conga line of dishwashers stood near the sink to clean up after breakfast. Kiko was drinking expresso on the patio. Sam ran by and stopped to give him a hug. A rarely expressive man, he set Sam down and greeted the other men with a broad smile. How lucky to find such contentment and warmth. Whatever this was he would never give it back.

CHAPTER 26
IT'S OVER

Between Christmas and New Year's, Andy began calling members of his former team who were abroad to update them on events and send good wishes for the holidays.

His message was straightforward. "There's no longer any need to worry," he told them. "The danger of discovery is over. The company has been unable to verify if all the bearer bonds can be found after the flood of the vault. An insurance claim for lost securities has been submitted."

His former team members had many questions. "Yes, you can go home to the U.S. whenever you want to. Yes, you can use your American passport to travel back and forth. Yes, you can keep your home overseas and go back and forth to your residence in the states. No one is looking for you and no one is tracking you.

"However, you need to keep your overseas identity, passport, and bank accounts. I'm told that any large movement of funds to the U.S. will be reported to the IRS and regulators. You do not want to invite this type of attention or questioning by authorities. Please keep using your local concierge or banker contact. They will help you move money without scrutiny. And they will arrange credit cards or credit lines you can use in the U.S. backed by your bank account overseas."

Once the initial message was delivered, Andy spent time getting updated on everyone's family. He wanted to know how they adjusted to living overseas. Most of the former staff said they would keep their homes, condos or apartments they bought in their foreign country of residence. Few of them had ever lived outside the U.S. They described it as wonderful having a vacation home far away. However, they also missed seeing friends and family back in New York. A few thought they might buy a residence in nearby New Jersey or upstate New York, or maybe move close to the New Jersey shore or look for something in Florida or Arizona. It was clear to Andy that having the experience living overseas had helped his team members see opportunities they never dreamed.

There was great relief once Andy told them the threat of discovery was over. Few had truly entertained the danger they faced. How the outside world worked and what might tripwire the discovery of the heist was too complex. They trusted in Andy's plan and the support they were given by Joey Testa. Some were surprised the danger would every truly go away.

Andy suggested one last team meeting in New York. "We have been blessed up to this point," he told them. "It's time for everyone to move on with their lives. But we spent so many years together."

During his calls, he found many team members would return home in spring. He asked everyone to join him for a late brunch on Sunday, May 5 at Smith and Wollensky's steakhouse on 3rd Avenue and 49th Street.

"Each of us now has the opportunity and the resources to chart a new direction. This may be our last chance to see and celebrate our time together."

The invitation was not a hard sell. Everyone was chomping at the bit to see others from the vault team. Andy was pleased to hear how excited folks were to have a reunion. He promised more communication would follow before the event.

After finishing his last call, he sat in his study for over an hour. It's over, he told himself. The danger he feared from the beginning had finally passed. In victory, he was not about to gloat. He felt like a burden had been lifted. His team could move freely back and forth to their families in the U.S. or to homes they had established overseas.

It was time for his former employees to start looking ahead to their futures. They now had resources. Team members like Jennie Li, Jose and Stella could begin to help their parents retire early, quit strenuous jobs, travel to places they only dreamed of and move to homes away far away. Giulia could find a broader range of counselors, and special needs programs for Giana. She could finally insist Mia go back to school and find a more satisfying career than being a waitress. Her income would no longer be a barrier or an excuse. Bea Siegel could finally make that trip to Israel she so desperately wanted but felt was out of reach. Her dreams included a family vacation together. Her parents always talked about a visit to Israel but never got there.

With Mei on the mend, Andy was certain Henry would see his way clear to venture out and travel through Europe. He led his whole life mindful of saving money and helping his children go to college. Reggie Seawright was most likely to start his own business in Brooklyn, while his wife continued her banking career. A larger home for his family, with kids who craved their own bedrooms, would climb the list of priorities. But Reggie also wanted to travel to the Grand Canyon and other national parks in America. His dream centered on his children seeing the world beyond big cities.

Later that afternoon, Andy briefed Ben on the call with Lincoln. He left out any mention of Boris. He had several long conversations with Stella during their time in Italy. He reminded her of Jennie Li's advice and encouraged her to always "keep your own money separate." Ben had worked many years, so he had resources. If it were up to Andy, Stella would never tell him about the heist of bearer bonds. She had found a guy with high integrity. Andy did not believe his values should be tested.

Ben was keen to hear Connolly was wrong as CEO to claim there were no losses after storm Sandy. Ben felt vindicated. Like Andy, they both still shared a strange feeling of loyalty to the organization. Ben hoped the insurance payout on lost securities would cover the company's exposure. Lincoln communicated the high regard most senior executives felt about Ben's calm and measured judgement. He reacted to this news with a smile. But he had already moved on from his job. It was now time to focus his energy and attention on Stella.

The next day, Andy decided to call Joey Testa. He made their escape possible. And in the process had become a good friend. Joey was almost out the door headed to the Caribbean for a week of vacation with his wife. His two children were staying with their grandparents. Joey was initially worried when his assistant told him Andy was calling. However, the update Andy shared restored confidence their plan had turned out profitable – and successful. He made a point to invite Testa to their brunch in

May so his team could thank him for safeguarding their freedom. Once again, Andy had made Joey feel as if he was a member of the family.

Villa life returned to normal two weeks after New Year's. Andy's children headed back to resume their careers and return the children to school. Stella's parents said their goodbyes to their daughter and grandson. It was especially hard to not see Sam as often as when Stella was working. Ben and Stella started to settle-in next door, with Andy's blessing. Andy still made a point of taking Sam into Florence once a week to visit historic sites. Sam didn't mind getting away from the country, especially if there was a promise of gelato before returning home.

On two occasions, he ventured further taking Sam by train to Rome's Colosseum and the Vatican. It was challenging trying to get an eleven-year-old to catch the 8 a.m. early train, but it gave them a full day, allowing them to arrive and return home at a reasonable hour. Andy's new friend, Santo, arranged express tours, which lasted only one hour and helped them avoid long lines waiting to enter.

At his age, Sam didn't need to learn Roman history. The tour guide just filled him with stories of gladiators who fought and sacrificed to entertain the public. He could see Sam's reaction to the enormous size of this amphitheater, one of the seven wonders in the world. Andy believed Sam would remember the feeling he had standing in the Colosseum. He was certain the visit would later spark his interest in history.

Likewise, rather than a boring lesson about religion at the Vatican, Andy focused on seeing the Sistine Chapel. For a kid from the South Bronx, the sheer size of the church and the magnificence of Michelangelo's paintings across the ceiling and the throngs of people filling the building would leave an indelible impression. Andy wanted Sam to see himself as part of a larger global community of worshippers guided by faith and a common bond. Whether seeing thousands of Catholics visiting the Vatican, Muslims converging on Mecca during the Hajj or Jews praying at the Western Wall, he hoped this young man would embrace a belief in God and serving mankind.

But while Andy felt responsible for Stella and Sam, he accepted they had to find their own way. His goal was to expose them to places and events that might influence and inspire them. He was always impressed by the insightful questions Sam asked him during their time together. Sam was endlessly curious about the world. It was such a wonderful quality to nurture in a child.

Meanwhile, Ben and Stella renewed their courtship. They spent time together touring neighboring towns: north to Lucca and Cinque Terre, south to Siena and Montepulciano and to Rome. As a couple they shared great chemistry but would that feeling endure the test of time? Their connection was driven by the enormous passion felt toward each other. But what was next? It was time to have frank conversations about their future, about Sam and whether they were ready to settle down together.

Ben wanted to take a year off to see if he could write a book. While he had made this decision when he left Americlear, he told Stella it might be time to reevaluate that move and instead go back to the job market.

"Stella, if we're going to be a couple, I can't just take off a year from work. Yes, I have resources and a year of severance to fall back on. However, being together means making these decisions together. Whatever I do has to work for both of us and for Sam. I don't want you to ever worry about whether we'll have money to live on."

"This is what I really love about you," Stella replied squeezing his hand. "I've never been with someone who puts me first. I've learned from my early mistakes in life, to make certain that a relationship works for me. I really do need to feel secure. At the same time, what we share together won't work if you can't express yourself. You've been doing the 9 to 5 job thing for a long time. Maybe taking a year will be a good thing for you – and for us."

Stella knew she could not keep her newfound wealth from Ben. In time, she had to trust him. But until they settled down, she wanted him to take the lead and feel he was the bread winner. Separately, she would ask Andy to help her direct money to make life easier for her parents. Giving Ben the time and space to write for a year would not put Sam at risk.

Their conversations about forging a life together would go on for weeks. Neither one of them was in a rush. During their travels exploring Italy, they would circle back to issues. Opening a bottle of wine at dinner or sitting at a café drinking cappuccino, they could talk for hours. Each of them was preoccupied with their partner's reaction and comfort level with decisions. Great love is like this. Great love is about sacrificing oneself joyfully, because it strengthens what they share together.

They decided to stay in Italy with Sam through the next year. Sam would stay enrolled in an American school near Florence. Ben would help her find tutors to ensure Sam was staying competitive with the expectations he'd find in private schools when he returns to the U.S. Stella and Ben decided to return home and attend Andy's send-off lunch in May.

During her visit home, Stella asked her parents to retire from their jobs. Her dad had enough years in the N.Y. Parks Department pension system for retirement. He planned to work longer, until his mid-60s. But Stella had set up an annuity to provide income for them to live on. Andy would help her immediately transfer a half a million dollars into the account. A longer-term deposit of $1 million would be invested in a portfolio of mutual funds to help secure her parents' future,

The renovated house next door to Andy's villa had plenty of room to accommodate grandma and grandpa. She wanted them to live one year in Italy, a vacation they had never considered. As they adjusted to their retirement, Stella planned to encourage her parents to explore the world. Her mom and dad had worked so hard and sacrificed so much, she wanted them to find a new purpose. And, if she and Ben had a child, they would be there to help and celebrate this joy.

Spring converged rather quickly. Andy was almost giddy at the response he received from his former team members. Everyone had confirmed they would attend the luncheon on May 5. Many had welcomed the chance to return home and see family in New York. Some planned to stay in the U.S. over the summer months. The heist had ended, but their new lives were just beginning. Each vault employee had to start thinking about the future. Where did they want to live? Did they want to travel? How would they invest their money to secure their children and their grandchildren.

In the countries where the vault employees hid for six months, Jimmy Valenti, at Andy's request, had insisted their banks come up with inter-generational plans that would further grow and safeguard their money. No one had to accept these plans, but he felt confident they would value professional help managing their investments. The bankers were shocked to find such wealthy customers could be so frugal. The employees and their families were cautious about spending money or acting in a frivolous manner, which seemed contradictory for folks who now had more than $8 million in their various bank accounts.

Back in New York, Andy and Stella greeted their colleagues at Smith and Wollensky's second floor private dining room, called the American room. How ironic these immigrants would celebrate their newfound financial freedoms here. Immediate family members were invited to join the luncheon. The room could handle seventy guests. Andy's eyes lit up when he saw Henry Wong approach with Mei holding his arm. Andy reached for Mei and hugged her. He kissed her cheek and held her hands. She had regained some of the weight that was lost after heart surgery. "Mei, it is so good to see you. How are you feeling?" Andy asked.

"We are all doing so much better," she responded. "Henry has finally taken your advice. He told the new executives in charge at Americlear that he would not be commuting to the New Jersey vault location. He has accepted retirement. Or perhaps it might be more accurate to say he has welcomed spending more time with me."

Andy nodded in agreement. He turned toward Henry and warmly shook his hand.

The line bunched up waiting to enter the room. Reggie waited his turn patiently with his wife and children. The Seawright family was moving to a new, larger home in a new neighborhood. His wife would have an easier commute. Reggie was still doing his due diligence before starting his own business. Sandra was trying to convince her husband that a job in banking operations might involve less stress and offer better medical insurance benefits. Reggie promised Andy he would try very hard to sit on the nest egg he had stashed in bank accounts overseas. His biggest extravagance after buying a new home was the money he and Sandra would pay for private school tuition.

Jennie Li strolled into the luncheon with Richard on her arm. Their relationship was no longer a closely guarded secret. She wore a flowing dress down to her ankles. Hollywood glamor had arrived. While her shoes had only a slightly raised heel, she easily stood over six foot tall. Richard didn't need to be told how lucky he was to be with her. Yet, he wore the milewide smile on his face without conceit. He may not have deserved to be with this beautiful goddess, but he felt certain they shared something that would last.

Like Stella, Jennie Li had spent time with her bankers in Singapore to set up accounts for parents and siblings. She knew Citibank had deep roots in Singapore, so she looked to leverage her New York relationship with the bank. She and Richard bought an apartment during their travels overseas. She hoped her parents would use their Singapore residence for visits and vacations. She convinced her parents they could travel between Singapore and Hong Kong to visit relatives in three to four hours. Jennie Li preferred using Singapore as her base. She didn't trust Hong Kong banks after China took back the territory in 1997.

Giulia warmly hugged Andy. Her daughter Mia and her granddaughter Giana came with her. Giulia updated her former boss. She insisted Mia quit her waitressing job and return to school. She didn't care if Mia took four years, six years or longer to finish a college degree. Giulia told Andy, "Just because my daughter will inherit money and have security does not mean she shouldn't have some sort of career. My parents believed work was just as important in life as going to church.

"Andy, you must come visit us. I want you to see what

they're doing with Giana. We now have an army of tutors and therapists working with her four days a week. Giana's comfort level and communication with me, her mom, and the play group she has joined are remarkable. She seems so happy these days. I finally have hope for her to be mainstreamed at school and enjoy a normal life."

It would take nearly 45 minutes for everyone to arrive and take their seats at the 10 tables Andy reserved. He encouraged his team members to walk around and keep talking while lunch was being served. He promised to send everyone new contact information so they could reach each other in their host countries or through email in the U.S.

As he stood up to make the opening toast, Andy publicly thanked Joey Testa and his wife, Gemma, for joining the luncheon – and for Joey's help during everyone's transition to retirement or career changes. "Look, I can tell you without hesitation that Joey and his staff took the needs of our team very seriously. They never wavered in their support of our well-being. In the years to come, I trust everyone here today will remember who guided and navigated us to this juncture.

"Ok, let's toast our good fortune. As I explained during my recent call, whatever anxiety you may have felt you can let go of it. It's over. Now, that doesn't mean being reckless. Considering how many of you took the subway to reach our luncheon, I'm relieved that none of you are taking your success for granted. Humility is the right answer to the blessings we've been given. Each of us has a responsibility in this group to be measured and mindful that what impacts one of us could impact all of us. It's over. Be grateful. Focus on moving forward – and doing good things with your lives.

"I also want to report that Bea Siegel has received commitments from our group for $250,000 in donations to a college scholarship fund named for our dear friend, Louise Taylor. Louise's daughter, Betty is here today sitting with Bea. Please let's acknowledge and remind her she is a part of our extended family.

The room erupted in applause. Betty stood and waved to everyone with tears in her eyes.

"Most of you know, the company reached a settlement with Louise's family. We are grateful her child is now financially secure. She is going to school now and her college tuition will be covered. However, Bea had the idea to set up a scholarship fund at the high school named after Louise Taylor. We want her daughter to have a lasting memory of her mom. Louise worked very hard during her life. This scholarship will give out awards each year to promising students who may not have resources to continue their education. For Betty and her extended family, it will be a living and lasting memorial. Can we all give Bea and the Taylor family a round of applause? And we are grateful that everyone on our team participated in donating money to this scholarship fund, including some of you who did not work at the company when Louise passed away."

While everyone returned to their seats when food was served, it was difficult to keep them there for long. Details about Americlear's move to New Jersey and plans to decentralize the vault were shared in conversation. The company was not surprised by the number of employees who did not return to work at the new location. The HR department had made this calculation when they considered the commuting required by employees living in the outer boroughs of New York City.

The restaurant was very accommodating. The lunch ran over by an hour. Andy made a point to generously tip the waiters, who would forfeit their break time before the dinner crowd showed up starting at five pm. When the lunch ended, the vault team continued their conversations in the hallway leading downstairs or outside in front of the restaurant. No one was in a hurry to leave. They clung to each other for as long as time would allow. Their daily routines seeing each other at the company had ended. Their family-like involvement in each other's lives would be lost now, except for periodic updates in emails.

Before the lunch ended, several of them asked Andy to consider gathering the group every two years. He wasn't certain how realistic it would be to stage reunions, with folks traveling and having second homes overseas. But he promised to try, at least in the short term. "Some of us are getting older," he jokingly told Edith Colon. "We'll have to see in two years if folks are still motivated as they are now."

Andy did invite Joey Testa and Gemma to come visit him in Italy. Both men wanted to keep their connection. They exchanged handshakes and a warm hug before saying goodbye. Andy was given an open offer to call if he ever needed help in the future.

CHAPTER 27
VISITING NANCY

In the days following their luncheon, Andy stayed at his home in Brooklyn. Very little had changed since he left for Italy. He told his daughters it was like being in this time capsule, where every piece of furniture, the carpet and the drapes on windows reminded him of his dear Nancy. While Emily encouraged him to sell the house, he turned away this suggestion. For the time being, he wanted to keep his option to return periodically. The house, the kitchen where he'd sit and drink coffee, the bedroom where he now slept alone, still brought back so many happy memories.

Andy wasn't certain if it was his imagination, but at night when he closed his eyes, he could smell Nancy on the blanket… or in the clothes he refused to remove from her closet.

"Dad, keeping the house as if mom were still with us, it's just not healthy," Anna told him. "We miss her too, but you shouldn't stay here anymore. It's time."

"Anna, I am moving on with my life. You saw that when you

came to visit me in Italy. But it's such a special feeling coming back to this house I shared with your mother all these years. I can move on and still enjoy coming back home to imagine hearing her voice when I'm standing in the kitchen. There's nothing wrong with keeping her closet filled with clothes. No, it's not morbid. I was just a kid when I met her. We shared so much joy together. And you don't dismiss or throw away the tangible evidence of memories. I don't ever want to lose her completely. I hope you and Michael will grow to understand how important this type of connection can be in life. I'm not turning away from my future; I just don't think I need to forget or erase my past."

Later in the week Andy went to visit Nancy's grave. He brought his lawn chair to sit and tell her about the changes taking place in the world. She would love his decision to buy the villa in Italy. He described in detail the renovations he made to the main house and the work underway next door. He tried to assure her that with Ben and Stella next door, she no longer had to worry he'd be alone.

He talked about Anna and Emily coming with their families for the holidays. Nancy always wanted the family to share Christmas together. Andy promised her he would continue honoring those wishes. He could also fund them to visit for vacations during the year.

"Nancy, I promise to keep our children close," he told her. "I also will stay involved in the lives of our grandkids. You don't have to worry."

He took his time explaining the events at Americlear. He knew she might not agree or approve.

He had skirted this conversation with Nancy for almost a year. It was time for him to come clean. Many of the issues he described happened long before Nancy died. However, he told her how often he kept his anger and disappointment bottled up inside. Whether he feared speaking out or lacked confidence in finding the right solution, Andy felt strongly that he failed the people who trusted him.

"Nancy, each time something happened, like the death of Louise Taylor, or when something was taken away from employees, I held back because I wasn't ready to sacrifice my standing at the company or the rewards I took home. It's embarrassing even now to admit I was a company man.

"I wish you could understand how much a burden these events have been on me. People I cared about lost their jobs during the market downturns, others lost bonuses and pay raises. Nothing impacted me and I kept telling myself it wasn't my responsibility. Even after they announced the elimination of pensions and retiree medical benefits, I initially thought these company decisions were okay. It was something that would not hurt me so why worry?

Andy was certain his wife would be shocked to hear about the theft of bearer bonds. Nothing he had ever done in life could have prepared her to truly understand this decision. Getting away with it could never justify committing a crime in Nancy's mind. Her absence did not absolve her husband. When you've lived a lifetime loving someone, death does not lower the bar of expectations. It doesn't waive the honesty you shared, an explanation, or taking responsibility for your actions.

At times, he rambled during their conversation. Then he experienced a burst of emotion he did not understand, and he could not control.

"Nancy, at the time, I wished you were here so I could ask your advice. I needed you. I tried to talk to you, but there was only silence. You were gone – and I felt so alone in my life. Then

Giulia had a heart attack. I realized she almost died. The stress of decisions by the company almost killed her. How could I stand by and do nothing to protect my family? When you left me, I couldn't sleep, I couldn't eat, and I did not want to continue living. But the people who have been my extended family for three decades – they saved me. They lifted me up. They stayed at our house so I wouldn't be alone. They brought me to their homes during holidays.

"When I almost lost Giulia, the same fear and anger swept over me as when I found you in our bed. My spirit had been broken, almost beyond repair. I cried and I prayed for Giulia. And suddenly, I realized I could no longer sit quietly on the sidelines. I couldn't ignore what was happening to people I cared about.

"Nancy, I could not save you. But I desperately wanted to save my team. I tossed and turned with sleepless nights for weeks. I was near exhaustion. It was the same feeling of desperation I experienced after your funeral. Then, in a moment of clarity, I chose to shape the future.

"I did what you so often asked me to do. I went to church that weekend. I wanted a sign. If my decision to cross the line in life was wrong, I needed someone to tell me. But the more I prayed, the more resolute I became. I could no longer move forward with my life, if the life I was leading did not count for something."

As a boy growing up in Brooklyn, Andy heard his parents often use the expression that you are "born into the world alone and you leave the world alone." Like so many other things you learn or hear along the way, he accepted that expression as the truth. But the world we navigate is so much more complex than that. We surround ourselves with family and people we love, because they fill the space and distract us from our solitude.

Yes, the people we love are mirrors into our souls. They try their best to see us and reassure us. In the end, however, it is rare they can give us answers where none may exist. We wander in the desert of life for years trying to figure out our destination, our purpose and whether we have the grit to survive the journey.

For over two hours, Andy talked with Nancy about the journey he had taken. It was the longest chat they shared since her death. His eyes were red with tears. The one person he trusted most in life could no longer give him the answers he was looking for. In the end, Andy wasn't certain if she had forgiven him. But life has a way of challenging us to press on. Before leaving her grave, he would gently lean down and kiss her head stone.

Andy never imagined how much his world would change. Nothing he experienced had prepared him for the sacrifices he was ready to make. Could he have succeeded if storm Sandy had not covered his tracks? He would never know the answer to this question. Perhaps he didn't need to know.

What drives someone to do the unimaginable? People in life are often motivated by greed and self-gratification. However, Andy's team were immigrants and first-generation Americans. They were different. They grew up only understanding humility, the value of prayer and personal sacrifice. Their hope was that this would be enough to allow the next generation to climb higher.

When he talked to his employees about his plan to steal bearer bonds, no one wanted to act out of malice. They feared for their families, for their dreams and the decades of hard work they had given to support and help their loved ones.

Yes, they struggled with misgivings and guilt when they crossed the line. These immigrants held onto their integrity and the values passed on to them. They refused to act out of avarice, entitlement or hate.

But truth be told, you can't hold people back forever. When hopes are beaten down and people feel oppressed, fear becomes septic, and people will take extraordinary measures to rebel; to break free.

Were the vault employees willing actors ready to deceive and commit crimes or were they victims of the company's long-standing neglect? Looking from the outside, some might judge them in a cold and unforgiving manner. However, Andy found peace by helping his team face the future and become resolute in changing it.

ALSO BY STUART Z. GOLDSTEIN

Moe Fields: The Special Bond Between Fathers and Sons

Moe Fields is a life affirming story for readers looking to find books that celebrate the strength of family bonds that can prevail over trauma and setbacks.

What readers are saying:

"This is a powerful book, a story about a man who fought and loved fiercely, and the impact he had on the lives of his three sons. If other men who read this book are like me, they'll find themselves reflecting on their own relationships with their fathers as well as with their sons."
— **Donald H. Harrison, editor and publisher of Jewish World Magazine**

“Every now and then, if you ‘re lucky, you read a book that stays with you long after you’ve finished it. *Moe Fields* is that book for me. It is beautifully written… I laughed, I cried, I cringed, I smiled, and most of all I wished I had known Moe Fields.” — **Charlene Wheeless, best-selling author of *You Are Enough***

Available now!

Scan to view below:

ABOUT THE AUTHOR

Stuart Z. Goldstein was one of the longest-serving PR spokespersons on Wall Street, having spent over two decades as Managing Director of Corporate Communications & Public Affairs at The Depository Trust & Clearing Corporation (DTCC) in New York. Prior to that, he served as a spokesperson for American Express and Citicorp/ Citibank. His communications journey began in college, where he wrote for the Trenton Times and played a key role in efforts to lower the voting age to 18, contributing to the ratification of the 26th Amendment.

Goldstein has continued his passion for writing through various projects, including the award-winning memoir *Moe Fields: The Special Bond Between Fathers and Sons*, and co-authoring two important works: *Guide to Clearance & Settlement 2009* and *Lifecycle of a Security 2010*, which detail the inner workings of U.S. capital markets. His bylined articles on public policy have appeared in prestigious publications such as USA Today, the Washington Times, the New York Times, the Star Ledger, and Global Financial Markets magazine, among others.

Residing near Princeton, New Jersey, with his family, Goldstein has been recognized as a prominent figure in corporate communications within the securities services industry. As noted by Global Custodian magazine, “Goldstein surely was the highest-profile corporate communications executive in the securities services industry.” In a field where most executives serve less than five years, Goldstein notably managed to exceed the average tenure, serving under three successive CEOs.

Made in the USA
Monee, IL
06 January 2025

a489d143-aa2e-4509-b01c-7bb120826267R02